"*A Timely Vision* grabbed my attention on page one . . . Puzzles are unraveled and secrets spilled in a fast-paced paranormal mystery full of quirky characters you'll want as friends."
—Elizabeth Spann Craig, author of *Pretty Is as Pretty Dies*

"A delightful yarn! Few amateur sleuths are as charming as this psychic-mayor sleuth in a small coastal town where murder stalks the dunes and ghosts roam the Outer Banks."
—Patricia Sprinkle, author of *What Are You Wearing to Die?*

PRAISE FOR

Wicked Weaves

"Offers a vibrant background for the mysterious goings-on and the colorful cast of characters."
—Kaye Morgan, author of *Ghost Sudoku*

"[A] new, exciting . . . series . . . Part of the fun of this solid whodunit is the vivid description of the Renaissance Village; anyone who has not been to one will want to go . . . Cleverly developed."
—*Midwest Book Review*

"Joyce and Jim Lavene have teamed up for yet another terrific mystery series . . . A feast for the reader . . . Character development in this new series is energetic and eloquent; Jessie is charming and intelligent, with . . . saucy strength." —*MyShelf.com*

"A promising new series set at a Renaissance faire . . . Interesting juxtaposition between the present and the past and the real and the fantastic . . . Entertaining and vivacious characters."
—*Romantic Times*

"I cannot imagine a cozier setting than Renaissance Faire Village, a closed community of rather eccentric—and very interesting—characters, [with] lots of potential . . . A great start to a new series by a veteran duo of mystery authors." —*Cozy Library*

continued . . .

Perfect Poison

"A fabulous whodunit that will keep readers guessing and happily turning pages to the unexpected end. Peggy Less is a most entertaining sleuth and her Southern gentility is like a breath of fresh air . . . A keeper!"　　　　　　　　　　*—Fresh Fiction*

"A fascinating whodunit with unusual but plausible twists and plenty of red herrings."　　　*—Genre Go Round Reviews*

"The book [has] so much . . . going for it . . . A feisty widow who exudes confidence . . . The plotting and pacing are cozy perfect."
—Cozy Library

Poisoned Petals

"A delightful botany mystery."　　　　　　*—The Best Reviews*

"A top-notch, over-the-fence mystery read with beloved characters, a fast-paced story line, and a wallop of an ending."
—Midwest Book Review

"Enjoy this pleasurable read!"　　　　　　*—Mystery Morgue*

Fruit of the Poisoned Tree

"I cannot recommend this work highly enough. It has everything: mystery, wonderful characters, sinister plot, humor, and even romance."　　　　　　　　　*—Midwest Book Review*

"Well crafted with a satisfying end that will leave readers wanting more!"　　　　　　　　　　　　*—Fresh Fiction*

Pretty Poison

"With a touch of romance added to this delightful mystery, one can only hope many more Peggy Lee Mysteries will be hitting shelves soon!"　　　　　　　　*—Roundtable Reviews*

"A fantastic amateur-sleuth mystery."　　　*—The Best Reviews*

"For anyone with even a modicum of interest in gardening, this book is a lot of fun." —*The Romance Readers Connection*

"The perfect book if you're looking for a great suspense." —*Romance Junkies*

"Joyce and Jim Lavene have crafted an outstanding whodunit in *Pretty Poison*, with plenty of twists and turns that will keep the reader entranced to the final page." —*Fresh Fiction*

"Complete with gardening tips, this is a smartly penned, charming cozy, the first book in a new series. The mystery is intricate and well plotted. Green thumbs and nongardeners alike will enjoy this book." —*Romantic Times*

A Timely
Vision

Joyce and Jim Lavene

BERKLEY PRIME CRIME, NEW YORK

THE BERKLEY PUBLISHING GROUP
Published by the Penguin Group
Penguin Group (USA) Inc.
375 Hudson Street, New York, New York 10014, USA

Penguin Group (Canada), 90 Eglinton Avenue East, Suite 700, Toronto, Ontario M4P 2Y3, Canada
(a division of Pearson Penguin Canada Inc.)
Penguin Books Ltd., 80 Strand, London WC2R 0RL, England
Penguin Group Ireland, 25 St. Stephen's Green, Dublin 2, Ireland (a division of Penguin Books Ltd.)
Penguin Group (Australia), 250 Camberwell Road, Camberwell, Victoria 3124, Australia
(a division of Pearson Australia Group Pty. Ltd.)
Penguin Books India Pvt. Ltd., 11 Community Centre, Panchsheel Park, New Delhi—110 017, India
Penguin Group (NZ), 67 Apollo Drive, Rosedale, North Shore 0632, New Zealand
(a division of Pearson New Zealand Ltd.)
Penguin Books (South Africa) (Pty.) Ltd., 24 Sturdee Avenue, Rosebank, Johannesburg 2196,
South Africa

Penguin Books Ltd., Registered Offices: 80 Strand, London WC2R 0RL, England

This is a work of fiction. Names, characters, places, and incidents either are the product of the authors' imagination or are used fictitiously, and any resemblance to actual persons, living or dead, business establishments, events, or locales is entirely coincidental. The publisher does not have any control over and does not assume any responsibility for author or third-party websites or their content.

A TIMELY VISION

A Berkley Prime Crime Book / published by arrangement with the authors

PRINTING HISTORY
Berkley Prime Crime mass-market edition / May 2010

Copyright © 2010 by Joyce Lavene and Jim Lavene.
Cover illustration by Robert Crawford.
Cover design by Annette Fiore Defex.
Interior text design by Laura K. Corless.

ISBN: 978-0-425-23475-4

BERKLEY® PRIME CRIME
Berkley Prime Crime Books are published by The Berkley Publishing Group,
a division of Penguin Group (USA) Inc.,
375 Hudson Street, New York, New York 10014.
BERKLEY® PRIME CRIME and the PRIME CRIME logo are trademarks of Penguin Group
(USA) Inc.

PRINTED IN THE UNITED STATES OF AMERICA

10 9 8 7 6 5 4 3 2 1

We want to thank our loving and supportive family, who daily put up with us having conversations about killing people. We love you all!

Joyce and Jim (Mom and Dad)

Chapter 1

It was right after the Fourth of July parade that follows the crowning of the new Miss Duck when Mildred Mason tapped me on the shoulder and sighed. I *knew* that sigh. It meant she'd lost something again. Usually, it was her purse or house keys. Nothing of earthshaking proportions to anyone else, but something important to her.

"Miss Mildred!" I pretended I hadn't seen the town's oldest citizen behind me on the boardwalk. "What are you doing here?"

"I'm missing something real important, Dae. I was hoping you could help me find it. You've always been so good at finding things that are lost. I remember when your mama was alive, bless her soul. She was always so proud of your gift."

I didn't mind Miss Mildred reminiscing about the past usually, but the hot July sun was beating down on us. I was wearing a heavy, old-fashioned coat that was a gift from the town to their first mayor since incorporation in 2002. It was hot and uncomfortable, not to mention tacky. Covered with red sashes and gold medallions, it was kind of something our pirate forefathers might have worn. Exactly what every mayor needed in ninety-eight-degree weather.

"Let's step inside." I invited her into my shop, Missing Pieces, as I grabbed two packages left out on the boardwalk for me. I'd recently become the sole agent for UPS in Duck. "I think I have some lemonade in the refrigerator. Would you like some?"

Miss Mildred wandered in as she always did, taking a few minutes to look around. I think she liked looking at the odds and ends that filled the thrift shop, even though she didn't come to visit very often. "No, thanks, dear. But you go right ahead. I love this shop, you know. It reminds me of people and places that are gone forever."

She admired a heart-shaped pin I'd found the day before, at a spot right off the edge of the boardwalk where it led into the Currituck Sound. The sunlight had glinted off of it as I'd walked by. It was fashioned from pink rhinestones. It took me an hour to get it cleaned up, but it was in good shape after being out there in the mud and sand for who knew how long.

Something about it told me it was an important find. I didn't know why yet, but my instinct for that kind of thing was never wrong. Sometimes it took me a while, years for some items, to figure it out. But I had time. It wasn't going anywhere.

I removed the heavy wool coat, revealing my white shorts and a patriotic red, white and blue tank top as she rambled on about her life. She could be a cantankerous old lady, but her many contributions to various charities around town had earned her a soft spot in everyone's hearts. She'd taught school here for many years, which meant at least half of the people still alive had her for one grade or another. They all remembered her as strict but fair.

She lived on the land her ancestors had settled some two hundred or so years ago. Miss Mildred traced her lineage back to a French pirate who'd sailed the Caribbean but decided to settle down on the narrow island that eventually became known as the Outer Banks of North Carolina. Duck is at the northern end of that hundred-mile strip of land.

"You should let Althea at the library record all those things you remember," I told her as I poured a glass of lemonade. "All that history is part of this area."

"I know," she said, as she always did. "I will someday, when I get old."

There was no convincing Miss Mildred that being ninety-two made her old. I thought about it when I was sixteen, never said anything, of course, and finally stopped thinking about it altogether at twenty-five. She didn't see herself that way. Who was I to argue the point? Besides, since I'd turned thirty, I'd begun to understand what she meant.

I tossed back half of the lemonade in a single thirsty gulp and went to join her. "Let's sit down, Miss Mildred. What are you looking for?"

We sat down on the old burgundy brocade sofa that had occupied too much space in the shop for too long. I should've gotten rid of it years before, but it was such a cozy place to sit and talk. Keeping it meant I had to occasionally put up shelves around it to hold extra merchandise that came my way, but I didn't mind. I couldn't bear to part with it.

"I'm looking for my mother's watch. I loaned it to my sister, Lizzie, last week. I've called her, but there's no answer." Her prim little mouth drew up even further. A wealth of cobweb-fine lines spun out along her face. "You *know* how she is, Dae."

I *knew* how Miss Mildred thought Miss Elizabeth was: irresponsible, reckless, careless.

"She's irresponsible, reckless. She's always been careless." Miss Mildred listed her younger sister's faults.

I would've asked *why* she'd loaned the watch to her if she felt that way, but I'd known the two of them all of my life. They'd been arguing since the day Miss Elizabeth took Johnny Simpson away from Miss Mildred in high school.

My grandparents had told me the sisters were never friends again after that even though Miss Mildred had married Frank Mason and done quite well for herself. Wild Johnny Simpson had left Miss Elizabeth crying and alone for the rest of her life. She never remarried, and Miss Mildred never forgave her.

So I didn't ask. I sipped my lemonade and let her run through the gamut of Miss Elizabeth's faults and vices.

"She's always thought she was better than me because we both ran for Miss Duck that year and *she* was chosen. Really, I think she let the judge feel her up a little, if you know what I mean. Otherwise I'm sure he'd have chosen *me*."

"This doesn't really sound like you've *lost* your mother's watch," I finally interrupted. "But I'll be happy to go by Miss Elizabeth's house and see if she's okay. I can check on the watch while I'm there."

"Oh, I'm sure she's fine." Miss Mildred waved away the idea that her sister *wouldn't* be fine with an impatient hand. "I can't help but feel that Mama's watch is lost. I need your help, Dae. I know you're busy being mayor and all, but surely you can spare me a few minutes."

I didn't remind her that this was one of the biggest days

in Duck. At least twenty thousand people were here for the holiday. They were looking for food and someplace to shop. Some of them might be about ready to run in and buy my treasures.

I glanced around at my collection of odds and ends, the precious and the ordinary. They had taken me a lifetime to find and might take a lifetime to sell the way things had been going the last few months. Sometimes I thought I should get rid of all of it and take to the open sea, as my Duck ancestors would have done. But visiting Gramps's old fishing boat always changed my mind. I was never crazy about the smell of fish.

I sighed and brought my thoughts back to Miss Mildred. It couldn't hurt to oblige her. Later, I could check in on her sister and find out what was going on. Miss Elizabeth, at the sweet young age of ninety, had been known to wander the beaches late at night and had often been escorted home by the police. "Okay." I took a deep breath and turned to face Miss Mildred on the sofa. "Give me your hands."

"I remember the first time you did this for me." Miss Mildred smiled. "You were such a pretty child. I was looking for my purse, and your mama told me to give you my hand and you'd help me find it. I didn't quite believe it then. But I do now."

Miss Mildred put her rough, dry hands in mine, her short nails dirty and cracked. She refused to wear gloves when she gardened, which she did a lot of the time. "Think about the watch." I closed my eyes and let the images form in my mind. I wasn't really expecting to see anything since the watch wasn't *really* missing. That seemed to be the way my gift worked.

But an image came seconds later, making me gasp. It was a gold wristwatch with tiny diamonds where the numbers should be. It was on a thin, wrinkled arm, presumably Miss Elizabeth's.

I opened my eyes and shook all over for a second. I'd come to think of the shaking as a reaction to being in someone else's mind. There's not much literature or research done on this kind of thing, so I had to go with what I knew.

"Did you find my watch?"

"I think so, yes." I let go of her hands and felt the link between us fade. "I think your sister is wearing it." I wasn't sure why that image would come to me since the watch wasn't *officially* lost. Maybe Miss Mildred *feeling* it was lost was enough for that part of me to latch on to it.

"Maybe you could drop by her place, if you wouldn't mind. I'd like to have Mama's watch back. She left it to *me*, you know. Not *Lizzie*."

I smiled as I helped her to her feet. "I'm sure your mother gave her something nice too."

"Not as nice as that watch." Miss Mildred patted my hand. "Thank you, Dae. You know, I voted for you, and you've done a very good job for us."

"You're welcome, Miss Mildred. I'll see if Miss Elizabeth will let me bring the watch back to you."

I was blessed with a string of customers after she left. I was always amazed at what visitors would buy and take home with them for souvenirs. Amazed *and* frustrated when the things I thought were most valuable were completely ignored for touristy lamps made from shells and little lighthouses that said "Outer Banks." Most of the lighthouses didn't even look like the ones you could find here—*and* they were made in China.

"Looks like you've got a good crowd," Trudy Devereaux observed as she sauntered in from the Curves and Curls

Beauty Spa next door. Trudy was showing off her signature tan with a short white dress that left her shoulders and most of her back bare. Of course, her pink nails and platinum blond hair were perfect, as always.

"Yeah, they finally found me." I watched one woman, badly sunburned, pick up one of my favorite pieces, a sugar bowl that looked like the Cape Hatteras lighthouse. She'd already picked it up once and put it down only to circle around and come back to it again.

"Lucky *you*! My place is completely empty. You'd think *someone* would want to have *something* done! It *is* the Fourth and everyone's off of work. *And* I have that bikini wax special going on."

The very idea made me wince. "Maybe it'll get better later."

"Maybe." She didn't sound too convinced. "But I think I might as well close up for the day and go to the beach like everyone else. A nice pitcher of margaritas sounds pretty good."

"Yeah. That sounds good." I was distracted, watching the woman with the sugar bowl start toward the cash register with the treasure. I wasn't sure whether I was happy or not. It had been in Missing Pieces for a long time. I'd found it at a flea market one weekend when I was visiting Charleston. It had called to me just like the pink rhinestone heart pin.

"Are you worried about her shoplifting that thing?" Trudy asked, no doubt noticing my preoccupation with the shopper.

"No. Of course not." I glanced away from the sugar bowl to Trudy's unhappy face. "I was interested to see if she'd buy it."

"You really love all this old junk. You're one of the missing pieces. You hate to lose any of them, don't you?"

"Don't be silly." The shopper caught my eye again as she picked up another treasure, a rosewood music box that had once belonged to Theodosia Burr, the daughter of the notorious Aaron Burr. This woman had an eye for the good stuff. "How would I make any money if I never sold anything?"

"Not being mayor of Duck, that's for sure. What do they pay you? Your grandfather said it was like a thousand dollars a year."

"Plus expenses," I added. "Anyway, nobody is mayor of Duck because they want to get rich."

"But in the meantime, you want to make sure all your precious junk goes to the right people, huh?"

"Something like that." The shopper had snagged the music box too and was coming toward me down the center aisle with both items.

"I don't know what you're worried about, Dae. You know how this junk seems to find you. There'll be plenty more where this came from." Trudy sighed and glanced at her nails. "I'm gonna go close up. I'll talk to you later when you can think about something besides your babies here in the shop. Bye."

I was glad she left. It sounds crazy, but I like to make sure the *really* important merchandise goes to a good home. I have a knack for finding things, but that doesn't mean I ignore them once I find them. My important treasures might not be treated right if that happened. I looked at it as part of the responsibility that went along with my gift. My mother taught me that when I was growing up.

My mother also used to say if there was a penny anywhere on the ground five miles around me, I'd find it. She was right. Not everything I found had great value. Sometimes a piece of junk was just a piece of junk.

"This is the most *interesting* piece." The shopper carefully placed the lighthouse sugar bowl on the counter. "I've never seen *anything* like it. And this music box! You know, I swear I've seen it before. Where did you get it?"

I looked at her. Assessing her, I guess. Hoping she'd be the one to take good care of these important items. The treasures I sold mattered to me, and they all needed good homes. For most of them, there came a time when they had to leave me. That's how we all survived.

I told her the story of how I came to have the sugar bowl and the music box. She listened in rapt attention until I'd finished. "I'm glad you like them. I think you'll give them a good home."

"Of course I will." She smiled, her even white teeth too bright to be natural. "How much do I owe you?"

I quoted her an astounding price, probably an *indecent* price, but one I knew she'd pay. I could see it in her eyes. When she handed me her Visa card, she met my third qualification for ownership. I didn't charge high prices for everything, but the really special stuff was too important to let go cheap.

"I hope you enjoy them as much as I have." I carefully wrapped her pieces in white tissue paper. "I've had them for a while. I'm glad someone finally noticed them."

Of course she gave me that you're-a-crazy-person look, but that was okay. She'd passed my tests. I didn't mind what she thought of me.

The other people in the shop bought trinkets, nothing of great value. Some of the things I collect for Missing Pieces are donations from people who want to get rid of stuff, like after the church rummage sale. I never develop feelings for those things, not like for the ones I find.

Once all the customers had left, I looked at the UPS

packages I'd picked up outside. Adding the UPS franchise to Missing Pieces was a way to bring in some extra money. There weren't a lot of shipments to and from Duck, but when they came through, they came here. I was proud of that.

I looked up from the boxes as I heard the shop door open. A scruffy young man with what my grandfather would call a roving eye walked in and asked about a job. I didn't recognize him as being a regular shopper or a Duck resident, but there was something about him that intrigued me. I shrugged it off after he asked me if something was wrong and I realized I'd been staring at him for too long. I told him I was sorry but I didn't have anything for him. He smirked and left the shop.

"It can't get much hotter out there." My grandfather came in right after him. "Who was that?"

"I don't know. Just somebody looking for a job."

He wiped the sweat from his forehead with a red rag before he replaced his straw hat on his thick white hair. "Lots of shoppers in Duck. Have you sold anything?"

"A few things." I couldn't keep it from him. "The lighthouse sugar bowl and the rosewood music box."

"I hope you got what they're worth."

I quoted him the price, and he whistled through his teeth. "You knew I wouldn't let them go for less."

"I knew." He hugged me as he reached the counter. "Ready for your close-up, Miss Mayor?"

"I suppose so." I smoothed down my shorts and picked up the oversized mayor's coat again. "I don't think they had this in mind for a woman mayor. I think the town council might need to consider changing this tradition."

He held one side of the coat for me. "You mean you

should get special treatment because you're a *woman*? I thought you hated that kind of thing."

"No. I should get a smaller coat because this one could fit Councilman Wilson, all six foot four, three hundred pounds of him. It's a *little* big on me by almost a foot and two hundred pounds."

"Come on now! The council had it tailored for you. It's not *that* big."

I wrapped the coat around me, flipped up the red ribbons and gold coins, then faced him. The sleeves were past my wrists, and my torso was swallowed by the coat. "I think they thought the first mayor would be a man, Gramps."

He laughed. "Maybe you *do* need something a little different, Dae. But not right now. You'll have to wow them with your personality."

"Thanks." I tried to adjust the coat again. No use. It was big and bulky, no way to make it less so. "I appreciate the vote of confidence."

"Never mind that." He ran his hand down the side of my hair. "You look like your mother. Those big blue eyes and your hair all bleached out from the sun."

"And a coat that's too big." I grinned so I wouldn't tear up. Talking about my mother always brought both of us to tears, even though it had been many years since her death. "I can't cry right now. You don't want my face to be all blotchy on local TV, do you?"

"You go ahead. I'll mind the shop. There's not much fishing going on right now with all the swimmers and surfers. Looks like a real high tide tonight. I hope there's not a storm coming."

"Nah. Not today. My storm knee isn't bothering me. Remember not to sell *anything* marked with a red tag."

"I know. Get their names. Get their phone numbers. If they pass inspection, you'll sell your treasures. If not, they'll have to find some others."

"That's right. I'll see you in a while."

I swept out the door with all the energy of a damp sponge. It was too hot for anything more. A breeze had come up from the Atlantic in the thirty minutes or so I'd been inside. Gramps was right. It smelled like a storm was brewing. So why wasn't my storm knee bothering me? Ever since I'd dislocated it surfing when I was fourteen, it had let me know when a storm was coming.

"Over here, Mayor O'Donnell." A friendly faced man beckoned me into the Duck Shoppes parking lot. Cars were starting to move again after the parade. "I thought we'd shoot out here. That way everyone gets a good look at Duck at the same time they get to meet you."

"That's a great idea." I looked around at the crowd swarming along Duck Road and across the sidewalk. The rough material of the large mayor's coat made my neck itch. It was too hot for anything except sandals and shorts, but this was what the people of Duck expected the mayor to wear on the Fourth of July. I reminded myself that it was probably no hotter today than it had been for the pirates who'd dressed like this and they'd survived.

"Mayor, we have to do something to protect the new crop of sea turtle eggs on the beach," Mary Lou Harcourt advised me as I stopped where the TV producer told me to stand. Her craggy gray eyebrows were knit together across her forehead like a headband.

"I don't know what we can do about them right now," I answered, distracted.

"There's an extra-high tide coming, and the eggs could

be washed away," she persisted. "We have to get everyone together. We'll save as many as possible."

"As soon as I get done here," I promised, knowing full well I'd have to go check on Miss Elizabeth first. "What time is high tide?"

"The paper said six P.M., but the almanac says five. I'd trust the almanac before the paper. Do you think you can get the volunteer fire department to help out?"

"That's a good idea, Mary Lou. You should go talk to Gramps. He's at the shop. I'm sure he'll have some ideas."

The producer of the news show that originated in Virginia Beach counted down as the cameraman prepared to film me with the show's host. A small crowd of people, mostly citizens of Duck, gathered around to watch what was happening. It wasn't everyday TV shows were interested enough to come down here.

"Just relax, Mayor O'Donnell." The show's host, Jerry Richards, was a reed thin man with gray-streaked black hair. He wore a white suit and a blue "Duck, NC" T-shirt. "You'll be fine."

"I'm sure I will." I tried to reach the spot on the back of my neck that began itching like fire as I started sweating, but it was no use. "I hope I don't look like an idiot."

"Not on *my* show!"

The taping went very smoothly considering people were giggling in the audience as I answered Jerry's questions. The questions were simple enough: Where was Duck located? How long had I been mayor of Duck? What was the Fourth of July celebration like?

After we'd talked, Jerry shook my hand and thanked me

for the interview. I was kind of impressed since I'd watched him on TV most of my life. But I couldn't wait to get back inside and change out of the mayor's coat. Even though the breeze had picked up, carrying with it the scent of the ocean, the temperature was still in the high nineties.

"How did it go?" Gramps swiveled on the tall stool behind the register to look at me.

"It went okay." I stripped off the coat, medallions and ribbons again. A person could learn to hate wearing that outfit. Thank goodness it wasn't something I had to wear everyday. "Sell anything?"

"Nothing important. You don't have to worry. Nothing you'll miss left the shop."

"Do you think you could manage for a few more minutes? I promised Miss Mildred I'd go check on Miss Elizabeth."

"I thought I saw Millie leaving the shop earlier." He shook his head. "What is it this time? Did she and Lizzie have another fight?"

"She's looking for her mama's watch. Miss Mildred loaned it to Miss Elizabeth and wants it back. Funny thing about that. She told me it was lost. I looked and saw it on Miss Elizabeth's arm. At least I *think* it was her arm. I didn't think I'd see it since it's not really lost."

"I wouldn't mess around with it, Dae. Let them hash it out. You know how they are."

"I know. But I already promised. And it might be something serious. Miss Mildred said she hasn't heard from her for a few days. I'd hate to ignore it and find out it was important."

"Go on then. Just don't blame me if someone buys your Roosevelt jelly jar by mistake."

"*Gramps!*"

He laughed. "You know I wouldn't let a thing like that happen. While you're down that way, you could stop in and welcome the new owner of the Blue Whale Inn. I hear he's from somewhere up north."

I checked my hair in a mirror I'd found in Cape Cod. It was a modern piece, probably not more than a few years old. It had intricate African carving around the wood handle and frame. I didn't know what the symbols meant, but I knew it was something special. I kept it behind the counter since I had no plans to part with it.

My hair was a mess from standing outside in the strong breeze. I ran my fingers through it, wishing I had a matching comb to go with the mirror. "Up north? You mean like Virginia Beach?"

"No. Like New York. Or Boston. I took him out for a cruise. He's an interesting man. Joined the Dare County Chamber of Commerce this week too."

"By interesting, you don't mean single, do you? I know you aren't *ever* planning on doing any matchmaking again after that last fiasco."

"What fiasco? You're too skeptical, Dae. And too picky. At this rate, you'll be too old to care when you meet that perfect man you've been looking for."

"I'll have to hope he's old too." I smiled and opened the door to the boardwalk. "You just mind the shop and don't worry about me finding someone. It'll take care of itself."

I closed the door before I could hear his retort. It was always the same anyway. I knew Gramps worried about me, especially about leaving me alone. I couldn't complain because he loved me. I only wished he was a little more careful about the men he tried to set me up with.

It was a short walk to the Atlantic side of Duck where Miss Elizabeth lived in a slightly less grand style than her sister. Of course, it was a short walk to *everywhere* in Duck. It's not a big place.

The roses swooned in the heat around the white clapboard two-story whose windows were shrouded with lace curtains. Johnny Simpson might've been wild, but he'd left a nice house for his abandoned wife. Atop the roof, spinning in the afternoon breeze, was an old lightning rod made to look like a fisherman holding his fishing pole with a dog yapping at his heels.

Now *that* was a treasure I'd like to get my hands on. I could feel it from where I stood in the front yard. My fingertips itched for it. But there was no way it would ever go anywhere as long as Miss Elizabeth was alive. The house and the lightning rod had been a fixture in Duck for longer than my thirty-six years. It was nice to know that some things didn't change.

I knocked on the front door, but there was no answer. I peeked through one of the ivory lace curtains. There wasn't enough room to see inside. I walked around back, looking at the whitecaps growing on the gray ocean not so far from the house. My storm knee might not feel it, but the weather was getting angry.

There was no sign of Miss Elizabeth around back either. A large pot of red geraniums sat near her neat, wrought-iron patio set. I looked in the kitchen window, pounded on the door and called her name. There was no answer except for the wind rushing through the old eaves.

I thought seriously about breaking a pane of glass in the kitchen door and opening it. But that wasn't something that sat well with the part of me that had taken the mayor's oath of office. Especially since Chief Michaels was only a cell phone call away. He could break a window or do something to get into the house. It was important to delegate to the right individuals, something I was still struggling to learn.

I turned back to take out my cell phone and almost walked into a man who'd been standing right behind me. I dropped my phone on the pink patio stones and watched it break into two pieces. It seemed to happen in slow motion. The whole slow-motion thing always took place right before an important find.

"You aren't trying to break in, are you?"

Chapter 2

"No. Of *course* not." As I spoke, the feeling passed. I looked around, but I couldn't see anything that even vaguely resembled my usual type of treasure. "I'm sorry. I didn't see you standing there."

"You were focused on getting in the house, I think. The lady who lives here hasn't been home for a few days."

I looked at him. He seemed fairly ordinary. Maybe late thirties, like me. Darker hair and bluer eyes. Maybe not blue, more dark gray, like the ocean after a storm. I didn't recognize him, but this time of year, there were plenty of people renting for the summer. "How do you know?"

"I live next door." He nodded, not taking his eyes off of me. It was an uncomfortable sensation. "I see her come and go all the time. A few days ago, she went out but she never came back."

His mouth was set in a firm line, giving him a kind of

tough expression, as though he'd seen hard times. He was taller than me, maybe six feet, like Gramps. I could see the muscles of his chest beneath his Blue Whale T-shirt. "Oh, you must be the *new* man." I put out my hand. "I'm Dae O'Donnell, mayor of Duck. I'd heard the inn had a new owner."

I wondered for just a breath if he was going to take my hand. Gramps was right. He wasn't from anywhere around Duck.

Then he put his hand in mine. "Sorry. Force of habit, I guess. It's hard to get over all of you people being so friendly down here. Where I come from, we don't shake hands unless we know we'll get our fingers back. Kevin Brickman."

Despite the tough expression, he had a nice face. Plenty of smile lines around his eyes. Maybe the slightest hint of sadness there too. "Where are you from?"

"I've lived in Washington, D.C., for the past few years. It's very different there."

"And what brings you to Duck?"

"I was looking for a career change. I saw the inn for sale in the paper. It sounded like the right place for me."

"You must be a do-it-yourselfer to take on the inn," I joked. "I think it was originally built by pirates in the 1600s and has never been restored."

"I like a challenge."

I bent down to pick up my cell phone. He was already there. "No damage done." He put it back together. "The battery popped out. Were you about to call the police? I thought about it this morning when I saw she still wasn't back. But I don't really know anyone well enough to know their habits."

I thanked him and took the phone. "Miss Elizabeth seems

to have gone missing. She likes to go for long walks, and she's a little forgetful about how long she's been gone. I'm sure she stopped off at a friend's house or something. But I think I'll call Chief Michaels. He's the head of the Duck Police Department. He'll find her."

"I was surprised to find out Duck had its own police department. How many officers on the force?"

"Five officers this year. Well, one of them is part-time. But as you can imagine, we don't get a lot of serious crime in Duck. Most of our problems happen over the summer when the renters are here. The rest of the time it's quiet. We like it that way."

"Me too. That's one of Duck's most attractive features. I like my privacy."

He smiled a little, and I could feel his eyes assessing me again. Not in a sexual way, like a lot of men might, but in a questioning manner, as though he were wondering who I *really* was. It occurred to me that if Gramps had met him he'd probably told him all about me, including what a marital catch I'd be. He was probably wondering what kind of woman lets her grandfather look for eligible bachelors for her.

"Well, if you'll excuse me, Mr. Brickman—"

"Kevin. It was nice meeting you, Mayor O'Donnell. I hope you find Miss Elizabeth before the storm."

"I'm sure we will." I glanced at the old hulk of the Blue Whale Inn next door. Only a hint of the slate blue color that gave the inn its name remained on the clapboard. "Call me Dae, please. Everyone does. Good luck renovating the inn."

With a mixture of interest and surprise, I watched him walk away from Miss Elizabeth's house and back toward the inn. There weren't a lot of good-looking, youngish (not high school or college students) single men who lived full-time in Duck. It was going to be fun to watch what happened once the ladies in the community met him.

I called Chief Michaels and asked him to meet me at the house. Then I sat on the wrought-iron patio chair to wait. It wasn't long before I saw Kevin climbing up on the inn's roof. He had a bundle of black shingles thrown over one shoulder and a hammer in a holster at his side. He turned around once he was up there and saluted in my general direction. I waved. That's what mayors are supposed to do.

The pretty blue sky that had made the Fourth of July parade so spectacular was being chased away by angry black clouds coming in from the south. The ocean responded with more whitecaps and thunderous surf. Mary Lou might be right about those sea turtle eggs. I realized that was the next thing on my list. Who knew being mayor would be so crazy?

I'd kind of fallen into it on a dare from Gramps. He'd been the sheriff of Dare County for twenty years before retiring fifteen years ago. He was a big believer in community service and asked what I'd done for my hometown since becoming an adult. Sometimes you have to be careful how you respond to people who want the best for you.

Fortunately, running Missing Pieces wasn't really a full-time job and Gramps filled in for me when I needed him. Being mayor was only a sometimes kind of job too, so they meshed together nicely.

Chief Ronnie Michaels came huffing around the corner of Miss Elizabeth's house. He always reminded me of the Marine sergeant on the Gomer Pyle sitcom. His uniform was immaculate, creases exactly where they needed to be. His patent leather shoes never had a scuff mark.

Officer Tim Mabry was at his heels, as always. Tim had

told me lots of times that he planned to become the next police chief when Chief Michaels, who was seventy like Gramps, retired. He was building a house on Duck Landing Road after inheriting a small patch of land his grandfather had left him. I knew all of this because he told me every time he proposed to me. Last week had made the sixth occasion this year.

"Mayor." The chief nodded at me, then turned narrowed eyes on the house. "You say Miss Elizabeth is missing?"

"I don't really know." I told him what Miss Mildred had said and threw in what Kevin Brickman had told me for good measure. "Mr. Brickman was here for a few minutes. He was concerned about Miss Elizabeth too."

"Are you saying you think he could be involved with this?" Tim lifted his police cap and let the breeze cool his sweaty blond head.

"No, Tim. I was saying he'd noticed she was gone and he isn't from here. Maybe that's odd. I don't know."

The chief laughed. "Yes, ma'am. It's real odd for people in Duck to know what everyone else is doing. No one *ever* knows what's going on around here."

I agreed, thinking he hadn't needed the sarcasm.

"But maybe if the mayor thinks something is up with that boy, we should check him out." Tim rushed in to defend me.

"No need. He came by when he moved in. Believe me, he's not involved in anything with Miss Elizabeth," the chief assured him. "But he'd be the kind to notice things, if you know what I mean."

"I don't," I admitted. "But if you think it's fine—"

"Not just fine, Your Honor," the chief continued. "I can't divulge everything Mr. Brickman confided in me on his move here to Duck. Suffice it to say, he's the kind of citizen we want to have here. We'll leave it at that."

Chief Michaels rarely spoke highly of anyone not born and raised in Duck, so his good word was enough for me. I'd known him all my life. He and Gramps had been friends since high school. I trusted the chief completely, and if the chief trusted Kevin Brickman, then regardless of the secret circumstances, Kevin Brickman was okay. I glanced back up at the Blue Whale Inn's roof. Kevin was nowhere to be seen, but I could hear his hammer.

"Anyway, as you can see," I continued, "we may have a situation here with Miss Elizabeth. I think we should search her house, and if we can't find her, we might have to issue a Silver Alert."

The chief scratched his head. "Silver Alert? I'm not sure I'm familiar with that term."

"It's what they call it when an older person is missing," I explained. "Like the Amber Alert when a child is missing."

"No need to panic, Mayor. We'll find her." The chief looked back at the increasingly angry horizon, where bright streaks of lightning were stabbing at the sky. "I suggest we do it before this weather hits too. Looks like a nasty one brewing."

Tim came over to hold my hand. "Don't worry, Dae. We'll find her."

I don't have anything against Tim. We went to school together and even kissed a few times back then. But I don't have *those* kinds of feelings for him either. Each time he's proposed I've told him as much. I don't think he was listening.

I smiled as I took my hand back. "I'm not worried. I'm sure everything will be fine."

* * *

But two hours later, things were far from fine. The storm was sweeping the town streets with rain and sand. A long line of visitors was snaking away from Duck to safer and higher ground. They represented at least a third of all the business we'd see that year. And Miss Elizabeth was still missing.

I put on a poncho and rain boots and locked up Missing Pieces. Gramps had gone to the fire station to help since he was a volunteer. I pulled the wood shutters closed over the windows to try to protect what I could. Even though the shop faces the Currituck Sound side of Duck rather than the ocean, there could still be damage. Everyone was meeting at town hall a few doors down on the boardwalk to coordinate efforts toward the storm and the search for Miss Elizabeth.

"It was going so well," Shayla Lily said on a sigh as she met me outside on the boardwalk. "I'd already done two tarot spreads and a couple of palm readings. They were lining up at the door."

Shayla ran Mrs. Roberts, Spiritual Advisor. Her business was located next door to Missing Pieces on the Duck Shoppes' boardwalk. She hadn't bothered changing the name of the popular tarot-card and palm-reading shop when she'd bought it from Mary Catherine Roberts last year. Shayla was an interesting person, with her slinky black clothes and sultry New Orleans attitude.

"I think everyone feels your pain. I guess we'll have to make it up this fall at the Harvest Festival."

"What about the fireworks?"

"I think they must be canceled."

"You're the mayor. Can't you do something about it?"

"I don't think I have that kind of power. We'll have to save the fireworks for next year."

"Or the Harvest Festival?" she asked with a brilliant smile.

"Maybe. I have to go. I'm looking for—"

"Miss Elizabeth. I know."

"Did you find that out using the tarot?"

"No. Someone came by and told me she was missing. It doesn't take a psychic to find out what's going on around here, Dae. Like that new man up at the Blue Whale Inn. I keep hoping he'll stop in and want me to read his palm."

"I don't think that's likely to happen. He doesn't seem the type."

"You met him already? What type does he seem?" She looked at me suspiciously, her finely drawn brows knitting together in her cocoa-colored face. "Have you been flirting over the UPS packages again? If I'd known what a babe magnet they'd be, I'd have taken them in *my* store."

The rain came down heavier, and I pulled my poncho hood down low over my face. I told Shayla we'd have to talk later. Miss Elizabeth might be out in the storm.

I kept seeing the image of Miss Mildred's watch in my mind. I wished those images came with better detail. Usually, the things I found were easy to locate. They were behind an oak bookcase or under a mirrored coffee table. The hardest-to-find item I'd ever looked for was some lose change Andy Martin—owner of Andy's Ice Cream—had somehow unwittingly dropped into a tub of his homemade vanilla.

But this was something else. Miss Elizabeth's life could be in danger, and all I could see was her mother's watch on her frail arm. Every time I tried to revisit the image, there was only darkness around it. Did that mean it was night?

Was Miss Elizabeth sitting against something black? I felt helpless and didn't know what to do. Having information that could save her life yet not being able to understand it was worse than useless.

It wasn't the first time my inborn abilities had frustrated me. It would've been nice if I'd been able to *really* see everything instead of bits and pieces. I'd wished for a long time that I'd be able to solve important, world-shattering problems with my psychic gift. But it was more finding missing earrings than helping hungry children. I tried to be grateful for what I had. My mother had taught me that.

By the time I reached town hall, a large group of searchers was there. Chief Michaels was coordinating the effort. He'd called up all of Duck's police force, including our part-time officer.

"We've already searched Miss Elizabeth's house and grounds," the chief explained. "We've searched the downtown area. That leaves the rest of the residential areas and the beaches. Obviously, the beaches are going to be dangerous for a while. All of you better be extra careful out there. We want to find her, but we don't want to lose any of you either."

I looked at the faces of the men and women I knew so well. Cailey Fargo, the fire chief, was there with her men. She'd taught fifth grade when I was in school. Carter Hatley ran Game World, the skeet ball and video game place down at the other end of town. I'd gone to school with his daughter. She married a musician she'd met in Manteo one summer and moved to New York.

My gaze snagged on Kevin Brickman, who was wearing a black poncho, his hood still pulled up on his head. He'd either been staring at me first or caught me looking at him and decided to look back. I couldn't be sure which. He nodded and I nodded back. Shayla was going to be very disappointed when she finally met him. I didn't see him as a tea-leaf, palm-reading kind of person. He reminded me of Chief Michaels in a strange sort of way. Maybe he'd been involved with law enforcement, and that's why they'd bonded so quickly.

"We'll divide up into three teams to search the beaches and the neighborhoods. Remember to keep in constant contact with this office. Mayor O'Donnell will be here taking those calls." The chief looked around at his task force. "Any questions?"

"I don't want to stay here and answer the phone," I complained, surprised he'd thought of it. "I want to help look for Miss Elizabeth."

"That's *not* a question, Your Honor," the chief responded. "We need you here to coordinate everything. Besides, we have to keep our mayor safe."

He sort of smiled and patted me on the head. I felt sure that if he'd had a lollipop, he'd have given it to me. The group started breaking up and heading for the door as though it were all decided. With Chief Michaels leading the pack, I had no one to complain to about it.

"Think you can handle the excitement?" Kevin asked.

"I didn't mean it would be less exciting. I want to do something more than answering the phone."

"You're the mayor." He shrugged. "Delegate."

He was right, of course. I saw Nancy Boidyn, our town clerk, at her computer. She looked up with terror written on her pretty features. We'd spoken before about her dislike of storms. Many times I'd wondered why she lived on the coast where we were famous for our violent weather.

"Nancy, would you mind staying here and answering the phone?"

"I'd love to, Dae. Thanks."

I'd already taken a breath to qualify why I thought she should stay, but it wasn't necessary. She grabbed on to the life preserver of coordinating the search and clung with both hands. "Great! Thanks. I'm going out to look for Miss Elizabeth."

"What will I tell the chief if he asks where you are?"

"Tell him I needed some fresh air. I'll call if I find anything."

I walked out of town hall feeling guilty for not doing what was expected of me. But I felt even more responsible for trying to find Miss Elizabeth, despite the chief seeming to think I wasn't up to the task. Just because I was mayor didn't mean I couldn't do the important things. Two of the men who'd gone out to search were on the town council. No one had tried to stop them.

The wind was gusting hard, blowing sheets of rain down the street. The sky had turned so dark it looked more like midnight than midafternoon. I turned to go toward the new housing development, a short walk from Miss Elizabeth's house, and almost walked into Kevin. He seemed to be waiting for me.

"Where are you going to look first?"

"Why? Are you afraid I can't take care of myself too?"

"No. Remember me? I'm the one who suggested your little rebellion."

"Why are you here then?"

"You know your way around. You were the first to report that Miss Elizabeth was gone. I thought you might be the one to find her."

His idea had some merit. "I thought I'd try looking

around those new houses being built close to where you live. Maybe the storm came up, and she ducked inside one of those for shelter."

"Sounds like a plan."

I didn't have time to question why he'd chosen to go with me instead of the groups of officers. I focused on finding Miss Elizabeth and tried not to think about him walking alongside me. The fact that I had to *try* to ignore him made me even more aware of him.

Once we got past the protected area between the businesses and the houses that made up downtown, the wind was stronger and louder. It battered us with gale force, making talking impossible. I hated to think of frail Miss Elizabeth out in this storm. I hoped she was somewhere with a friend the chief had missed in his initial search. The sisters didn't have any relatives that I knew of. Neither of them had children.

I glanced over the dunes covered with various plants and prickly shrubs. Mary Lou Harcourt's little group was down by the turtle nesting area. The tide was rushing in with a fierce vengeance to reach the shore. Already the water was crashing close to where the turtle eggs were hidden in the sand.

Mary Lou waved to me, the relieved smile on her face telling me she thought we'd come to help her save the eggs. With the wind and the surf banging between us, there was no way to make myself understood. I yelled, but she kept beckoning to me. I couldn't walk off without telling her why I couldn't help.

"I have to go down there." Kevin leaned closer to hear what I'd said, and I yelled it again. "I have to tell her about Miss Elizabeth."

I could see by the look on his face that he didn't under-

stand. I tried yelling again and this time, he yelled back.
"Why?"

"I can't just walk away. I have to explain."

He shrugged and followed me down the well-worn path
between the sea oats. The town had planted them there
years ago to prevent beach erosion. The huge plants
whipped at us in the wind. I could see the sand shifting
from the rough water. Each year the town had to work to
keep Duck's shoreline intact. It was a never-ending task.
Someday, people said, Duck would be gone, lost under the
gray Atlantic and Currituck Sound. But not on my watch.

Mary Lou had two other older ladies with her. I thought
they were members of the Ladies' Sewing Circle who made
the quilts that were auctioned off at Christmas. They were
all throwing themselves across the area where the turtles
had laid their eggs in the moonlight a month past.

"Thank goodness you're here!" Mary Lou hugged me.
She was soaked despite her poncho and vinyl pants. "We
can't protect them. The sea is going to wash them away."

"We can't stay," I told her. "I'm sorry, but we're looking
for Miss Elizabeth. You haven't seen her, have you?"

"No, I haven't. But the eggs . . ."

"Everyone is out searching for her." I felt bad about having to desert Mary Lou. I wanted to help the turtles too, but
Miss Elizabeth needed my help more. "We'll come back if
we find her."

I could see she wasn't happy with my decision, but it
was the only thing to do. I smiled again and turned to walk
back up the path the way we'd come. Kevin had moved to
the right of me, and I took a step forward. The rain and
wind had shifted the usually solid sand into a gooey mess
that caught at my foot and tugged hard.

I pitched forward, face-first, into the sea oats. A few of the sharp leaves scratched my cheek and chin. I guess I must've closed my eyes as I fell because when I opened them, it wasn't sea oats that I saw. It was Miss Elizabeth's fragile wrist, with her mother's watch on it, half buried in the sand.

Chapter 3

I scrambled out of the sand and sea oats, breathing hard. I didn't need my psychic sense or the police to tell me that Miss Elizabeth was dead. I looked around at Mary Lou and her friends trying to save the turtle eggs from the incoming surf, which was already lapping at my feet. If the tide rose much higher, it would wash Miss Elizabeth's body out to sea. I had to stop that from happening.

I glanced at Kevin. He was trying to help me up. How would he react if I asked him to help me move the body? I had no doubt Mary Lou and the turtle savers would lose it if I asked for their help. I was going to have to take my chances with Kevin. Maybe if he had some kind of police training, as I'd considered earlier, he'd be okay.

"I need your help," I yelled at him against the mind-numbing crash of the waves and shriek of the wind.

"What?" he yelled back at me.

I moved closer to him and cupped my hands. "I found Miss Elizabeth. I need your help to move her."

I could tell by the expression on his lean face that he understood me that time. I tried to smile encouragingly, tried to stay calm. I was a public official, after all. People expected it of me. Inside, my heart was jumping up and down while a terrible pain squeezed my chest. I was already crying. It was hard not to panic and run screaming up the hill back to town.

He leaned closer, gray eyes serious. "Where is she?"

I pointed to the sea oats. "I saw her when I fell. I'm afraid the water will take her if we don't do something. I don't want to think what would happen if I tell the others."

"Show me where."

We both got down on our knees and I looked around in the sea oats again until I found her wrist. Her arm was sticking out of the sand, but the rest of her was nowhere to be seen. *Someone buried her here*. There could be no doubt of it. If it hadn't been for the storm pushing at the sand that made up the dunes, we might never have found her.

I put my head down and prayed for the strength I needed. I looked at Kevin's face, very near my own. He was focused on the body. He looked calm, not squeamish or ready to panic.

"You're right," he acknowledged. "We have to get her out of here. The crime scene is damaged beyond repair anyway. It'll be better than losing the body."

Of all the things he might've said, *that* wasn't what I'd expected to hear. It cemented my position on his law-enforcement training. "We have to put her in something. We can't take her out of here like this."

"I don't know if we have time." He'd already started using his hands to move the sand away from the rest of Miss

Elizabeth's body. I could see she was wearing her favorite black dress with the little pink embroidered hearts on it.

The reality of it hit me like a rock. First the pink rhinestone heart pin I'd found, half buried in the sand on the other side of the island. Now, this. *This is what I saw when I tried to help Miss Mildred find her watch.* I'd seen the watch on her sister's arm with the black dress behind it. I felt lightheaded and nauseated. The very idea that I'd found a watch on a dead woman's arm was unbearable.

"Are you all right?" Kevin looked intently into my face. He'd stopped moving the sand and put his hand on my arm. "Take a deep breath. You look like you're going to faint. Put your head down."

And I'd been worried about *him*! I put my head down and took a deep breath. There wasn't time for me to panic. Everything else had to wait until we could move Miss Elizabeth. The water was still rising toward the dunes. "We should call someone. This is too much for us to do alone."

"Look at the water. There's no time." He began throwing the sand away from the body, revealing more of her dress and legs.

I caught a glimpse of one of the Fourth of July banners being blown by the wind. "Let me grab that sign. We can wrap her in it."

I ran up the path, which by now was mostly underwater. Mary Lou and her friends had their arms full of turtle eggs and were trying to get off the beach. It was just as well they were leaving. I didn't know if the banner would cover all of Miss Elizabeth or not.

I pushed against the wind and took out my cell phone. But there was no service. Why was it that there was never service when you *really* needed it? I continued across the parking lot where visitors could find free beach access, chasing the red, white and blue banner. I finally grabbed it with both hands and then fell on it so it couldn't blow away again. Still struggling against the wind, I scrunched the banner into a ball and hurried back to where I'd left Kevin.

But he was already coming out of the sea oats with Miss Elizabeth in his arms. Her poor, dead face had a look of terror on it that I'd hoped never to see outside a movie theater. There was a large red gash in her forehead. *Is that what killed her?* Who could do such a terrible thing?

"Put her down," I screamed at Kevin. "We have to wrap her in this. I don't want everyone to see her this way."

"We have to get away from the beach," he yelled back. "Bring the banner. We'll do it over here in the parking lot."

I'd never been hysterical, but I could feel a torrent of wild emotions flooding through me, like the ocean flooding the beach. I wanted to scream and rip at my hair. My hands shook as I fought to maintain my self-control. *Hold on for Miss Elizabeth's sake*. I'd have to fall apart later. It couldn't be right now.

I put the banner down in the parking lot and tried to hold it in place long enough for Kevin to lay Miss Elizabeth on it. It was an almost impossible task as the wind kept threatening to rip it from my hands.

He finally put her wet, sandy body down. The banner would barely cover her face this way. I looked at him, not knowing what to do next. I'd run out of ideas.

He stripped off his poncho and tenderly laid it over Miss Elizabeth's face. If I hadn't already been sobbing at the time, I would have broken down at that gesture of human understanding. I wanted to say thank you, but there wasn't

time. The water was coming up fast toward the parking
lot. My gratitude would have to wait, along with all of my
questions.

He stooped down and lifted Miss Elizabeth again. The
rain was coming down so hard we could barely see as we
crossed the street. Water was ankle deep on the blacktop
and was punctuated by floating debris that was washing
away with the storm.

I kept glancing at Miss Elizabeth's arm sticking out from
under the poncho and the banner. It was her watch arm, a
dread reminder of what I'd seen from her sister. I couldn't
think about what that meant right now. Instead, I focused on
pushing myself forward as Kevin and I slogged through the
water. Finally, we reached Duck Road. We crossed the
empty street and walked up the ramp to town hall. Every
shop, every home, was shuttered against the storm. *At least
no one would see her this way.*

I kicked open the door when we reached the office. Despite the overhang that protected the shops, rain propelled
us inside, out of the storm. Nancy got up from her desk,
took one look at Kevin and sat back down. She didn't say
anything, just stared at the terrible burden he held.

He dropped to his knees and put Miss Elizabeth on the
green and white tile floor we'd had installed last year. I
could see he was exhausted. In normal conditions, it was a
short walk from the ocean-side beach to the sound. These
conditions had been anything but normal or easy.

"There's no phone service—at least I don't have any," I
told him. "I tried to call Chief Michaels from my cell. We
need to get the medical examiner out here. Maybe the State
Bureau of Investigation too. I can't even remember the last
time someone was killed here."

"I have the radio," Nancy said. "I could call the chief."

Kevin and I both looked at her. She hadn't moved from her place at the computer. "It would be good for you to call the chief," he replied.

"All right." She blinked a few times before pressing the button on the radio. "What should I tell him?"

"Tell him to come back to town hall," I said. "Tell everyone else to go home. We don't need the whole town here for this. Try to call the medical examiner and the sheriff too."

"She hasn't been dead long." Kevin wiped sand and saltwater from his face. "She was wearing this dress when I saw her leave Tuesday morning."

"You have some experience with this kind of thing, don't you?"

The pain I'd seen earlier in his eyes intensified. "Yeah. Too much experience."

He didn't seem like he wanted to say anything else about it. I didn't want to push him. "Thanks for your help. I'm glad you were there with me." I didn't even try to stop the tears from coursing down my cheeks. I was a wreck, covered with sand and salt, my hair plastered to my head and eyes red from crying. "I couldn't have done it without you."

His eyes narrowed on my face. "You *knew* it was her."

"I did. I was looking for the watch." I nodded toward her arm. "It really belongs to her sister. I was helping her find it."

I couldn't explain it any better at the moment. I didn't have time, as it turned out. Chief Michaels and his officers swept through the door. He was followed by the Dare County sheriff and an EMS team. I didn't want to be there to see anything they might do to Miss Elizabeth, but I couldn't quite follow Nancy's lead and run out of the office.

"I think I noticed the coffee shop was still open when we walked past," Kevin said. "I don't know about you, but I could use something hot to drink."

It was a lifeline and I took it. I felt guilty doing so, as though as the mayor, maybe I should stay where I was, with the chief and the EMTs, but I convinced myself that I would only be in the way. I'd done as much as I could to help Miss Elizabeth. At least for now.

By the time Kevin and I left town hall, the storm had abated somewhat, as storms always do. They come up fast and change everything, then the sun shines and people try to figure out what to do next.

I soon found myself sitting across from a man I barely knew, drinking a hot mocha with shaking hands while I dripped all over the floor. I waved at Phil, the owner of the Coffee House and Bookstore. I couldn't summon a return smile even though that's what the mayor is *supposed* to do.

"You've never found a dead body before," Kevin guessed.

He knows about me. Gramps must have told him. "No. I find lost *things*, not *people*. I'm sure it was the watch. It led me to her."

"That could be a valuable service to anyone in law enforcement." He sipped his double-shot latte. "Have you ever done that kind of work?"

"*No!* I do what I can for friends and neighbors when they lose their car keys or their rings. I don't hire out, if that's what you mean."

He nodded. "Sorry. I was wondering. Your grandfather mentioned it when I met him. I'm missing a key for a room upstairs at the inn. He said you might be able to find it."

"That explains it."

"Explains what?"

"Why you were looking at me so funny when we met. Why you waited for me to look for Miss Elizabeth."

"I suppose so. You seemed like the most likely person to find her since you find lost things. I'm sorry it happened that way."

"At least we found her." I dared a glance at him. "What do you think happened to her?"

"I'm not sure."

"I guess it's my turn. Chief Michaels spoke very highly of you, but you aren't from Duck. You didn't freak out when we found Miss Elizabeth. Were you a police officer in D.C.?"

"FBI. For twelve years. I think someone hit her in the head with an edged weapon, maybe a shovel. Then they buried her. It might've been a perfect crime except that someone asked you to find that watch."

I took a deep breath, fighting back a sudden wave of nausea. "I'm glad this doesn't usually happen to me. I like finding things for people, but I'd have to give it up if the things I found came attached to dead people all the time. Is that why you gave up the FBI? Too much death?"

I could tell I'd crossed an invisible line. His face became shuttered, and he sat back in his chair, engrossed in drinking his coffee. It was one of those too-early-in-the-friendship kind of things. He obviously wasn't ready to talk about it yet.

"Anyway," I continued when he didn't respond, "I'd be glad to help you find the key you're looking for. I only have a couple of rules I work with."

"Such as?"

"What I'm looking for has to belong to the person who

asks me to look for it. You wouldn't *believe* how many people have asked me to look for things that don't belong to them."

"That doesn't surprise me." He smiled a little and put his coffee cup on the table again. "And the other rule?"

"It's not illegal. In high school, a friend of mine asked me to find his lost marijuana stash. I made up that rule for him."

"Another wise rule." Kevin defrosted a little more. "How does it work? Is it like a séance or something?"

"Nothing like that. It's really very simple." I was about to explain that we could do it sitting right there in the coffee shop when Chief Michaels came in and told me he needed my help.

The chief nodded to Kevin and then spoke to me. "I'd like you to come with me when I talk to Millie. You seem to get along real well with her. I think she'd like to have you there representing the town and all."

"Of course."

"Maybe we can look for the key when you're not so busy." Kevin got up from his chair and handed me a business card. "Just give me a call. Let me know if there's anything I can do, Chief."

I wanted to be with Miss Mildred when Chief Michaels told her about her sister. I really did. But I almost chickened out when I went home to change out of my dirty, wet clothes. It would be so easy to stay here. I took a look at myself in the mirror, though, and knew I couldn't back out. My pink T-shirt had the Duck emblem on it, a big yellow duck holding a sailboat. I had to go for the town and the sisters.

The chief and I drove in silence over the drenched, sand-covered road to Miss Mildred's home. Her house was every bit as large and interesting as her sister's home, but there were dozens of tinkling fountains here. Both women had done all right for themselves, mostly through marriage. I didn't want to speculate on how Wild Johnny Simpson had made his money. No one did. Now, despite their wealth and standing in the community, one of them was alone.

The chief nodded to me (I think sort of asking if I was ready), then knocked on the door. Miss Mildred greeted us with a sweet smile. "I hope you've come to tell me the power will be back on soon. You know, Dae, this doesn't look very good for you as mayor. That wasn't even much of a storm and already my lights have been out for hours."

"I'm sorry." I couldn't meet her eyes. "I'll try to light a fire under the power company."

"I think we should sit down, Millie." Chief Michaels took her arm and helped her to a chair with a crochet-covered back.

"Why?" She stared at him as though she *knew*, her lower lip already trembling.

"The mayor found your sister a little while ago," he explained.

"Oh good! May I have Mama's watch back now?"

It was too hard. I'd known these women all my life. Tears were sliding down my cheeks. I hiccupped on a sob, and she stared at me. "You haven't lost the watch, have you, Dae?"

I was about to blurt out the whole thing when the chief put his hand on Miss Mildred's shoulder. "Your sister is dead, Millie. We think she might be the victim of foul play. Let's call someone from the church to come over."

She glanced back and forth between us, a slow frown puckering her forehead. "What are you saying, Ronnie? Did you find Mama's watch or not?"

I tried to keep my voice from cracking, but it didn't work. "It was where I saw it. Miss Elizabeth had it on her arm. I don't know if the water damaged it or not."

She nodded, smiling again. "Maybe you could have Barney over at the jewelry store take a look at it before you bring it back. I *knew* I could count on you, Dae. You've always had the gift."

The chief and I glanced at each other again. Neither one of us seemed to know what else to say. He told Miss Mildred to have a nice day and awkwardly patted her shoulder. She smiled at us, and we left her rocking in her chair. Using her kitchen phone, I called the deacon at her church and explained what had happened. He arrived at the house less than ten minutes later.

"I didn't like the way she sounded," the chief said as we walked out to his car.

"It'll sink in on her," I assured him.

"I hope so. She scared me. I don't mind admitting it. I'd hate to see her taken out of her home. She might not be able to live alone anymore after this. I've seen it happen with folks her age."

We climbed into the car and headed back to my house, weaving around fallen tree branches and patio furniture that had been swept into the street by the storm. I looked out the side window at the ocean. There were still some whitecaps, but the surf was mostly calm and the tide level was back where it belonged. "She knows what we were saying. She's not crazy or senile. She couldn't take it all in, but she'll be fine."

"In the meantime, we've had a murder." He shook his

head. "Those SBI boys are gonna come down here and tear up our community."

"If they find out who killed Miss Elizabeth, I guess it'll be worth it."

The storm had caused substantial damage up and down the Outer Banks. Duck was hard hit, but we'd seen worse. As soon as it passed, everyone was out cleaning up the mess and putting the town back together. It was a way of life for us. This coast wasn't called the Cape of Storms for nothing.

I was lucky there was no real damage to Missing Pieces. Rain had come in through a broken window in the back storage room, but the water hadn't reached anything of value. Gramps and I used a wet-dry vac and a mop to clean it up. The power came on shortly after we'd left Miss Mildred's house. I was glad she had that much anyway.

Everyone was devastated by the news of Miss Elizabeth's death. After the weekend, I sat in the town hall listening to people talk about it as they waited for the town meeting to begin. It had been the topic of conversation on everyone's lips for the past two days. No one could believe anyone in Duck would hurt Miss Elizabeth. But there were always outsiders here. The same tourists who provided so much of our livelihood came from across the world. There was no way of knowing anything about them.

"I heard she was robbed and raped," Althea from the library in Manteo whispered loudly to Trudy. "She didn't have her purse on her. No one's found it either."

I didn't tell her that Chief Michaels said it didn't look like robbery at all. Whoever attacked Miss Elizabeth had left her mother's expensive watch on her arm when he or she had buried her. That wasn't like a robbery. It was true they hadn't found her purse. But the ocean could've taken that away before we got there.

"Did you hear anything about Miss Elizabeth being raped?" Trudy asked me after Althea had moved on to have the same conversation with Mary Lou on the other side of the town meeting room.

"No. I haven't heard anything other than what Chief Michaels announced two days ago. I think he's waiting for the medical examiner's report before he releases any more information. Althea's only speculating—she doesn't know anything for sure." As I spoke, I kept one eye on the rapidly growing group entering town hall for our monthly meeting. This large of a crowd was unusual. Normally only a handful of residents showed up. No doubt it was a sign of how worried everyone was about what had happened to Miss Elizabeth. With no real answers, the whole town was on edge.

I was on edge too, worried about who'd do such a terrible thing, of course, but also heartsick because I was the one who'd found her buried in the sand. My gift led me to her. The idea of that frightened me.

Since the storm, I'd spent some time sitting alone in the dark, wondering whether this was the start of something far worse than being a finder of lost things. I didn't want to find dead bodies. I hoped never to see another corpse outside of a funeral home.

There was no one I could talk to about it. According to my mother, my grandmother had been able to find things when she was young, but she had died before I was born. Though my mother had never had the gift, she'd understood it, and her unique perspective had helped me as I grew. But she was gone too—thirteen years this past April. It was only Gramps and me.

I *knew* Gramps understood about finding things, but I was having a hard time working up to explaining exactly what had happened at the beach during the storm. I'd hoped to make peace with it in my own mind before talking to him. I didn't want to burden him with the information. He'd been there for me through some terrible dark places. I was old enough now to figure this out for myself.

Chapter 4

The other members of the Duck Town Council were all in place around the big, U-shaped table before I sat down. There weren't enough chairs to accommodate the crowd of people who'd gathered for the meeting, so many were standing at the back of the room. One of them was Kevin. I waved to him through the crowd. He didn't wave back, but he nodded and smiled.

I took the gavel that had been donated by the League of Women Voters and brought the room to order. Everyone quieted for the Pledge of Allegiance and the reading of last month's minutes. Then we came to the public forum part of the agenda where citizens were allowed to speak.

"What are we doing about finding Miss Elizabeth's killer?" Mark Samson, owner of the Rib Shack, called out.

The room erupted with loud chatter. I banged my gavel, but no one paid any attention. The whole town seemed to be talking at the same time, demanding answers I knew the chief didn't have. The other council members looked worried and kept sneaking furtive glances toward the door, as though they wanted to leave. Nancy calmly typed all of it into her laptop.

"Someone is out there stalking people in Duck," yelled out Carter Hatley, owner of Game World. "What are we going to do about it?"

I got to my feet. If the gavel wasn't going to do any good, maybe yelling back would. "The chief is doing everything he can," I explained loudly. "The SBI is here investigating. I know you all are upset. I understand your anger and frustration. But coming in here and disrupting the town meeting won't help."

I noticed as I spoke that a few strangers with TV cameras were sneaking into the back of the meeting room. I guessed I'd see myself on TV later that night.

"Mayor, this is bad for business," Carter yelled back. "We need an answer *now*. We can't afford to wait."

"*You* can't afford to wait? Mr. Hatley, with all due respect, you didn't lose a loved one. How do you think Miss Mildred feels about now? She's been wronged more than anyone in this room. You're worried about *business?* She lost her only sister. I think you should sit down and think about that."

I wasn't sure my reprimand would work, but Carter finally nodded and sat back down. No one could've been more surprised than me. The rest of the group followed his lead, and the meeting progressed as it should after that. The council cut the proceedings short, recessing until the following week when we all hoped things would be calmer. The only business we conducted was to approve sending Miss Mildred a condolence card and flowers for the funeral.

Afterward, people stood around talking, debating whether everything that could be done was being done. Chief Michaels brooded over it for a few minutes before gruffly thanking me and leaving the building.

"You did a good job," Tim Mabry said as he approached me with a big grin plastered on his face. He took out his nightstick and patted the palm of his hand with it. "We could've handled it. There was no reason to worry."

"I don't think two police officers launching themselves on a group of townspeople in front of TV cameras is such a great idea. It's best this way." I gathered my papers and folder together. There was no reason to hang around.

"I'd be glad to walk you home if you're scared," he said.

"I'm not. But thanks. I'll see you later." I smiled as I made my retreat. A group of people were holding a candle-light vigil in Duck Municipal Park. I couldn't avoid the town meeting since it was part of my job, but now that it was over, I wanted to head down that way. Maybe going through the grief process with the group would be good for me.

"Mayor O'Donnell!" Jerry Richards called out. "Remember me? From the interview after the Fourth of July parade?"

"Of course." I shook his hand, not looking at the TV camera over his shoulder but aware of it.

"The death of Elizabeth Simpson, of course. It's such a tragedy. I thought we might talk about it."

"I don't think so. Excuse me, Jerry."

"But, Mayor—"

I didn't answer and didn't turn back. Talking about what had happened on TV wasn't my idea of helping anyone. I hoped he wouldn't follow me. Luckily, I managed to avoid the second TV crew outside. I checked my watch. It was slightly after eight P.M. The vigil had already begun. I had a white, gardenia-scented candle in my purse from Shayla's shop. It was supposed to help with grief and give peace to Miss Elizabeth's soul.

I'd barely stepped off the boardwalk outside of town hall when someone came up beside me. I turned to face the person, ready to fend off another reporter, and was surprised to see Kevin there instead. "I hope you don't have any questions."

"Not me. I saw you inspecting that candle in your purse before the meeting. I thought you were probably headed for the vigil."

"Is there anything you *don't* see?" I slowed my pace. Silly, actually, since he could've probably kept up without any problem. "What brought you to the council meeting? I've never seen you here before."

"I've been meaning to come, but I've been busy. You did quite a number up there with that gavel."

"A good mayor has to know when to be firm. I know everyone is upset about Miss Elizabeth, but we still have to conduct the town's business."

"And how are you holding up, Dae?"

"I'm doing as well as I can given the circumstances." I didn't want to mention my fears about finding more dead bodies. "I'm not afraid to be out on the streets. Just because one bad thing has happened doesn't mean the whole town is bad."

"That's true."

We walked along Duck Road in companionable silence as cars crept by us, caught in summer traffic on the two-lane road. Kevin wasn't a nervous, chattering kind of person like Tim. I was grateful for that.

"I guess everyone in Duck knows that you find things," he said as we passed Andy's Ice Cream.

"Everyone who lives here full-time anyway. My grandmother found things too. The older folks remember her. People here accept that I find things the same way they accept that I have blue eyes. It's part of who I am."

"You've never been tested for the extent of your psychometric abilities?"

"No. I didn't even know it was called that until we had the Internet." The night was warm but clear, stars twinkling down at us from the dark sky. Pieces of tree branches still littered the street. I made a mental note to get after the town maintenance people. Sand was everywhere, of course. It wasn't easy keeping that where it belonged.

I could hear Reverend Lisa leading the singing in the park. Lisa is a large woman who lives life in a big way. She has a booming, unmistakable voice that could probably carry from one end of Duck to the other. Tonight, it sounded like the angels singing from beneath the trees. The lights in the park glowed softly around the candles held by at least fifty hands.

"We can talk later, maybe when you come by to find my lost key." He nodded toward the group. "I know you miss your friend. I'm sorry for your loss."

"Thanks." Realizing all over again that Miss Elizabeth was gone, I sniffed and wiped my eyes. "I was able to pull the council meeting together, but I'm kind of a mess when I'm not being the mayor." I took out my candle and searched my pocket for the match I must've dropped.

Kevin lit the candle for me with his cigarette lighter. "I used to smoke. I never got over the habit of carrying a lighter."

I thought he'd probably drift away, like sea foam, as I

walked up to the group, but to my surprise, he stayed with me. We found a spot near the edge of the crowd, and I took a moment to glance around. The candlelight illuminated the tears and anger on the faces of the people I'd grown up with.

It was hard dealing with Miss Elizabeth's loss. Maybe it would be easier if there was someone to direct our anger at. But so far, there was no one. I guessed it was too much to expect the guilty party to come forward and turn themselves in. All we could do was wait.

"Our good friend and neighbor, Miss Elizabeth Simpson, would not want to see us standing here feeling bad about her death," Reverend Lisa was saying. "She'd want us to go out and tell people about her and her life here in Duck. She'd want us to carry on. That's what we have to do, folks. We have to put on a smile Miss Elizabeth can see all the way in heaven, because we all know that's where she is."

"We don't know that." Suddenly Miss Mildred's voice filled the silence after Lisa stopped speaking. "Why do we always assume people go to heaven, even bad people like Lizzie?"

"She's overwrought," whispered a woman beside me. "She doesn't know what she's saying."

The group moved aside as Miss Mildred's frail form continued past them until she was standing beside Lisa under the streetlight. It created a halo around her white hair but left her face in darkness. "Lizzie wasn't the good person you all think she was. She took Johnny Simpson from me. She was fast with the judge in the Duck beauty pageant. She took things from me all of my life. She was my sister, but she did evil things. I don't think God wants her in heaven."

Lisa smiled and tried to gloss over Miss Mildred's harsh words. "I'm sure we could all judge the people we love. We know their strengths and their weaknesses, don't we? But in the end, Miss Elizabeth was a good person who didn't deserve to die alone out there on the beach."

The group of mourners agreed with her, and Lisa started singing again, probably hoping she could change the mood and help Miss Mildred out of the awkward situation she'd created.

"She doesn't sound like she loved her sister the way the rest of you did," Kevin commented.

"She's old and she's in shock," I reminded him. "They feuded and fussed like all sisters. But they loved each other."

"You're right. I wish I'd had a sister, but I was an only child. What about you?"

"I'm an only child too. I wish I would've had a sibling when I was growing up. Even a brother would've been okay." I joined the others in singing, putting my whole heart into "Amazing Grace," and smiled as I heard Kevin's baritone beside me. Chief Michaels was right. Kevin might be from somewhere else, but he belonged here in Duck.

I watched as Mary Lou took Miss Mildred's arm and led her back out of the crowd, toward home. Miss Mildred was tearful and seemed confused. She went with Mary Lou, but she wasn't happy about it. The two ladies were swallowed up in the darkness as they left the park, and the group came together again. I was glad Mary Lou had rescued Miss Mildred. I guessed that's what she did best—rescuing. Kind of like how I found things.

The singing ended and was followed by an emotional moment when we were all supposed to blow out our candles at the same time to signify the passing of Miss Elizabeth. But before anyone could exhale, a brisk breeze blew up off of the water behind us and snuffed out the tiny fires. There were murmurs of ghostly visitation as the crowd began to break up. In Duck, there were always rumors of ghostly visitation. It was part of our culture, like pirate folklore.

"That was spooky." Shayla sidled up to me, then looked at the sky. "I feel like she was here, Dae. What do you think?"

"I think breezes come up off the water all the time."

"I can't believe you of *all* people don't find that kind of spooky. I mean, you're psychic and all. You and I can see into that other world that most people miss every day."

"I don't have powers beyond the grave or anything. My ability is like teleportation or telekinesis. It's a science of the mind."

"Whatever," she argued. "You found Miss Elizabeth's body. Her spirit cried out to you. You can't deny that."

"Her *watch* cried out to me. That's it. It had nothing to do with her being dead."

"Dae is right," Kevin chimed in. "There's a lot of exploration into the field of psychometry for security reasons."

I didn't need decent lighting to see Shayla's big brown eyes focus on him. "And *who* are *you?* I think I'd remember if you were Dae's beau."

I introduced him to Shayla. "He's not my boyfriend."

"Hallelujah! You're the new man from the Blue Whale, aren't you? I've been hoping to meet you." Shayla wrapped her arm around his. "You have to buy me a drink after all this grief and spooky stuff. I think Curbside should still be open. You got anything against buying a girl a drink?"

I thought Shayla's considerable powers of seduction and persuasion (part of her stock-in-trade as a palm reader) might be wasted on Kevin, who seemed too worldly and hardened by his time in the FBI. I found myself holding my breath and hoping it would be so. But I was disappointed. He drew her closer and smiled down at her like a sailor on leave for the first time in weeks.

"You two go on ahead," I said right away. "I'm tired and I'm going home. I thought Gramps would be out here, but I don't see him. He might not be feeling good. I better check on him."

"That's good, honey," Shayla said without bothering to look at me. "We'll get on fine without you."

"After we walk her home," Kevin intervened.

Shayla giggled. "*Of course* we should walk her home. Even with Dae's command of the supernatural, she could be in danger with a killer stalking the streets of Duck."

"You *must* be an actress," Kevin said. "You have such a command of the language."

And of course Shayla was too smitten by him to realize that he was subtly insulting her. At least I thought that's what he was doing. I sure wasn't going to tell her, though. She'd wanted to meet him, and she'd practically thrown herself at him. She'd have to take what she got.

"I'll be fine." I started to walk away. "You two go on. I'm not worried about anyone stalking the streets except a stray dog or two."

"I insist." Kevin derailed my best efforts to get away gracefully. "It's the least we can do."

The three of us set off down Duck Road toward my house. We passed several large groups of people walking to the open restaurants and bars. Walking was a common form of transportation here. It was better than waiting in summer traffic.

"Are we one hundred percent sure Miss Elizabeth was

murdered?" Shayla asked as we ambled awkwardly down the road. I say "awkwardly" because it's never synchronous for two people to walk together as a couple and have a third person tag along.

"Someone had to bury her in the sand," Kevin responded.

I looked at one of the hundreds of horse statues that are spread out across the Outer Banks in honor of the wild horses in Corolla. This one was blue with butterflies on it, but there are pink horses with wings and black horses with gold stars. I doubted that the wild horses would recognize any of these statues as kin, but people were trying to do something nice by putting them up.

"All the same," Shayla continued, "maybe it was an accident. We may not be looking for a killer exactly. More someone clumsy or having a bad day."

"A bad day? Whoever did this *killed* Miss Elizabeth and left her buried out there in the dunes. That's more than a bad day." I couldn't believe she'd even consider making excuses for this nameless person.

"Sor-ry." She scooted closer to Kevin, if that was possible. "You were there. What do *you* think?"

"I think the ME will be able to answer all our questions in a few days. Until then, we're just guessing." His voice was level and calming.

I turned my head away from them and instead looked at the lighted businesses on Duck Road. The neon sign from the Rib Shack reflected on something in the street. That familiar slow-motion feeling came over me as I bent down to pick it up. It was no bigger than a quarter and had letters embossed on it. I couldn't read what it said, so I put it in my pocket for later.

The house Gramps and I shared was the first one out of

the business district. The cheerful yellow clapboard and green accents were shadowy, even with the yard lights on, but it was good to be home. I rounded the mailbox with the duck sitting on top and the sign that said "Duck's Landing." I sort of hoped Shayla and Kevin would head back to the Curbside right away. No such luck.

"Nice place," Kevin said, catching up with me. "I wish the Blue Whale was in this kind of shape."

"The Blue Whale is a lot bigger. Once you get it fixed up, I'm sure it'll be worth a lot more than our house."

"Not that Dae's would ever be for sale," Shayla added. "She's home safe, Kevin. Let's head back before the bar gets too crowded."

But we'd already reached the path between the bushes that led to the front door. Gramps must've been watching because he opened it as soon as he saw us. "There you are! I've been worried about you, Dae. That's why they make cell phones, you know. You could give an old man a call."

I apologized for making him worry. "I have Kevin Brickman and Shayla with me, Gramps."

"Of course!" He shook hands with Kevin. "How are you, Mr. Brickman? How did those pictures turn out?"

"Just fine, thanks. I think I got a good feel for the land looking at it from out there."

I'd forgotten our conversation at Missing Pieces. Hopefully, Gramps would too and not try to do any matchmaking. Although Shayla wasn't holding Kevin's arm anymore, she was practically standing on his shadow. She was definitely doing some matchmaking of her own.

"I just finished making dinner," Gramps said. "You'll stay, won't you? There's plenty. Dae eats like a bird, and I can only pack away so much now that I'm older. When I was younger, I could eat a whole swordfish by myself! But those days are past me now."

I could see the uncomfortable, disappointed look on Shayla's face as Kevin took Gramps up on his offer and the two of them went into the kitchen. "What's wrong with men anyway?" she whispered. "Why don't they ever know when to leave a thing alone?"

"I can't believe you think Kevin is *that* interesting."

She smiled, catlike. "I can't believe you *don't*."

During our dinner of fried rice, cornbread and garden tomatoes, the conversation turned to Miss Elizabeth's death, as had all conversations over the last few days. We sat around the scrubbed wood table and tried to imagine what had happened.

"I think she was robbed," Gramps said. "She was an old busybody, that's for sure. And she loved to go out walking. How many times did someone have to end up taking her home? But she always had her purse with her. She wouldn't leave without it. No one can find it now."

"It could've gotten lost in the sand," Shayla added, playing with her food. No doubt wishing she was at a dark table at the Curbside with Kevin. "There *was* a storm, you know. Maybe it was swept out to sea."

"Or you could be right." Kevin glanced at Gramps. "She could've been robbed. Maybe she put up a fight and got hurt. It wouldn't take much to kill a woman that age."

"We have a few break-ins every now and again. We even had a robbery last year at the convenience store. But I have a hard time with the idea that someone murdered Miss Elizabeth." I said my piece, then sat back from the table.

Food didn't taste so good when you were talking about murder.

"Maybe you could touch something she was wearing and tell us all what happened," Shayla suggested.

I stared at her—if only looks could kill—and finally said, "No."

"Could you do that?" Kevin asked.

"I can't form images from things," I explained, softening my tone a little. "I have to touch the person."

"Maybe you could touch Miss Elizabeth," Shayla continued. "Maybe you could pick up a vibe that way."

"I've already touched her. I didn't see anything." I felt a little uncomfortable defending myself, but I went on. "I've thought about this again and again since finding Miss Elizabeth. But I get nothing. No image. Nothing."

"It's probably because Lizzie isn't able to form a picture in *her* mind." Gramps started clearing the table. "I think Dae's ability has always been like her grandmother's. She could only see a picture of something a person visualized in their mind."

"What about Dae finding all that junk she puts in her shop? She can find *that* without touching anyone." Shayla sounded as though she was daring me to deny it.

"That's different. I can find odds and ends by myself. But I have to touch someone to find things they've lost. I don't see them getting married, giving birth, or dying. I wouldn't want to even if I could." Why was she being so antagonistic? I knew she liked Kevin, but this was ridiculous.

"I'm sure Kevin is right, and we'll all know what happened shortly." Gramps brought that part of the conversation to an end. "I've got a little pecan pie left in the fridge. Anybody up for dessert?"

He took Kevin out on the porch that overlooked Currituck Sound while Shayla and I got out plates and forks. "What's wrong with you tonight, Dae?" she demanded. "I know all of this has been stressful, but there's no reason to look at me like you'd like to strangle me."

"I wasn't looking at you like that." I sliced the pie in four even pieces. "I wasn't looking any way at all. What about you? I felt like the accused at the Salem witch trials!"

"It's Kevin, isn't it? If you have a thing for him, you should tell me."

"I don't have a thing for him. I just met him." I glanced toward the back porch. "If you want him, you can have him."

She giggled. "Maybe you *should* have a thing for him. You know we don't have that many good-looking, single men who live here year-round. And no one wants more than a one-nighter with a tourist."

"It's not like that." I licked my finger after putting pie on all the plates. Gramps has won ribbons for his pecan pie at the county fair. It's the best. "He talked to Gramps before he met me."

She looked around me as she picked up two plates. "So he knew all about the psychic thing. Was he weird about it?"

"No. Not really. It's why he was with me when I found Miss Elizabeth. I was glad he was there. He asked me to help him find a missing key. That's it."

"You're sure he didn't want to hold hands with you? It might be his idea of a good pickup line given how you find things."

"It didn't seem that way to me."

She nudged me with her elbow as she walked by. "Then it's every girl for herself. As the pirates used to say, no quarter."

I laughed as she walked toward the back porch, picturing the two of us sword fighting over a captive Kevin. For some reason, that reminded me of the piece of metal I'd picked up on the street. I told her I'd be out in a minute and took it out of my pocket.

It was old, an award of some kind. I could barely make out the name . . . Amanda. The shield shape was clear. It had a date on it, 1964. It seemed to be made of gold. It looked like the lapel pins people wear on blazers, but there was no pin on the back.

A knock on the front door interrupted my examination of the pin. I put the medal back in my pocket, left the two slices of pie on the kitchen table and went to answer it. It wasn't unusual for Duck residents to come up to the house when there were problems. I hoped whatever it was would be easily resolved. But the man at the door was a stranger. "Can I help you?"

"I saw your house, and I was wondering if you'd ever thought about selling." He smiled broadly, showing big, even white teeth. His brown hair was carefully tousled, and his handsome face shone with a sprayed-on tan. *Definitely not a resident.*

"No. Thanks anyway. We like it here."

"I could offer you some good money for it. Land is scarce out here, as I'm sure you know. It goes for a premium. I have some wealthy buyers looking for places all the time. I could get you at least two million for this house and land. Just imagine what you could do with that kind of cash!"

"Buy another house because I'd be living in the street?" I started to move back from the doorway. "I'm not interested. Thanks anyway."

"Wait!" He put one large, pudgy hand on mine. "Let's not be hasty! I have some information here about my real estate firm. Let me leave it with you along with my business card, which includes my 24/7 cell phone number. You can call me day or night if you change your mind."

The contact from his restraining hand felt odd, but the vision it brought was very clear. I had something that belonged to him. He'd been thinking about it enough that it was in the forefront of his mind even as he tried to get me to sell the house. "You can't have my house"—I glanced at his card—"Mr. Sparks, but I do have something that belongs to you. Please come inside."

Chapter 5

A grin spread across Sparks's face. "I'd love to, ma'am. Please call me Chuck."

"Okay, Chuck. I'm Dae O'Donnell." His obvious eagerness made me uncomfortable. "I meant what I said. You can't have the house. But I found something I think you've been looking for. Would you like some iced tea with your pie?"

By that time, the new voice had brought everyone in from the back porch. Chuck shook hands with all of them and passed out business cards. "Are one of you gentlemen the owner of this property? I think you'll find the offer of two million dollars I made Dae to be a real incentive. Do you mind if I take a look around?"

He didn't wait for actual permission but took our silence as a go-ahead. He investigated the living room first, smiling and nodding when he saw the stone fireplace.

"Who *is* this man, Dae?" Gramps asked.

"Did he really offer you two million for your house?" Shayla demanded.

"He's a real estate person," I explained. "And yes, he offered me that much. Not in writing, but as a throw-out number to get the ball rolling. You know how real estate people are."

"Why is he in the house instead of in the street?" Gramps wondered.

"I picked something up tonight. It belongs to him. I'm trying to get around to telling him that I know it's his."

"Nice half bath down here." Chuck came out of the hall. "Any closets?"

"Dae," Gramps warned. "Get a move on telling him."

"Let's all sit down for a minute." I smiled at Chuck. "Tea? Pie?"

He joined us at the table, smiles all around at each of us, as he dug into his pie and slurped his tea. "This place is great! I might be able to go as high as two and a half. What do you think of that?"

Gramps's face darkened, like a thundercloud ready to burst. I saw a storm coming and decided I'd better step in before he let loose. "Chuck, we *really* don't want to sell the house."

He nodded. "I understand. Things are tough. Sometimes we have to do things we don't want to do. Believe me, I've been in that spot."

"Young man," Gramps bellowed, "I have no inclination to sell my house to you."

Chuck's smile faded. "But you wanted me to come in and eat pie."

I took out the medal and put it in his hand. "I have something of yours. Something you've been looking for."

"Where did you find this?" Chuck stared at the medal.

"On Duck Road coming back here through town. I wasn't sure what it was, but I realized it was yours when you came to the door."

He looked at me as though he'd wandered into an episode of *The Twilight Zone.* "How did you know?"

"It's difficult to explain."

Shayla made an impatient clicking sound with her teeth. "It's not *that* difficult. Dae finds things, you know? She's psychic. She knows who things belong to. Understand?"

Chuck looked even more uncomfortable. "This medal belonged to my mother. It was the first award she ever won after she became a real estate agent. She lost it twenty years ago. No way she dropped it *then,* and you found it *now.*"

"I'm glad I met you so I could give it back." I smiled and hoped it would ease some of his discomfort, but it didn't help. He pushed back his chair and left his pie half eaten. His eyes were wild. He looked like he wanted to say something but couldn't. He picked up his brochures and let himself out the front door.

"You're welcome," Kevin called, an annoyed smile on his face.

"Aren't you going to call him back?" Shayla demanded. "The next man might not offer you so much. I wonder what *my* house is worth."

Conversation lagged after that. The pie was gone and the coffee was cold. It wasn't long before Shayla convinced Kevin to take her out for that drink. He asked politely if Gramps and I would like to come. Both of us said no, and I waved good-bye to them from the front door.

"They make a nice couple." Gramps came up behind me and waved too.

"You think so?"

"If you aren't interested in him, I do. Any chance you might be interested in him?"

"I don't think so. He's okay, I guess. For an outsider."

"I can't believe you're so prejudiced, Dae. I know we didn't raise you to be that way."

"He might decide to move back to D.C. someday." I closed the front door and turned off the outside light.

Gramps let out a grunt as he pushed himself back in his recliner. "You know how to ruin an old man's fun, don't you?"

I sneaked out of the house early the next morning. Gramps didn't have a charter, so he'd stayed up late and was sleeping in. It was nice escaping without eating breakfast. He's kind of a good-breakfast nut. I love him, but sometimes our lives clash a little.

Duck is beautiful early in the morning. It's the one time the town resembles the way it was when I was growing up. When I was in my twenties, the place went through a kind of growth spurt, like people suddenly discovered Duck was here. Since then, it has to be cold for there to be any peace and quiet. Except in the mornings. Combine that peace and quiet with a good cup of coffee and the morning paper, and I was in heaven. There was always a little town gossip too. I liked that with my coffee.

Some of the other shopkeepers said good morning to me as we passed on the boardwalk overlooking the sound. A few joggers were out, along with some hungry seagulls scavenging for food. I settled on a bench, ready to sip my coffee and enjoy that lazy, satisfying feeling that comes from sitting on the boardwalk, watching people go by.

My mood was shattered when I opened the paper and took a good look at the front page. In broad headlines, Miss Elizabeth's death became public property. It seemed wrong somehow to share all the intimate details of the tragedy with strangers. How did reporters find out she was wearing that black dress with the little pink hearts?

I half expected to see a picture of her body being carried to the medical examiner's office. Thankfully, that didn't happen. The paper ran a much younger shot of her from when she was crowned Miss Duck seventy years ago. I glanced at the caption. The photo was courtesy of the Duck Historical Museum and Max Caudle.

I could tell from the growing heat of the sun and the crowd beginning to build that it was time to open Missing Pieces. But my heart wasn't in it today. My mind was too preoccupied with thoughts of Miss Elizabeth. What had happened to her out there, alone in the dunes? Imagination can be a terrible thing.

I was so caught up in thinking about the tragedy that I completely neglected Chief Michaels's number-one rule for keeping safe: Be aware. I'd even gone to his safety refresher course over the winter, yet still I wasn't keeping track of my surroundings.

As I opened the door to the shop, someone brushed by me, knocking me against the side of the building and grabbing my purse at the same time. It took me an instant to realize what had happened. I looked up to see the purse snatcher running down the boardwalk toward the parking lot. "Hey! You can't do that!"

I couldn't remember whether the chief had said you were or weren't supposed to chase someone who took your purse. It was my first thought, though, and before I knew it, my feet were following. I ran after him, taking a shortcut through the midsection of the Duck Shoppes to head him off. I kept yelling, hoping someone might stop him before my lungs exploded. I hadn't run anywhere for a long time.

The thief was tall and thin, kind of scruffy looking from the back. He looked familiar, and I suddenly realized he was the young man who'd asked me about a job on the Fourth of July. He must've been setting me up. And if someone didn't do something to help me stop him, he was going to get away with my purse.

I yelled again and tried to speed up. He was passing the Coffee House, and I saw him run around the back of the Dumpster on the side. Was he trying to hide or trying to double back to confuse me?

I had my answer a second later as he ran out from behind the Dumpster and headed back in the direction from which we'd come. There was a small runoff ditch beside the parking lot that he plowed through, water splashing everywhere as I followed him back to the blacktop. I was closer now because I'd waited for him to make his move, but he was still faster than me. I was going to lose him and with him, my credit cards, driver's license and a very expensive tube of my favorite lipstick. Lucky my keys had been in my hand to open the door.

We kept running through the parking lot. I wasn't sure which way he'd turn. One way went up to the boardwalk again and the other way went right down into the sound. He might lose me in the gathering crowds starting to shop. If he ran down into the water, I had him.

Then something amazing happened. Tim Mabry jumped down from the boardwalk right on top of the purse snatcher. The boy crumpled under his weight. Suddenly everyone noticed what was going on and took an interest. Where were they when I was trying to save my property?

"You need this boy for something?" Tim grinned as he hauled the young man to his feet.

"H-he . . . stole . . . my . . . p-purse." I tried to catch my breath, but couldn't seem to get enough air into my poor lungs. I leaned against the side of the stairs with a dozen people staring down on us.

"Purse snatcher, huh?" Tim yanked my purse from the thief's hands. "You know, we may have to have a little talk about where you were Fourth of July. We have a purse missing that might be part of an important murder case."

"Should you tell him that?" I wondered, gratefully accepting my purse from him. "Won't that mess up the investigation?"

"I don't think that's a problem, Mayor. You don't worry your pretty head about it. We'll take care of everything."

His tone set my teeth on edge as it always did, but I couldn't complain. He'd stopped the purse snatcher and rescued my lipstick. I knew what was coming next, and I accepted it graciously. When he asked me out for dinner, I said yes. How could I say no even though I knew another marriage proposal waited for me after the last course?

Tim handcuffed the young man and then led him to his police car parked on the far side of the lot. As I watched him put the purse snatcher in the backseat and then climb into the driver's seat, I thought about how desperate the young man had to be to steal my purse. I was far from looking like someone who had money. Maybe everyone had turned him down for a job, and stealing was his only recourse.

"I'd like to weigh in on that," Trudy said after I'd told her about the incident later that morning. "You're going to have to suck it up and testify against that little weasel. He could've hurt you when he took your purse. Don't feel sorry for him."

We were in Missing Pieces, and I was watching my customers pick things up and put them back down. "No one starts out bad. He was desperate. I could see that in his face."

"Maybe. But everyone's desperate at one time or another. It doesn't give them the right to steal. And I heard what Tim said. He thinks that boy could be involved in Miss Elizabeth's death. How can you even think about his motives?"

I had already heard that speech from Gramps and Shayla earlier. News traveled fast in Duck. By eleven A.M. everyone had heard the story, and by noon had added their own embellishments. The young man had become a large, muscular brute who'd picked me up and slammed me against the wall. He'd left me there to die, taking my purse and most of the money from the cash register in Missing Pieces. That's the way small-town gossip works.

Nothing they said changed my mind. I still felt sorry for the young man. And I felt a little guilty that I hadn't given him some kind of job when he'd asked me. It might've made a difference.

Trudy finally got tired of trying to convince me she was right. She had a client under the hairdryer and left a few minutes later. Despite the crowd of shoppers around the boardwalk, the day was slow for me. Souvenirs and beach clothes seemed to be moving a lot faster than treasures.

But there was one astute shopper who was looking at a garnet necklace I'd bought from an old woman in Wilmington one winter. It was one of my special finds. The research I'd done on it pointed to its owner having been the wife of

Jefferson Davis, the president of the Confederacy during the Civil War. My fingers had tingled when I had touched it. The garnet was good and the chain was old gold, but the real value lay in its ownership.

The woman, her white hair piled high on her head, sunglasses hanging around her neck, pointed to it in the glass case. "What's that?"

I held my breath, then slowly let it out. "It's a necklace that once belonged to Sarah Knox Taylor Davis."

"But what is it? Is it a ruby?"

"No. It's a garnet."

The woman smacked her gum a few more times and scratched her arm where her sunburn was peeling. "Is that like a ruby?"

"No. It's completely different."

"So who's this Davis woman? Does she live around here?"

This was painful. I didn't want this woman to buy my garnet necklace. "She's dead. She's been dead for a long time. There's a jeweler right up the road. I'm sure he has some nice rubies you can look at."

Smack. Smack. Smack. "Naw. I think I want this one. How much is it?"

I quoted her an awful, *outrageous* price. "I can't let it go for less than that."

"That's crazy! I'll give you a hundred dollars. That's what I've got. Do you gift wrap?"

Since I'd quoted her five *thousand* dollars, I laughed. "I'm sorry. You can't have it."

She looked at me as if she thought she'd misunderstood. "You *can't* be serious. That piece of junk isn't even worth a hundred. You can't make that much here in a day."

We both surveyed the empty shop. "That's not the point. I told you the price. I won't take less."

"I am so out of here. You're crazy, you know?"

Watching her leave, her pencil-thin legs wobbling on high-heeled sandals, I agreed. She was the closest thing to a real sale I'd had that day. I had sold a few trinkets I'd gotten at the Presbyterian church rummage sale last spring but nothing of any great value. A few people came in for their UPS packages and dropped a few off. Not much to live on.

As I was about to call it a day at four P.M., Kevin came through the door and stopped to admire the place. "Wow! You really have a lot of junk."

"Some of that is very good junk," I told him. "Some of it is even very expensive junk."

"Sorry. I didn't come to make you angry. I have a warning."

"That sounds ominous." I gravitated toward the burgundy sofa in the middle of the shop.

"Well, since you haven't done anything wrong, it won't be a big deal. The SBI had me come in this morning to talk about finding Miss Elizabeth and about *you*."

"What about me?" I scooted over so he could sit down on the sofa. "I told Chief Michaels everything I know."

He shrugged, and I noticed the Blue Whale Inn T-shirt he was wearing. "It's standard procedure. If I were investigating this case, I'd bring you in too."

"Should I say anything about finding Miss Mildred's watch?"

"That's up to you." He glanced toward a painting of a dog running up the seashore. "Hey! I like that. It might look good in my lobby."

"In other words, you already *told* them I find things."

"I didn't have to. They talked to Chief Michaels, and he filled them in. It was really only a matter of time anyway. I couldn't deny I knew you were psychic. How much for the painting?"

A little annoyed that I'd be in a defensive position when they talked to me, I rolled my eyes and answered, "Fifteen thousand dollars."

He smiled, then looked at the painting again. "For real?"

"How much do you think my privacy is worth?"

"Look, Dae, everyone here knows about you. It might be a little more uncomfortable for you talking to the SBI with them knowing you're psychic, but it will be fine. I'd be happy to tag along and help out if—"

"Great! What time do they want to see me?"

"There's nothing to worry about."

"But I'll feel so much better with you there. I'd call my lawyer, but he's working off a DUI picking up trash on the roads. What time did you say?"

"I don't know. Chief Michaels might come for you. Or he'll call. I don't know which."

I took out my cell phone. "I'll call you then. Thanks for volunteering."

"Sure. So how much for the painting?"

We settled on three hundred dollars. I was only asking four hundred. It wasn't one of my special finds, but I was glad to see how much Kevin liked it. I'd know if it was a pity purchase (to make up for his talking about me to the SBI) if I didn't see it hanging in the Blue Whale lobby.

"Thanks. You made my lackluster sales day much better." I nodded at his T-shirt. "I like the color and the new design on that. I'd be glad to sell some of them here if you like. I have a community board over there too where you could give out information."

"That would be great! Speaking of the Blue Whale, when can I expect you to come over and help me find my key?"

I thought about it. I could've done it right there in the shop on the brocade sofa. But I had never been in the Blue Whale. I was barely six years old when it closed. I thought this would be a good excuse for a tour. "I can come anytime. I was about to close up for the day."

"Fantastic! Let's have some dinner and look for the key."

I started to agree, then remembered my promise to Tim. "I can't today. Maybe tomorrow. I have a date, sort of."

"A date! That's worth not finding my key. Anyone I know?"

"Probably not since you're new here." I went on to explain about the purse snatcher and how Tim had saved the day. I didn't go into how the evening would end with another marriage proposal.

"I know Tim. You can bring him along. I'll call Shayla, and we'll make it a foursome."

The smile on his face seemed devilish to me, as though he already knew about Tim's infatuation. Adding Shayla to the mix was like scratching a fingernail on a chalkboard. "I don't think so. Thanks anyway. I'm sure we'll have time to look for the key later. If not tomorrow, the next day."

"I guess that'll have to do." He followed me out of the shop after I turned off the lights. "I heard you chased down that guy who took your purse. That wasn't very smart."

I locked the door with a loud click. "I got my purse back."

"He could've turned around and shot you."

"But he didn't. I'm safe and sound and probably in better shape after running all over the parking lot. I appreciate you letting me know about the SBI."

He held up his painting. "And I'm glad I came in. I guess I'll call you tomorrow."

"Unless you hear from me in the middle of the night when the SBI comes for me."

I smiled as we walked in opposite directions. Kevin seemed to be on his way to the General Store or Wild Stallions, the little bar and grill tucked into the corner of the boardwalk. I headed down to the town hall to check my messages with Nancy.

Kevin was much different than I'd imagined when I first met him. He was a little trickier than I'd originally thought. I don't know why he struck me originally as being a straightforward kind of man. Not a bit like Chief Michaels, Gramps or Tim, the three other law enforcement men I knew well. They were always to the point. I kind of liked the difference.

Chief Michaels was in my office when I arrived at town hall. Nancy got up from her desk with a worried frown on her thin face. "He's been here for an hour already. I think he wants to take you down to meet with the SBI people. They want to question you about finding Miss Elizabeth."

Since I knew about the meeting (*thank you, Kevin*), I was calm and collected as I took my mail and messages and went through to my office. I'd decorated it myself. It had been a storage room, but it had a good window overlooking the sound. I'd painted the room blue and brought in all the sea paraphernalia I could find, including a ship's bell from a freighter that went down in a storm in the early 1800s. I felt relaxed and calm when I was here. Even now, Chief Michaels's worried face didn't upset me.

"You wanted to see me?" I sat behind my white oak desk and picked up my letter opener.

He put his hands on the desk. "The SBI wants to talk to

you, Mayor. It's routine. Nothing to worry about. Except for the part about you finding things. I don't know how *that* will play out. Tell the truth and everything will be fine."

My heart started pounding a little faster. "What do you mean? Of course I'll tell the truth."

"I don't think you should mention your gift for finding things, or that Millie had asked you to find the watch. You *know* what I mean, Dae. We understand that kind of thing out here. Other places, not so much."

I put down the letters and the opener. "Kevin already told me that they know about me finding things. What do you want me to do?"

"He did?" He looked uncomfortable. "For your own sake, don't emphasize it. Tell them you were out looking for Lizzie like the rest of us. They don't have to know anything else."

"That would be lying, Chief. You told me to be honest."

"Not exactly. There's a fine line between lying and telling a partial truth, Dae. I've known you since you were a little girl. Take my word for this. None of us wants to go through what they might start if you tell them *everything*."

I got up from my desk and started pacing around the room, mulling over what Kevin had said. I looked out at the sound where the seagulls were whirling and dipping in their quest for food. How bad could it be? The SBI might not understand what I had to say about Miss Mildred's watch, but there wasn't much they could do about it. "When do they want to see me?"

"First thing tomorrow, eight A.M. Out of deference to your position, they'll come here. Nancy can hold the phones, and you'll answer their questions—to a point, I hope. Take my advice, Mayor, and know when to stop."

The chief nodded to me, then put his cap on and left the

office. I sat back down at my desk and called Kevin to tell him about my coming date with the SBI. He didn't answer, of course, but I left him a message about the meeting. I hoped he'd be there. If nothing else, he'd be good moral support.

I didn't know him well enough to be sure I could rely on his judgment. But the chief's request that I skirt around the truth about myself made me more uneasy than I would've been. What was I supposed to say if they asked me point-blank if I could find lost things with my mind?

Kevin seemed to be familiar with abilities like mine. Maybe the SBI agents would be too. I hoped they wouldn't try to recruit me or something because I definitely wasn't interested. Finding Miss Elizabeth had been a terrible experience. It had destroyed any thoughts I'd had about using my gift for something more important than locating lost trinkets.

Thirty minutes later, Nancy popped her head into the office as I was getting ready to leave. "Are you okay?" she asked.

"I'm fine," I assured her. "But if Tim proposes again tonight after supper, I might lose it."

"Sweetie, why don't you marry the boy? Have a nice little family and live your life?"

I could tell by her kind smile that she meant well. Nancy was divorced and had two beautiful daughters. I'm sure that's what she meant by living my life. "If it was somebody other than Tim, I might consider it. But he's been asking me to marry him since I stuffed sand in his mouth when we were kids. Maybe I'm looking for someone else. Or I'm meant to be alone with my lost treasures."

"Very dramatic. And very lonely. What about the new guy at the whale place? I heard he's a darling."

"He's also taken. Shayla has her hooks in him. At least right now. We'll see. Good night, Nancy."

"Good night, sweetie."

I headed out the door into the early evening air. The streets were crowded. Duck nightlife was bustling and noisy in the summer. The music of at least three different bands was spilling into the streets from various establishments as I made my way home.

Gramps had left me a note on the kitchen table. He was out for the night playing pinochle. He loved his games. I took a quick shower and changed clothes, wondering what I should wear in the morning to be interrogated by the SBI. Was that a formal thing or more a shorts-and-tank-top thing? I might call Kevin and ask his opinion later.

By the time I had changed into a short, mint green sundress and embroidered sandals, Tim was at the door. He gave me my obligatory (*his idea, not mine*) bouquet of daisies from the local supermarket. I smelled them, pretending they had a smell besides that strange refrigerator odor, and said thank you.

"I was thinking we could go over to the Rib Shack. They have a special tonight." He grinned and swayed back on his heels with pleasure.

If he'd said *anyplace* else in Duck or Southern Shores, I would've been impressed. But it was always the Rib Shack. Oh well. I owed him for catching the purse snatcher. I smiled and tucked my arm in his. "Sounds great!"

Chapter 6

I've noticed that people can be incredibly devious when it comes to getting what they want. Take Martha Segall, for instance. She wanted the town to clean up a drainage ditch for storm water behind her house. It had been created by the city then storms had dropped debris and branches into it. The town council's position was that the ditch was on her private property and, therefore, was her responsibility. Martha blocked the ditch with a load of sand. When the water backed up on the street, she argued that the property obviously belonged to the town since it caused problems with the street, so the town should take care of it.

Other nearby property owners affected by the water (mosquitoes build up fast) demanded the town do something. The town council voted to clean out the ditch but only after voting to fine Martha. It was only a twenty-five-dollar fine. Martha won the battle, since cleaning up the ditch would've been a thousand dollars.

I mention this because I felt the same way when I looked up and saw Kevin and Shayla standing next to our table at the Rib Shack. We hadn't even had a chance to order yet. I didn't have to be psychic to know why they were here: Kevin wanted me to find the missing key for him sooner rather than later.

"Kevin!" Tim got up and shook his hand. "Hi, Shayla."

Shayla rolled her eyes and didn't say anything. She wasn't part of or happy with this plan.

"Hey, it's good to see you guys! Mind if we join you?" Kevin didn't wait for a response as he grabbed two chairs for him and Shayla.

I scooted over closer to the window as Kevin came in next to me. "What a surprise," I said. "Imagine seeing the two of you here tonight."

"Yeah, well, it wasn't *my* idea." Shayla pouted.

"We were here anyway," Kevin said. "Might as well have dinner together."

"You're right." Tim grinned at me. He didn't care. He'd proposed once in front of the whole town council.

After we'd ordered, the men started talking about police procedures, the SBI and Miss Elizabeth. Shayla and I excused ourselves to go to the bathroom. "You can't have Kevin, Dae," Shayla stated flatly when we were standing in front of the wide bathroom mirror.

"I don't want Kevin." I smoothed my hair down and put on a little more lipstick. "What makes you think I do?"

"He came in here looking for *you*. As soon as he saw you, he made a beeline right for your table. I don't think he wanted to talk to Tim, do you?" She spritzed on some exotic perfume.

"I *know* what he wants. He lost a key to a room in the Blue Whale. He suggested we go over there tonight. I said no. I guess he doesn't take no for an answer."

"He wants to go over there?" Shayla's eyes got brighter. "I like that idea. I haven't been over there in a hundred years."

"That was your previous life, right?"

"Don't sound so skeptical. You know what you know. I know what I know."

"Whatever that means."

"It means I like the Rib Shack, and I'm willing to go look for an old key, even if it is with *you*."

And that was that. We went back to the table where Kevin had cleverly engaged Tim in the hunt for the old key. Everyone looked at me as the last holdout. "All right," I said, giving in. "But you better be there at eight A.M. tomorrow when the SBI comes to interrogate me."

"I'll be there," Kevin said. "I got your message."

"But it won't be an interrogation." Tim took a gulp of his beer and lounged back in his chair. "They want to corroborate a few things. That's all."

"Like whether or not I'm psychic." I glanced at Kevin. "Chief Michaels said I shouldn't offer that information."

Kevin's eyes narrowed, and his face took on a different personality. I guessed this was his professional law enforcement face. "Why would he say that?"

"I'm sure you didn't understand what he meant," Tim said. "The chief would never tell you to lie."

"He didn't tell me to lie," I clarified. "He told me not to go into any explanation about finding Miss Mildred's watch on her dead sister. He said to tell them I was out looking for her like everyone else."

"I'm sorry, Dae," Kevin said. "But they already know.

Believe me, it's not as big a thing as the chief is making it out to be. Maybe he's afraid it will call into question his investigation skills. No one in local law enforcement likes it when the state or federal government comes in on a case like this."

That didn't make me feel any better. "I don't know what to say now."

He put his hand on mine where it rested on the red and white checkered tablecloth. "Just tell them the truth. You didn't do anything wrong. You have nothing to hide."

The contact lingered and I felt my mind clouding over, exactly as it had when I saw Miss Mildred's watch. If a person isn't concentrating on looking for something in particular, I don't see anything. In this case, Kevin had the key in the forefront of his mind. I saw where it was right away. "It's in the drawer behind the cash register," I blurted out.

Everyone looked at me. Kevin moved his hand away slowly. It made me wonder if he'd held my hand to comfort me or to see if I could find the key.

"Are you talking about the key?" he asked.

"Yes. It's an old skeleton key. And it's in the drawer behind the cash register in the bar." I smiled at him and ate a few French fries as our food arrived. I was showing off a little, but it was exciting.

Shayla groaned, and Tim complained, "I wanted to go over there, Dae."

"Me too," Shayla added.

"You guys can still come over," Kevin assured them. "I think Dae might be a little quick on the draw anyway. There's no drawer behind the cash register. It's up against the wall. There isn't anything behind it. I sanded and repainted that whole area. There's nothing there." He held out his hand. "Want to look again?"

I realized then that he *had* held my hand to see if I could tell him where the key was. It made me a little surly, I'm afraid, since I realized something else when he was touching me. I felt more than friendly toward Kevin, despite my protestations to Shayla. "I don't need to look again. It's in a drawer behind the cash register in the bar. Take it or leave it. Once I see something, I don't need to look again."

"Okay." He put his hand down. "We'll all go look after dinner."

"No thanks to you, Miss Kill Joy," Shayla hissed across the table.

"No need to be so hard on Dae," Tim said. "Speaking of which, there might not be anything for the SBI to ask you about tomorrow. When we arrested the boy who took your purse today, we searched his motel room and found a hundred purses stuffed in the closet. He's been here a few weeks from Virginia Beach. Seems like he has a record there for doing the same thing. The chief and I figure he might have gotten a little rough with Miss Elizabeth when he stole her purse."

"So you found her purse in his closet?" I asked, hoping he was right and it was an outsider who had killed her.

"Not exactly. Not yet anyway. It's taking a while to go through all of them," he explained. "But by this time tomorrow, we could have all the answers."

I recalled the way the purse snatcher had shoved me against the wall when he'd taken my purse. If he'd done something of that nature to take Miss Elizabeth's purse, I could understand how she could have been hurt—or worse, in this case.

"And that's how it goes from a simple purse snatching to armed robbery," Kevin said. "They find out they can do it, and it escalates."

"Poor Miss Elizabeth. I hope he killed her dead before he left her out there." Shayla sighed as she nibbled at a barbecue chicken leg.

"Shayla!" I couldn't believe she'd say something like that.

"What? I was only hoping she wasn't left out there, unable to get any help. I'd rather be dead than out there in the dunes barely alive with the gulls and the turtles eating me. You ever see what they can do to a body?"

"Well, we don't know for sure yet what happened," Tim said. "I hope we can get a confession from this boy and put it all behind us. The chief and I don't like loose ends."

He smiled at me and winked. I'd lost my appetite after Shayla's remark. The conversation turned to the upcoming dance in the park and other less gruesome things. Everyone was done eating a few minutes later. Shayla and I stepped outside while Tim and Kevin paid for dinner.

"I hope Tim's right about this kid being the killer," Shayla said after taking a deep breath of night air, which was sweetly perfumed by the roses blooming near the restaurant entrance.

"So do I. It's bad enough it happened. I don't think any of us wants to think someone who lives here did it."

"I guess it was a close call for you today," she suggested. "I mean, that boy could've killed you too."

"If he had, I promise I would've come back and told you." I knew Shayla's one earthly goal (besides money, great boyfriends and everyone's respect) was to find proof that there was an afterlife. We'd talked about it many times. Shayla and I believed the souls of the dearly departed were never far away. Proving it was another thing.

"You're a good friend, Dae O'Donnell. If I go first, I swear I'll come back and visit you too."

I smiled and encouraged her. We didn't write anything in blood, so I was probably safe. I believed in the afterlife too, in ghosts. But I didn't need to prove anything. There was only one person I wanted desperately to see again.

Duck Road was crowded as we walked down to the Blue Whale Inn, on the Atlantic side of town. It took a good fifteen minutes to get there from downtown Duck, a long walk compared to the five minutes between my house and Missing Pieces.

We passed the walk-through where Kevin and I had found Miss Elizabeth. I couldn't keep from shivering as we neared the spot. The wind off the ocean stirred the sea oats, some of them still smashed flat from the investigation. They'd have to be replanted. I made a mental note to put the public works guys on it.

"The real estate agent said the inn is close to two hundred years old," Kevin told Shayla as we approached the front of the impressive structure. A large fountain with a mermaid in it splashed in the middle of the circle drive. There was still a place to tie your horse right off the big, wide veranda.

"He's probably right," Tim agreed. "This place has been here forever. My grandpa told me it had a speakeasy in the basement during Prohibition. People came out here from all over, even with the long ferry ride from the mainland."

"Every place out here had a speakeasy," I added. "We were famous for bootleg rum. Some of it was smuggled in, but some of it just washed up. People out here have always taken advantage of what the sea brought them."

"It's a great old place," Kevin said proudly as he opened the front door. "I found ledger books and old trunks full of stuff in the attic. I don't think anyone moved anything out of here when the last owner left."

"Probably because he died and there wasn't an heir."
Tim followed Kevin into the inn. "It was years before it
could go on the market. Then it sat empty for at least twenty
years. Must've been a mess to clean up."

"Not so bad." Kevin flipped on the lights.

Shayla and I toured the old-fashioned lobby. There was a
high desk on one side and a large, circular seat in the middle. A few chairs were scattered on the expensive-looking
rugs.

"Good furniture," Shayla observed. "It looks like it's
straight out of the fifties."

"I suppose he could leave it this way and advertise it as
a retro place to stay." I went behind the tall desk where a
bell still sat on the counter. The telephone was one of those
heavy black landlines everyone used to have out here.

"Are you two coming into the bar to look for the key or
not?" Tim demanded from the doorway.

"This is like a treasure hunt." Shayla picked up an old
Tiffany lamp from the marble-topped table. "You could use
some of this stuff in Missing Pieces, Dae. Maybe then you
could sell something."

I made a face at her and thought about the dog painting
I'd sold to Kevin. I didn't see it in the lobby. Maybe he
hadn't had a chance to put it up yet. Not that I was worried
about it. It wasn't one of my important pieces. Still, I like
to know the things I sell are appreciated.

I followed Shayla and Tim into the bar area. The bar itself was amazing. It was a large wooden slab, smoothed and
polished to a mirrorlike finish. It appeared to have come
from a single tree. There were cute old bar stools with rat-
tan seats set up to it and a large number of tables near a big
bay window that overlooked the Atlantic. The faint smell of
cigar smoke permeated the entire room. I could almost hear

the tinkle of ice cubes in glasses of bootleg whiskey and the laughter of the Blue Whale's patrons enjoying themselves.

"Wow!" Shayla circled around the room a few times. "Look at this! This place could become the hot spot for the whole community. I hope you're going to have food too."

"I hope to," Kevin assured her. "I have a lot more work to do before I open. I've been living on the ground floor. I haven't done any work on the other two floors yet."

"What are you going to call the place?" Tim asked, playing with an old dartboard.

"The Blue Whale. No point in looking for a better name. I like the sound of the one it has." Kevin ran his hand down the polished bar top, then glanced over at me. "I'd also like to find that key so I can open the locked room on the third floor."

As I stood by the window overlooking the seashore, I nodded my head toward the ancient silver cash register that rested between antique bottles of whiskey lined up against the mirrored back wall. "The key is behind the cash register. Honestly, either you believe me, or you don't. That's where I saw it."

Tim shrugged. "I think she's always right."

"Give me a hand," Kevin said. "Let's see."

Together they moved the heavy cash register to the bar behind them. Shayla let out a little screech as they started to put it down on the glossy surface. Before the metal could come down on the wood, she'd thrown a towel under it. "Geez Louise! You don't have any idea what it costs to refinish wood, do you? The two of you are such *men*."

"Maybe so," Kevin replied. "But I still don't see anything back here. There's no mysterious drawer."

I was looking out the window, not really paying attention to the goings-on by the bar. There was something on the beach—a figure or object that faded in and out as the moonlight came and went with the clouds. I stared, trying to determine what it could be besides one of the legendary ghosts said to prowl the Outer Banks from time to time. I'd never actually seen one, but I knew plenty of people, including Gramps and Shayla, who had.

"Dae? Are you still with us?" Shayla demanded, waving her hand in front of my eyes.

I blinked and whatever was out there was gone. "I thought I saw something on the beach. Maybe a ghost."

"*Duh*! Where are we? If there wasn't a ghost out there looking for its head or some pirate treasure, we wouldn't be in Duck." She turned my head toward the bar. "This is much more interesting than some old ghost. Help the man find his key."

"You know, you see ghosts all the time. You might give the rest of us some consideration."

"You see treasure all the time," she countered. "You might give us the same consideration."

"Did someone mention treasure?" Tim asked with renewed interest in his voice.

"We don't know what's in there, do we?" Shayla nudged me toward the bar. "And we won't if Dae doesn't find the key."

Kevin had been systematically poking and pushing at the section of mirrored wall behind where the cash register had been. "I don't see anything."

"It's there." I sighed, walked across the room and stepped behind the bar. "I can still see it very clearly. These old places used to have hidden panels and rooms. The owner probably built them to hide things from pirates. During Prohibition, they used them to hide profits from liquor sales—as well as the liquor. You just have to know what to look for."

I stood before the mirror and closed my eyes so I could picture the space I'd seen in the vision from Kevin.

"Do you need to hold my hand again?" he offered.

"*Hey!* She already did that," Shayla protested. "Let's remember which side of this double date you came in with."

"Nope." I opened my eyes and stared at the ornate molding that separated the mirrored area from the wood paneling beneath it. "It's right here."

I pushed at the molding, but nothing budged. It was there, cleverly disguised. It didn't help that Kevin had painted over it. I couldn't make out where the sides of the drawer were hidden.

"It's here." I puzzled over it and stuck my fingers under the bottom of the molding. I heard a popping sound and my fingernail snapped off. "Ouch!" I cried as the drawer opened. "There was a little lever at the bottom. And here it is!" I turned around and held out the old key.

"Great!" Shayla snatched it from me. "*Ick!* This thing is revolting." She handed it to Kevin, then wiped her hand on the edges of the towel that was protecting the bar.

"Anything else in there?" Kevin wondered. He wiped off the key on his jeans.

"There are a few receipts, I think." I opened the drawer all the way. "And a list of different kinds of alcohol. Maybe a shopping list. And an old gun."

"A gun?" Tim and Kevin were instantly at my side.

I lifted the gun out of the drawer and looked it over. "It's an antique derringer. Pearl handle. Probably one shot. Ladies and gamblers liked them."

Tim whistled. "You know your guns."

"In my business, it pays to know a lot about everything." I handed the derringer to Kevin since he was its owner now. "I'm sure it could tell some stories."

"Any money in there?" Shayla tried to see in the drawer too.

"This is a beauty!" Kevin appreciated the piece. "No telling who it belonged to."

"Or what it was used for," Tim added.

"Who cares?" Shayla was done with the find. "Let's go upstairs and open the door."

Kevin pocketed the derringer after examining it to make sure it wasn't loaded. "That was completely amazing, Dae! I know everyone says you find things, but you really have to see it to believe it."

"Blah. Blah. Blah." Shayla tugged at his arm. "Wait till I read your palm, Kevin. Now *that* will be something amazing. What Dae does is okay, but nothing compared to what *I* can do."

I ignored the double meaning behind her words. Shayla could be so needy sometimes. I'm not a psychologist, but I'm sure her insecurity had something to do with her childhood. Her mother had abandoned her and her fisherman father when she was very young. If I hadn't known that about her, I would've stopped being friends with her a long time ago.

"Now ladies," Tim said, "you don't have to fight over Kevin. I'm here and willing to do whatever is necessary to keep you happy."

Now *that* surprised me. In all the time I'd known Tim, I'd never heard him say anything like it. He always focused on me. Perhaps there was more to him than what I already knew. I still didn't want to marry him, but it gave me some food for thought.

"All right." Kevin smiled at Shayla. "Let's go upstairs. Do you want to take the elevator?"

She giggled. "An elevator? That sounds great! Maybe

Tim and Dae would like to take the stairs and meet us up there."

I knew how to take a hint. Besides, I'd seen the old wrought-iron elevator cage in the lobby. I got the creeps when I looked at it. "We'd *rather* take the stairs," I told them. "Third floor, right?"

Tim puffed out his chest. Clearly he thought I wanted to be alone with him. "Don't be scared, Dae. I'll take care of you, like I always have."

I could hear the elevator motor pulling the cage up to the third floor as we started up the stairs. The stairwell was dark and probably filled with things I'd rather not see. Every so often, I heard a squeaking sound and wasn't sure if it was a bat or a rat. In a building that had sat empty for so long, anything was possible.

"This is *some* place." Tim huffed a little as we climbed to the second floor. "I think we should've taken the elevator."

I looked out the window on the second-floor landing. This side didn't face the beach. Bushes were spread out along the drive and down to the road. Their shadows seemed to move as the clouds passed through the moonlight. A few cars went by, their headlights fading quickly into the distance.

"I hate elevators. Even the safe ones with music and lights. I wouldn't go in that elevator for anything." I stepped on something hard and bent to retrieve it. The feeling of time slowing told me it was something important.

In the dim moonlight, I made out a tiny key. It was too small to open a room. It looked like the kind of key that would open a jewelry box or diary. No matter, it would belong to Kevin like everything else here. My fingers itched to explore everything in the Blue Whale and discover its treasures. I shoved the key in my pocket and started up the last flight of stairs.

"I might be having a heart attack, Dae." Tim wheezed up behind me. "Slow down. This was supposed to be romantic."

"If you got out of that police car and walked like everyone else in Duck, you wouldn't be having such a hard time on these stairs," I taunted him. Honestly, the mileage on those cars was incredible considering how small Duck was. More than once, I'd pushed the town council to buy bicycles, but the police had threatened to go on strike.

"Are you two *ever* going to get up here?" Shayla yelled down the stairs. "I don't even want to think what's going on down there."

The fact that she was yelling down at us made me think nothing much was going on with her and Kevin up on the third floor. That lightened my heart a little, but I put it down to jealousy.

"You know," Tim huffed, "I wanted to ask you something important while we're alone, Dae."

I knew it was uncharitable of me, but I couldn't help but grimace.

"I know I've asked you before," he continued. "I don't know if you've ever taken me seriously. I'm a stable man, Dae. You've known me all your life. I'd make a good husband. I cook and clean up after myself. I've been doing laundry since I was nine."

It always went the same way. I wished he'd take no for an answer. I felt cruel having to refuse him over and over again. But better to be alone than with someone I didn't love.

"And someday, your grandfather will be gone, and you'll be alone. You should marry me before that happens. We can live with him and take care of him. That house is plenty big for all of us *and* a few kids. So what do you think? Will you marry me, Dae?"

At that moment, a flashlight beam played over us. I realized Kevin had been close by, close enough to hear Tim pop the question. "Sorry. I thought you guys might be lost," he said.

Kevin's voice had that strange tone people use when they're curious about something they've heard or seen but they don't want to pry. I wanted to assure him that there was nothing intimate about the moment, but I couldn't do that to Tim. It was one thing for me to make fun of him in my own mind but another to help someone else make fun of him.

"No, we're fine." Tim's breathless voice came from behind me.

I couldn't really see Kevin's face because the flashlight beam was pointed in my general direction. It was an awkward moment, at least for me. I didn't want Kevin to get the wrong idea about me and Tim. "Did you open the door yet?"

"Not yet," Kevin assured me. "We were waiting for you."

Maybe he'd think I felt embarrassed about him overhearing the proposal and not mention it again. I certainly hoped so as I started up the stairs, without answering Tim's still-lingering question. Tim followed, a bit more slowly, and we met up with Kevin on the third-floor landing. Here, the window overlooked the ocean. The light rippled on the waves coming in at low tide.

"I'm glad you finally found them," Shayla said as we approached her. She was standing next to the door of the locked room, one hip resting against the wall. The sarcasm in her tone was obvious, at least to me. She hadn't wanted Kevin to come back and look for us.

"Well, we're all here." I walked up to the door and pretended an excitement I wasn't really feeling. There was a damp, moldy smell to the place that I hoped Kevin would be able to get rid of before he tried to rent out rooms. It was the smell of decay and neglect, maybe even dust and cob-webs. I wanted to be out walking the beach, trying to find that elusive ghost that Shayla took for granted. "Let's see what's inside."

Kevin stepped up and inserted the key in the lock. It made a grating sound as it turned. The door swung open on stiff old hinges. There was a strange whoosh of air that carried an unpleasant odor. I supposed any room would smell bad after being closed up for thirty years.

This room faced the ocean too. I could see the beach through the dirty panes. The moonlight flowed in like a spotlight, illuminating the room. A desk with an old crook-neck lamp was barely visible in one corner, a simple bed and chest of drawers completing the room.

"Is this it?" Shayla asked in a very quiet voice.

"What were you expecting?" I responded.

"It looks like someone's sitting at the desk over there." Tim pointed. "Must be a trick of the light."

Kevin walked closer to the desk. The beam from the flashlight shone on something I'd hoped never to see again—a dead person. But this time, it was only the skeletal remains. Empty eye sockets stared back at us. Bony fingers rested on the desk.

I heard Shayla gag beside me, and we both stepped back from the grisly scene.

"Someone's sitting at the desk, all right," Kevin said. "I think he or she has been here for a long time."

Chapter 7

Tim and Kevin hustled Shayla and me out of the room before calling the police. When Chief Michaels finally arrived, he came trudging up the stairs rather than using the elevator. Who knew the chief and I had a fear of elevators in common? Not that he'd admit it.

"I don't understand why we couldn't look around a bit," Shayla complained from the floor where she'd plopped down at least half an hour earlier. "You both have police training. They wouldn't have known we were in there."

"It's about crime-scene preservation," Tim began. He paced up and down the dark hall ranting about people who disturb crime scenes and how difficult it makes life for police officers. "Don't you agree, Brickman?"

"Yes. Otherwise I'd be in there cleaning out that mess."

"Imagine whoever it is being in there all this time," I

added. "We *thought* Duck had a low homicide rate. Instead, dead people are lurking everywhere."

"I'm sure that's not the case, Mayor." The chief came out of the room as another man came up behind him. "This is Agent Brooks Walker of the SBI. He's here to check this out with us."

Agent Walker shook my hand briefly. He was a short man, barely five feet. I could see his graying brown hair in the flashlight beams as several other Duck police officers joined us. "Mayor O'Donnell. It's a pleasure to meet you. I wish it were under better circumstances. You seem to have a knack for finding dead people."

I was about to vigorously defend myself when Kevin stepped in and shook hands with him. "It looks like we meet again, Agent Walker. Whatever bad luck Mayor O'Donnell is going through right now, I seem to be part of it too."

Agent Walker looked up at Kevin, and a small smile appeared on his mouth. "Yes, that much is evident. Who are these people?"

Tim introduced Shayla, then said, "We already met, Agent Walker. I'm Officer Mabry, the chief's assistant."

"That's right. I knew I recognized you." Walker shook his hand, then glanced around the crowded hall as he put on some latex gloves. "Let's take a look at what we've got here, gentlemen."

Two hours later, Shayla and I were still waiting to find out what was going on. The chief had informed us as delicately as he could that he didn't want us to leave the Blue Whale until they'd had a look at the crime scene, in case he had any questions. Kevin and Tim had become part of the group investigating upstairs while we waited downstairs in the bar.

"You think they like us for the murder?" Shayla asked as she sipped a Coke.

"You watch too much TV."

"There's nothing else to do out here in the winter. I'm lucky if I have one or two tarot readings a week. What do *you* do?"

"I read. Books, not palms or cards. Once in a while, I watch TV or help Gramps work on the boat. Last winter, I painted the house. You *know* that."

"Sounds to me like your life is as boring as mine. Without tourists, we're nothing."

It was a depressing thought but one I knew many permanent residents (especially those with businesses) agreed with. People talked all the time about ways to bring tourists down to the Outer Banks in the winter. It never quite seemed to happen. I was glad I didn't make it a campaign promise.

"How long does it take to do this anyway?" Shayla whined.

I heard the squeak of the old elevator. "Sounds like it must be done. Quit slumping over that drink and sit up straight."

"Yes, Mom."

Kevin, Tim and Agent Walker entered the bar as we heard the elevator heading back up to the third floor. "Where did you say you found that gun, Brickman?" Agent Walker asked.

"It was behind the old cash register." Kevin showed him the secret drawer. "I was fooling around and found it."

I started to speak but managed to catch myself. This might be one time where showing off *wasn't* to my advantage. Kevin seemed all right with the idea of me telling the SBI the full truth about finding Miss Elizabeth. Why was he protecting me now?

"We'll have to keep the gun until ballistics has a look at it." Agent Walker barely glanced at the secret drawer. "I expect there are plenty of secret passages and places in here. My granddad used to help raid these old hotels regularly during the twenties and thirties. Probably found a still or two out here too."

"I haven't done much on the upper floors," Kevin said. "This is the only secret compartment I've found so far."

Agent Walker nodded, obviously beginning to get bored with the conversation. "Well, it's a nice place, Brickman. I don't know why anyone would give up your position with the FBI for this, but to each his own, I always say."

Shayla and I were apparently not to be questioned by the SBI. Probably because we were with Kevin and Tim when we found the dead person. It probably helped that the person had been dead for a long time. I shuddered, thinking about the skeletal form at the desk.

When Agent Walker had left the bar, Shayla pounced on Kevin. "What happened? Who's dead now?"

"A man by the name of John Simpson, according to his wallet," he said. "It looked like he'd been shot once in the back of the head. Whoever did it was secure about leaving his personal possessions with him. All his personal effects were intact."

Tim frowned. "Why didn't Agent Walker tell *me*? You're not even a *real* FBI agent anymore."

"Are you saying that's Wild Johnny Simpson up there?" I demanded in disbelief. How often is it that you come face-to-face with a legend?

"You mean, you know that guy?" Shayla seemed amazed. Of course, she wasn't from Duck and hadn't grown up with all of the stories I'd heard about the two sisters and their lover.

"Not personally," I explained. "It's like folklore around here. Everyone knows about Miss Elizabeth and Wild Johnny Simpson."

"Well, I don't know about it, and Kevin probably doesn't either. I think we should go get a drink and discuss it." Shayla smiled at her date.

"I could make us a drink right here," he said.

"*Please!* There's a dead guy upstairs. It was bad enough that I had to *see* him. *And* smell him." Shayla grabbed her purse. "Let's get out of here."

We decided to walk back to Wild Stallions since it would be the only place open this late. Somehow as we walked down the narrow road between the heavy bushes, Shayla ended up in front with Tim, and I found myself in back with Kevin. Except for the sound of the ocean, the night was quiet. Most of the traffic on Duck Road was already gone.

"I hope you don't mind that I took credit for finding the hidden drawer," he said.

"I was a little curious about why you did it. You were the one who told me I should be honest with Agent Walker tomorrow." I corrected myself: "I mean, today."

"I know. But it's my place, and I felt like I should take the responsibility. I can correct it, if you want me to."

"That's all right. I guess I'll have enough to talk about with Agent Walker at our interview."

"That's what I was thinking." He glanced around as the steady breeze stirred the bushes near us. "This place has atmosphere, doesn't it? Even without finding a thirty-year-old corpse in the inn."

"He wasn't thirty," I corrected. "He had to be in his sixties when he was killed. He would've been about the same age as the sisters."

"That's not what I meant. We'll have to wait for the ME

to know for sure, but I'd be willing to guess he's been up there since the Blue Whale closed thirty years ago. He was already almost mummified."

Thankfully, our exit off the side street and onto Duck Road saved me from having to think about that last comment. We switched partners as we crossed the road and headed for the bar.

It had been a long day, beginning with the purse snatching and ending with yet another homicide for Chief Michaels to investigate. I yawned as we went up the stairs to the boardwalk that led to the bar. I wasn't looking forward to a drink, instead wishing I were home in bed. It was only a few hours until my interview with Agent Walker. I wanted to be awake for it. I'm not much of a night person.

Someone must've heard me because Cody, one of Wild Stallions' owners, was already closing up. "Sorry. I have to close early. My wife is in labor. Rain check?"

"Of course!" I hoped I didn't sound as relieved as I felt. "Give Sally my love."

"Thanks, Dae. We'll let you know how it turns out."

We seemed to be at a loss for something to do. We were close to Missing Pieces, so I offered to make coffee at the shop. Shayla wasn't happy about being denied her rum (she seems to be part pirate), but Kevin and Tim were happy to accept.

Shayla made up for her disappointment by sitting between Kevin and Tim on the brocade sofa, leaving me to make the coffee and haul out the chair from behind the counter for myself. By that time, Tim had already told the story about Miss Elizabeth and Wild Johnny Simpson. I poured four cups of coffee and put cream and sugar on the table. It was almost anticlimactic for me to sit down.

"Wow! What a story!" Shayla laughed and rolled her

eyes. "Do you think Miss Elizabeth or Miss Mildred killed Johnny and left him up there at the Blue Whale?"

Tim shrugged. "I guess it could've been either one of them if they did it with that little gun. Anybody could handle that."

"First, one of them would have to have some connection with the owner," Kevin said.

"If it's only been thirty years," I reminded them, "Johnny's death happened well after the sisters fought over him. I can't imagine either one of them going up there and killing him."

"I don't know," Tim said. "Those two always had that between them. If Miss Mildred knew Johnny was here, I wouldn't put it past her."

Shayla put down her cup and yawned. "As interesting as all of this is, I have to go. I have a bikini wax at seven thirty. I'd hate to mess that up."

Tim offered to take her home. "I've got the car out front. I have to go past your place anyway."

"Okay." Shayla glanced at Kevin, no doubt to see if he had any reaction to Tim's proposal. "I guess I'll see you two tomorrow."

"I could take you too, Kevin," Tim offered as an afterthought.

"No, that's okay. I'd rather walk. See you later, Shayla."

Shayla's disappointment was written on her pretty face. "Yeah. Maybe tomorrow?"

"Maybe." Kevin showed no sign of remorse at letting her go with Tim.

As Tim and Shayla called out their good-nights, I carried the coffee cups over to the small sink in the back of the shop and began washing them out. Kevin brought the coffeepot over to me. I thanked him, and then my mind immediately leapt to small talk. "I think the Blue Whale will be nice when you finish it."

"Thanks. I won't be able to do much until they get done with the investigation. It's hard to believe that guy was up there all that time and nobody knew."

"Except the killer." I took the coffeepot from him.

"That's true," he agreed.

"I can't believe there are two deaths being investigated in Duck at the same time. It will be on everybody's blog and the topic of conversation for years. That's the way we are."

"I like it. I like Duck. I'm sorry I didn't retire years ago." He glanced around Missing Pieces. "Can I walk you home?"

"No. That's okay. I might hang around a while and do some straightening up." I was lying, of course. I could hardly keep my eyes open. All I wanted to do was lie down and not get up until morning. But I needed him for the interview with Agent Walker, and it didn't seem right to impose on him anymore. We didn't know each other *that* well. "Good night, Kevin. I'm glad we found your key, even if it did lead to something terrible."

He smiled. "It was good that we found him. Someone probably misses him. I guess you *are* good at finding lost things. Good night, Dae."

I locked the door behind him, stuck my hand in my pocket and remembered the key I'd found on the stairs. It was too late to call him back. I'd have to give it to him later. I took it out and looked at it again in the light. I was right about the size and shape of it. Someone had probably dropped it years ago before the Blue Whale was closed. I knew from the way I'd felt when I picked it up that the key was important. But right now I was tired and couldn't think about it anymore. I opened the cash register and stashed the key inside.

It had been a very eventful day, *too* eventful. I still hadn't recovered from finding Miss Elizabeth. I didn't need the added anxiety of finding another dead person. I turned out the lights and sat down on the old brocade sofa.

I wondered what Johnny Simpson had been doing back in Duck after all those years. Had anyone known he was here? Obviously, *someone* knew. It was likely that person was the one who'd killed him. Could it have been one of the sisters?

I pulled my feet up on the sofa and closed my eyes. Shayla might feel that ghosts weren't important, but they were more important to me than a lot of the tangible things that went on every day. I *believed* in the afterlife. I'd grown up on stories of ghostly visitations that predicted storms and of spectral lights that led people to safety during pirate raids.

There was one ghost in particular I wanted to see. My mother had died in a car accident as she was crossing the bridge to the mainland thirteen years ago. I was a rebellious twenty-three-year-old at the time who'd wanted to camp out on the beach with a group of hard-drinking bikers.

We'd argued fiercely about it, the end result being one of those not-while-you-live-under-my-roof kind of things. I promised to move out as quickly as possible. She didn't back down.

She'd gone off without me that day. It was raining hard, and the bridge was wet and slippery. They said she had a blowout and lost control of the car. It pitched over the rail and into the sound. They never found her body, as so often happens in the waters off the Outer Banks.

For the first few months after she died, I hardly slept, waiting for her, torn apart by guilt. I quit college and spent most of my time staring out at the sound. There was unfinished business between us, the hallmark of most ghostly happenings. Every sigh in the eaves, every unusual creak in the old wood, sent me out into the hall looking for her.

I was desperate to apologize and try to make amends. But after six months, I realized it might take something more than waiting around. That's how I met Shayla. She didn't have a shop on the boardwalk then. She'd recently moved to Duck and was working out of her home. She tried to contact my mother during a séance. Shayla and I became friends, but there was no message for me from the other side.

Part of me gave up then and reasoned that one unresolved argument wasn't a big deal. We knew we loved each other. We'd always been close. Talking to her one last time would've been great, but it wasn't necessary.

Part of me *still* believed. Sometimes, in the deep night, when I thought I heard her voice in the wind, I'd sit up for hours, waiting for her. I'd learned most of those island ghost stories from her. She'd come back, if she could. How many times had I repeated those words to myself? *She'd come back, if she could.*

I pulled up the blue afghan she'd knitted for me and snuggled down under it, pretending I could still smell her perfume. She'd made this for me on my twelfth birthday. I had many things that she'd given me through the years, but none that I cherished more than this.

It was the death and despair that made me long for her again. Tears slid down my face. I told myself to get up and go home before it got any later. Gramps would be worried. Sitting here crying wasn't going to make that interview in the morning any better.

I closed my eyes, just for a second, to clear them. I'd get up in a minute and drag myself home. It had been a long day, that's all.

When I opened them again, it was morning. Don't ask me how that happened. Sunlight rushed in through the shop windows, blinding me, and someone was pounding on the door. "Dae! Are you in there?"

I wasn't sure if I was there or not. I recognized Kevin's voice and sat up straight on the sofa. My face felt pushed in on the right side where I'd been lying against it, and my hair was standing up on my head. Added to that, my clothes were wrinkled and smelled like the old inn. I wasn't a fit sight for man nor beast, as Gramps frequently says after a long night playing pinochle.

I hoped Kevin would go away, but he kept yelling and pounding. The headache I'd woken up with pounded with him. There was no other way to get rid of him. I was going to have to answer the door.

I tied a blue scarf around my hair on my way to the sink, where I splashed some water in my face. I didn't have a toothbrush so I used my finger and some water to freshen up my mouth. Finally, I shouted, "I'm coming! *Please* stop yelling."

He stopped yelling *and* pounding. I opened the shop door and found him standing there in a gray suit and black tie. Gramps was beside him, still wearing his flannel pajamas with the fish on them. I couldn't imagine a more unlikely duo. It almost made me laugh.

"*There* you are! You promised you wouldn't sleep here any more." Gramps rushed toward me. "We've looked everywhere for you. I tried calling here a dozen times. You weren't answering your cell phone. Kevin and I have been scouring Duck for you. Martha Segall assured me that you were attacked and left for dead like Lizzie. I told her to mind her own damn business."

The story, and the large, coffee-scented bear hug, was almost too much. I swallowed hard and looked past Gramps to Kevin. "You're out looking for me too?"

"I was *supposed* to meet you at town hall at eight, remember?"

I suddenly realized what had happened. I glanced at the teapot clock in the shop. It was almost ten thirty. "I fell asleep! What am I going to do?"

"You're going to go home, take a shower and change clothes," he said with all the authority his gray suit could muster. "I'll tell everyone, and we'll meet you at town hall at eleven. Can you do that?"

"I think so." My brain was still not functional. Maybe my reasoning was a little fuzzy too, but it occurred to me that there was a *long* time between eight and ten thirty. "You were *late* for the SBI meeting too! Even if I'd been there on time, you'd just be getting there now."

He nodded. "Guilty as charged. When I went back to the inn last night, I got caught up in looking for other secret places, so I overslept this morning too. Oh well, all's well that ends well. So . . . are you going to change clothes or not?"

I realized he had the right idea. Kevin hadn't shown up, but neither had I. I could hardly hold that against him. I glanced at Gramps. "Did you bring the golf cart?"

"You know it. Let's hop to it, Dae. I don't think you should keep these men waiting again."

With a murmur of thanks to Kevin for taking care of contacting Chief Michaels and Agent Walker, I left with Gramps, and we drove down to the house in record time. At least record time for the old golf cart.

I grabbed the black suit I usually reserved for important mayoral duties, then jumped in the shower. There was no time to really fix my hair, so I tied it back in a ponytail, put on the black suit, shoved my feet into black sandals and ran back downstairs again. Gramps held out a piece of toast with orange marmalade and a bottle of water. I took it, said thanks and raced out the door.

It was only ten fifty when I reached my office in town hall. Kevin was there with Chief Michaels and Tim. Agent Walker was absent. I didn't mind getting there first. I took a deep breath, plastered a polite but apologetic smile on my face and sailed behind my desk.

"Gentlemen, I'm sorry I was delayed."

"Delayed?" Chief Michaels demanded. "You're almost three hours *late*. I hope you have a good story to tell Agent Walker. I don't want Duck to be the laughingstock of the state."

"I hardly think a late mayor will cause that, Chief." I tried to calm him down. "I got caught up doing . . . *inventory* . . . last night and fell asleep in the shop. I don't know if that's a good story or not, but it's what I've got."

While the chief scowled and mumbled, Kevin came up to the front of my desk. "I think you have a little jelly on your mouth," he whispered, his lips flirting with a smile.

I picked up a tissue from the desk and dabbed at my lips. He nodded when I finished and walked to the corner of the room again. I was beginning to see a pattern in the places he chose to sit and stand. They were always the best vantage point to keep an eye on the room and the door. Maybe something left over from his FBI days?

As Kevin took up his chosen post, Agent Walker and several of his officers walked into the office. I had to give the same speech all over again, minus the marmalade on my mouth. I suggested we all sit down, and Nancy brought in coffee for everyone. I was never so happy to see a cup of coffee in my life.

"I'm glad to see you're all right after everything that happened last night, Mayor O'Donnell," Agent Walker said.

"Call her Dae," Tim offered. "Everybody does. We aren't too formal here in Duck."

Agent Walker cleared his throat. "I hope you're not too uncomfortable, *ma'am*. I didn't foresee having such a large audience for our interview."

I could tell Agent Walker was having a bad day too. I took a sip of Nancy's awful coffee, then put down the cup before I spilled it and managed to look even more ridiculous. "As I said, Agent Walker, I apologize for the delay in the interview. The audience doesn't bother me. I guess you can consider them advisors."

He lifted his eyebrows before he put on his reading glasses but didn't comment further. "Mayor, if you could describe the attack when you had your purse taken. Include where you were at the time, your reaction and everything that ensued until the arrest of Brian McDonald."

So that's the name of the young man. I settled myself in my chair and told him what had happened from the time Brian McDonald had pushed me into the side of Missing Pieces until Tim jumped on him from the boardwalk in the parking lot. "He didn't have time to take anything."

Agent Walker scribbled my words into a notebook. "Did you ever notice him around town before that event?"

"Yes. He came to my shop on the Fourth of July and asked about a job. I told him I didn't have anything."

"So we know McDonald was hanging around the area, scoping out his prey." Agent Walker looked up at me. "Was

Mrs. Simpson in the habit of walking through town with her purse?"

"I never saw her without it," I answered. "Not until that night when Mr. Brickman and I found her in the dunes."

He nodded. "Did you feel threatened by the purse-snatching incident, beyond losing your purse?"

"I suppose so. He shoved me pretty hard. Mostly I was angry and determined to get my purse back."

"I'm sure Chief Michaels and Officer Mabry have both scolded you for chasing McDonald. It ended well this time, but it could've ended badly for you."

"I know. Several people have mentioned it." I glanced at Kevin. "More coffee, Agent Walker?"

"No, thanks. Mayor, I'm going to tell you something that can't leave this room. It would jeopardize our investigation if it got out to the media."

I sipped my coffee. "I understand. I won't tell anyone."

He removed his glasses. "We believe Brian McDonald may be responsible for Mrs. Simpson's death. Our scenario is that he came upon Mrs. Simpson. She fought him for her purse, and he hit her with something. Then he buried her in the sand."

"How awful." I thought about what Shayla had said. "Do you think she was dead when he buried her?"

"We don't have that information yet," he admitted. "We found his motel room in Kill Devil Hills. He had a lot of purses stashed in there, hundreds of them. We're still going through them, hoping we find Mrs. Simpson's. That would connect him to the crime without a confession. If not, we may have to charge him on the strength of the circumstantial evidence. Either way, we may need you to testify against him."

I swallowed hard. "Of course. Whatever I can do to help."

He leaned toward me. His voice dropped to a whisper. "Can *you* find the purse?"

I wasn't sure what to say. Obviously he was alluding to my gift. "I'm afraid it doesn't work that way. I would have to be able to *touch* Miss Elizabeth to find something she lost."

"We could drive up to the morgue today."

That made me uncomfortable. This was definitely not what I'd expected from him. "I think she'd have to be alive. In order for me to find a missing object, the person who's looking for it has to be thinking about it. I know it seems complicated, but I didn't make the rules. I think I came with them."

"Have you ever tried touching someone who *wasn't* alive, you know, to experiment?"

"No!"

"Just a thought." He pulled out another notebook, identical to the first one—black, cheap and a little worn. "As to this new development, I assume Mr. Brickman filled you in on the identity of the dead man found at his establishment."

I glanced at Kevin. He didn't appear to be upset that Agent Walker knew he'd told me—not to mention Tim and Shayla—about Johnny. "Yes. I could hardly believe Wild Johnny Simpson came back to Duck to die."

"It wasn't quite as simple as that, Mayor. Someone *killed* Mr. Simpson. It was a long time ago, but there is no statute of limitation on murder. He was shot in the head. Do you think his wife might have been responsible?"

"I don't know." *Miss Elizabeth as a murderer?* "I guess anything is possible. Isn't it ironic that she was killed before we could ask her?"

"Ironic . . . or *timely,* at least for her?" Agent Walker put away his black notebooks and got to his feet. "Thank you for your help, Mayor O'Donnell. We'll be in touch. And if you change your mind about wanting to try out your talent on Mrs. Simpson, give me a call." He handed me his card.

I didn't tell him there was no chance I would change my mind, but there was no chance. I smiled, nodded and saw him to the door. His men followed him out.

Chief Michaels closed the door after them. "Well that was a fine howdy-do!"

Chapter 8

"That fella sweeps in here from Raleigh and takes over not one but *two* homicides. My boys and I could've handled the situation. We're trained. I was with the Dare County Sheriff's Department before Walker was old enough to carry a gun. I've been chief here in Duck longer than most people can remember. I *know* what I'm doing."

Tim laughed a little at the chief's humor. "That's right. Who collared that boy for them anyway? Without me and Dae, they'd still be out knocking on doors looking for Miss Elizabeth's killer."

I wasn't sure how much of that was true. As far as I knew, the Duck Police Department had never investigated a murder. I wasn't sure they had the manpower to do everything that needed to be done. But I smiled and nodded, wishing they would be on their way. I wanted to sit on the boardwalk for a while before I had to open the shop. It was nice outside. Warm, with a steady breeze blowing off the sound.

"That reminds me." Chief Michaels put down his empty coffee cup and looked at me. "I had a call last night from Millie. Seems she's been seeing her sister's ghost over at the house. I told her to go back to sleep and call in the morning. She called again at six A.M. on the dot. I guess I'll go over and check on her."

Tim volunteered to go over for him. "You shouldn't have to do something like that, Chief. Let me take care of it."

"No, that's okay. I offered to go, and you know what she's like. I'll end up over there anyway if I let you go." The chief looked at me again.

"Would you like me to go with you?" I offered, even though I knew I should be getting over to the shop to open up for the day. But the chance to talk to Miss Mildred about her ghost was too tempting. Treasure hunters would have to wait until I got back.

"That would be real nice of you, Mayor. I'm sure she'd like to see a friendly female face too. Losing someone in your family does strange things to you. But I don't have to tell you that, do I?"

I didn't comment on his remark. I'd had a few bad times after my mother died. As long as I lived here, there were going to be people reminding me of it.

Kevin came out of the corner and smiled at me as though he understood. He couldn't possibly, of course. He hadn't been here, and I felt pretty secure that no one had told him about it yet. If he stayed for a while, he was bound to hear about those times. I didn't fool myself into thinking otherwise. "If you don't need me to be here anymore, I'm going home to work on the roof," he said.

"Need *you* to be here?" Tim asked. "She has me and the chief. We've known her all of her life."

I extended my hand to Kevin. "Thanks for coming. It wasn't as bad as I thought it would be."

"Even with that part about touching dead people to find their stuff?"

"Even with that." I shivered. "No way that's going to happen."

"I figured as much. I'll talk to you later." He nodded at Tim and the chief. "Gentlemen."

The chief nodded back, but Tim looked away. When Kevin was gone, he had his say. "I can't *believe* you asked him to be here."

"He was with the FBI." I defended my action. "I thought he might know more about the way the SBI does business."

"More than *us?*" Tim followed the chief and me out of the office. "Come on, Dae. You wanted him around because he's new and all mysterious and everything. I saw the way Shayla was with him last night."

"I'm not Shayla." I turned to the chief. "Are you driving?"

"Yes, ma'am." He took my hint and told Tim to go out on patrol. Then the chief and I headed to the parking lot and got in the car. It was already hot as only July can be in the South. "You know, you should give that boy a break, Mayor. He's loved you all his life. Why don't you make an honest man out of him?"

I was used to people in town talking to me about personal things. They'd been doing it since I was born. "I'm not ready for anything like that, Chief. Tim's nice, but he's not for me."

"And Brickman is?"

"I didn't say that. I don't know what Tim's talking about. I was with *him* last night. Shayla was with Kevin. We were all together at the inn to look for the key. That's it."

The chief nodded and smiled as he turned out of the lot and headed toward Miss Mildred's street. "So he's *Kevin* now, huh? I guess you two are moving fast. Poor Tim. He never saw it coming."

I didn't answer that. Thankfully, we were in Miss Mildred's driveway before he could think of anything else to say. It's not that I mind people discussing my personal life. Well, I do, but short of moving away, there's not much I can do about it. And not that I don't talk about other people's lives. But I wasn't really ready to share any more information about Kevin. Not that there was any more to tell.

Andy Martin of Andy's Ice Cream was trimming the hedges in Miss Mildred's yard. He shut off the electric trimmer when he saw us. "I'm glad you're here, Chief. Miss Millie has been frantic for you all morning."

"I know. I brought the mayor with me to help with the situation."

Andy smiled. "Better the two of you than me. Miss Millie can be hard to handle, bless her heart. And she *did* just lose her sister. Is it true you all found Wild Johnny Simpson up at the Blue Whale yesterday?"

"That's right," the chief responded. "Does Millie know about it yet?"

"Probably. She still reads the paper. That's where I got it."

"Damn newspaper people!"

"Think they'll have a reunion since both of them are dead now?"

"Doubtful. Johnny has been dead a good thirty years, according to the SBI. Don't start spreading rumors, Andy. Mayor, let's go inside."

I knocked at the big front door, bougainvillea draping across it in pink splendor. I didn't hear any movement inside, so I turned the handle and pushed it open. "Miss Mildred? Where are you?"

The front hall closet door opened, and she popped her head out. "Do you see her out there?"

"There's nobody out here but me and the mayor, Millie," the chief assured her. "Come on out of there."

Carefully looking around the room, the old lady did as he requested. "Thank God you're finally here, Ronnie. Lizzie has been here all night long. She probably heard you pull up, and it scared her off."

"Come and sit down, Miss Mildred," I coaxed. "Have you eaten? Let me make you some tea."

"Tea?" She made a spitting sound. "Child, I need some strong coffee with a little brandy in it. It keeps my heart beating."

"I'll get that for you, if you'll eat something. I don't think you should have brandy on an empty stomach."

We all walked into the spotless, sunlit kitchen. Lines of copper pans hung alongside large copper utensils on the yellow wall. I found some eggs and butter, then slipped bread into the toaster. Chief Michaels helped her sit down at the wooden table, then sat beside her.

"I know you're going to think I'm crazy," Miss Mildred began, shaking her head.

"I don't think any such thing," the chief assured her. "You're just agitated. Who wouldn't be with their sister dying that way and all?"

She sniffed. "And Dae still hasn't brought my watch back. You know, this whole thing started when I asked her to find Mama's watch."

"Millie, you can't have the watch back right now. It's evidence. There was a boy who snatched Dae's purse yesterday. He's not from around here. We think he might've taken Miss Elizabeth's purse too. She may have been killed in the process. I'm sorry."

"That doesn't make any sense. My sister was strong, Ronnie. You know that. I think she gave you a paddling one day when you wouldn't pay attention in Sunday school. She wouldn't let anyone knock her down and take her purse."

"I'm sorry, Millie. But we think that's what happened. We haven't found her purse yet, but we think we have the man who took it from her. I know it's hard for you to hear."

I'd finished the eggs and buttered the toast by the time they were done talking. I could see Miss Mildred impatiently pushing at tears as they ran down her cheeks. She didn't want to admit how this was affecting her, and that was a bad thing. She needed to open up about it to someone. Maybe not me, or the chief. I made a mental note to call Mary Lou. Maybe someone closer to being her contemporary could help out.

There was no one left in Duck with the mythological status of Miss Mildred and her sister. When Miss Mildred finally passed on, the story of her and her sister would live on only in the words of others. Of course, Miss Elizabeth's terrible death and the discovery of Wild Johnny Simpson's body would fuel some gossip for a while. It seemed to me that after thirty years, no one would ever be *quite* sure who killed Johnny.

"Maybe you should have someone come in and stay with you," I suggested as I put the plate in front of her.

"Don't be silly. I'm fine. Or at least I *would* be if Lizzie would stay dead." Her pale eyes looked deeply into mine. "Why is she haunting me, Dae? I know we had some problems when she was alive. But I swear I thought we always loved each other. Despite Johnny and everything else."

I put my hand on hers. It trembled beneath my touch, as cold as if she'd come in from a December storm. "I'm sure she loved you, Miss Mildred. Maybe she has something she needs to tell you." I couldn't help it. The chief frowned at me for encouraging her, but who was he to say her sister *wasn't* visiting her?

"That's exactly what I was thinking." She patted my hand and picked up her fork. "Maybe you know someone who could help me. There must be someone left who can talk to the dead. If you could bring someone like that here, maybe we could get things sorted out. I don't like that the police can't find who killed Lizzie. I bet she's impatient with it too."

"We're doing our best, Millie." Chief Michaels shook his head. "There's not much to go on except for that purse snatcher. If we could find Lizzie's purse in that mess he has, we could make an arrest."

"Well why didn't you say so?" Miss Mildred pushed back her chair, scraping the legs on the wood floor. "She brought it to me yesterday. Maybe she knew you were looking for it."

Chief Michaels looked at me as though waiting for me to explain that what was happening *wasn't* happening. I shrugged and shook my head. I had no idea what Miss Mildred was talking about.

"You don't understand, Millie," the chief struggled to

explain. "We think she had her purse with her when she was killed. That's why the purse snatcher killed her, to get her purse."

"Nonsense." Miss Mildred went to a shelf by the back window. She picked up a black purse and brought it back to the table. "Here you are. Go out and find Lizzie's killer. If I would've known you needed it, I would've brought it to you. Maybe that's why Lizzie brought it here. She probably knew you wanted it."

I looked at the purse on the table. I was afraid to do anything more. Chief Michaels hadn't moved. I knew he felt the same. What did it mean? Had Miss Mildred had her sister's purse the whole time?

Chief Michaels finally broke the spell by taking latex gloves from his pocket and putting them on. "When did you say Lizzie brought this?"

"Just yesterday. I told her I'd keep it safe. You know she never went anywhere without her purse. Isn't that right, Dae?"

"Th-that's right."

Carefully, Chief Michaels opened the purse and looked through it. One by one, he placed Miss Elizabeth's ID, embroidered handkerchief and other personal items on the table as he searched. There was no doubt that this was her purse.

Just when I thought he'd finished, the chief glanced at me and then leaned the opened purse toward me, so I could see into it. Pushed down into the bottom was what looked like a pair of blue gardening gloves. They seemed to be covered with blood. Chief Michaels didn't pull them out. Instead, he sighed heavily, then said, "Millie, I'll have to take this back with me. I'll need to take a look around the house and in the garden shed too."

With a large, cheerful smile, Miss Mildred gave him her permission to search her house and land. "Whatever I can do to help Lizzie rest, Ronnie. Maybe she led a wicked life, but the Bible says we should forgive."

My heart was racing against my mind, searching for answers that made sense. He was taking advantage of an old lady who didn't understand what was going on. "Chief, if I can have a moment outside."

"I'll finish up these eggs before they get cold." Miss Mildred excused us like the children she'd taught in her youth.

When the chief and I were outside, I whispered, "You can't *really* think she killed her."

"I can't think she didn't, Mayor. Dammit, she has the *purse*! We've accused a man of killing Lizzie because we thought he had her purse. Millie has said from the beginning that Lizzie didn't deserve to go to heaven. And you saw how calm she was when we told her about her death. It was staring us right in the face all the time."

"No. There's no way. All sisters fight. They weren't any different than other sisters. Miss Mildred was in shock when we told her about Miss Elizabeth. And you know she's not always here"—I pointed to my head—"when you talk to her. That doesn't mean she killed anyone."

"I'm sorry, Mayor. But it's my job to find the truth. Right now, I think the truth might be that Millie finally lost it with Lizzie. She hit her with something, left her out there on the dunes and brought her purse back with her. I'll know more once we check everything out."

"This is wrong. You know it's wrong."

"If you really want to help out, Mayor, you'll go back in there and tell Millie to think about what she used to kill her sister. Hold her hands and find it for us. That's what *you* can do."

If possible, I was more horrified than when Kevin and I had found Miss Elizabeth on the beach. This new scenario made me physically sick. I watched the chief go back to his car, my stomach clenched in nausea and fear. I rushed back inside and locked the front door.

But what could I do? This wasn't a fortress. I couldn't bar the gates and not let him in. Miss Mildred needed help, but not the kind I could give her. I pulled out my cell phone and called the only person I could think of. "Gramps, you have to find a lawyer and get over to Miss Mildred's house *fast*. Chief Michaels wants to accuse her of murder."

I quickly dead-bolted both doors into the house. I waited for help as Chief Michaels came back to conduct his search and found he couldn't get inside. He pounded on the door and shouted my name. There was a penalty for keeping the police from doing their job. I didn't care. Someone had to protect Miss Mildred, and I was the only one around. I wished Mary Lou and her turtle rescuers were here. They might have known better what to do.

"You have to let us in sometime, Mayor," the chief yelled. "This is obstruction of justice, you know."

"What's going on outside?" Miss Mildred asked. "Ronnie sounds angry."

"Just a little disagreement," I answered with a smile. "Maybe you'd like to lie down for a while since you were in the closet all night."

"That's a good idea, Dae, thank you. I'll go outside and check the mail first."

"*No!*" She stared at me with troubled eyes when I caught her hand as she reached for the doorknob. "I mean, not right now. Maybe after your nap. The mail isn't here yet anyway."

"Are you feeling all right?"

"I'm fine. Thank you." I resumed my guard at the front window. Would they call in the SBI and use a battering ram to break down the front door? Would I be led away in handcuffs with Miss Mildred while Jerry Richards tried to ask us questions for his next TV news feature?

I was scared *and* paranoid. I didn't know what to expect. I wanted to do what was right for Miss Mildred, but the consequences might be awful. I squared my shoulders, prepared to face the worst. Then I heard the first siren.

I knew the entire Duck Police Department was already outside. Chief Michaels had made sure of that. There was only one other group with sirens—Gramps had called on his volunteer firefighter friends for help. Within seconds, there were trucks, cars and firefighting vehicles everywhere. They outnumbered the police five to one.

I laughed out loud. Miss Mildred frowned with concern. I didn't care. At least Gramps was there. I looked out again and saw that Kevin had joined the group too. I wasn't sure how I felt about that. He could either be there to help me save Miss Mildred or to add his expertise in helping Chief Michaels.

Gramps and a tall man with a sandy-colored buzz cut spoke to Chief Michaels and Kevin for a moment. I held my breath as the men talked in the yard, glancing at the house occasionally. Finally, Gramps and the man I didn't recognize approached the house. The chief and Kevin stayed where they were, arms folded resolutely across their chests.

I stood behind the door until I heard Gramps call my

name, then I slid back the dead bolt, opened it quickly and let them in the house. "I'm so glad to see you!" I hugged him. "I didn't know what else to do. I'm sorry to drag you into this."

"I'm not sorry you called me, honey." Gramps patted my back. "I'm sorry you decided to take a stand on this. I don't know there's much I can do to help."

"But maybe I can do something," Sandy Buzz-Cut said. "I'm Luke Helms. I used to be a prosecutor in Wake County before I retired to my fishing boat this month."

I shook his hand eagerly. "Thank you so much for coming. I don't know exactly how I got into this mess. I wanted to help Miss Mildred."

"Let's sit down for a minute of the five they gave us and tell me what happened." Luke took off his bright yellow jacket. "You're lucky they let us in at all. They didn't have to."

"She's *my* granddaughter and the mayor of Duck," Gramps protested. "The chief did the only rational thing he *could* do. Now, tell Luke the story, Dae."

So I spilled it, everything from Miss Mildred putting Miss Elizabeth's purse on the table to the chief saying he was going to search her house and land. "It's not right. She didn't realize what she was giving him permission to do."

Luke nodded. "She's incapable of making that kind of judgment?"

"I don't know if I'd say that about every circumstance, but—"

"What Dae is trying to say is that she fears for my sanity because my sister visited me last night," Miss Mildred added. "She's a very sweet girl with remarkable talents. But I'm not senile. I *know* what I saw. And I have nothing to hide from Ronnie. He's welcome in my house anytime."

I tried to think of a nice way to say it, but there wasn't one, so I blurted it out—"Chief Michaels thinks you killed your sister."

Miss Mildred's eyebrows disappeared into the cloud of her white hair. "Why on earth would he think something like that?"

The sound of Chief Michaels's voice, amplified by a bullhorn, interrupted us. "Your five minutes is up in there. We're coming in, even if we have to break down the door."

Chapter 9

"What do we do now?" I looked at both men with something like panic beating in my chest.

Luke shook his head. "Well, if Miss Mildred is okay with the chief searching her house—"

"I didn't know he wanted to put me in prison," Miss Mildred protested. "I didn't kill anybody. I wouldn't hurt my sister for anything. Please help me."

"In that case, he needs a search warrant," Gramps said. "That's clear as glass."

"He may not see it that way," Luke added. "But you're right. We can hold him off for as long as it takes to get a warrant. He'll be in here sometime. You can't keep him out forever since he found evidence here."

"What about if we hide the purse?" I suggested.

"That's tampering with evidence. That will make the

124

police angrier and could land you in jail, Mayor," Luke explained. "There's no point in making the situation worse."

"So we hand it over?" I couldn't believe there was no way to protect Miss Mildred.

"That would be the best thing. If she didn't kill her sister, there won't be anything to hide." Luke glanced at Miss Mildred, discomfort written all over his face. I attributed it to his giving advice to possible law breakers instead of prosecuting them. "Are you sure you don't remember *anyone* visiting you who could've dropped off your sister's purse?"

"No. No one has been here, except for Andy. He was working outside and didn't come in. Lizzie brought me her purse," Miss Mildred insisted. "I know how that sounds. I've never been much of a believer in this kind of thing. But I swear on my mother's Bible, that's what happened."

The front door burst open. I hadn't replaced the dead bolt when I let Gramps and Luke in. Chief Michaels stood there glowering, with Kevin, Tim and several other Duck police officers at his side. "Miss Mildred, you're under arrest for murdering your sister, Elizabeth Simpson."

Luke shot to his feet. "That's a mighty big jump, Chief, going from wanting to search her house to accusing her of murder."

"Stay out of the way, lawyer boy." The chief took out his handcuffs. "Now you know I'm as sorry as I can be about this."

"I can tell since you plan on handcuffing a ninety-two-year-old woman," I berated him, moving to stand in front of her. They weren't taking her without knocking me down. What good was it to be the mayor if I couldn't protect someone who needed my help?

"Dae, you can't interfere with this," Kevin advised.

"Stay out of this," I responded. "I'm not letting *anyone* take her to jail."

It was a standoff. Clearly no one knew exactly what to do. The chief lifted his cap and scratched his head, his face already bright red. Kevin folded his arms against his chest and stepped back. Gramps and Luke stood on either side of me. I couldn't help but wonder how this would end. I knew they could force us out of the way and take Miss Mildred, but I thought that was unlikely.

An answer came in the form of Jerry Richards, who barged in with his cameraman. "All right, pan on those three over there, then back on the chief and his men."

"What the hell is going on?" Chief Michaels demanded, looking at Tim.

"I don't know." Tim looked at Jerry Richards, then at the officers behind him. "Escort Mr. Richards back outside."

"I'm not going anywhere," Jerry said. "We have a right to see what's going on. Mayor O'Donnell, tell me what's happening in here."

I opened my mouth to do just that, but the chief got between me and the camera. "If I could have a word in the next room, Mayor. Maybe we can resolve this issue."

I glanced at Gramps, who assured me nothing would happen while I was gone. I noticed as I followed the chief out of the room that Gramps and Luke stepped closer to Miss Mildred, who was holding up very well in the face of so much drama.

In the kitchen again with Miss Elizabeth's purse still open on the table, Chief Michaels confronted me. "Why'd you have to go and make this so complicated? We both love Millie, but she did something wrong. Maybe she isn't mentally responsible. She may not even realize she did it. If that's the case, they'll find a place for her. Don't be so stubborn. Let the process work. You're the mayor. You're sworn to uphold these laws, Dae. You can't pick and choose when it's comfortable for you."

I knew he was right. At least the *rational* part of my brain knew he was right. But after finding Miss Elizabeth, and everything else that had happened, the *emotional* part of my brain was on overload. "You know her sister didn't drop off this purse. But you also know Miss Mildred didn't kill her. You can't take her in on the strength of that evidence."

He drew a deep breath that threatened to burst the buttons on his blue uniform. "What if I told you there was more?"

I swallowed hard. "*More?* Like what?"

"She gave me permission to look around. I think we have the murder weapon. It was out in her garden shed."

"That's not possible." I sat down. "What makes you think it's the murder weapon?"

"It's a small shovel. There appears to be hair and blood on it." He put his hand on my shoulder. "We have to take her in, Dae."

"Why? She isn't going anywhere. She's not a flight risk. Couldn't she stay here while you continue investigating?"

"That's what bail is for. But someone not so involved with her should make that decision. You know if it was up to me, I'd walk away from it. But *we* can't do that. I can't, and neither can you."

There was no argument with that logic. "Can you at least not handcuff her? Her wrists are so delicate. I don't want to think what this will do to her."

As compromises went, it was the best we could reach. The chief treated Miss Mildred with dignity and kindness as he led her outside, no cuffs, to the police car. Gramps didn't

ask what changed my mind. Neither did Luke. I assumed
Tim or Kevin filled them in while we were in the kitchen.

Agent Walker and his SBI agents arrived a moment later
and took charge of Miss Elizabeth's purse. They began
searching the house and yard (again). There wasn't anything else I could do. I didn't want to watch the procedure.
Andy promised to lock up the house after they were gone.

"If she doesn't have legal representation, I'll see what I
can do," Luke offered. "It might be strange to be on that
side of the courtroom."

He didn't seem as though he thought that would be a
good thing, but I took his phone number and thanked him
for offering. "What will happen now?"

"The court will probably set bail for her. I can't imagine
they want to continue this publicity." Luke nodded toward
Jerry and his cameraman as they got in their van to follow
Chief Michaels to the police station. "She'll be evaluated
by a doctor to see if she's fit to stand trial."

I thanked him again and smiled. He hugged me awkwardly and promised to keep up with what was happening.
It seemed like a strange reaction from a man who looked
like an ex-Green Beret. He'd spent his whole life (or, by my
best guess, at least the last twenty years—he didn't appear
over fifty) sending the bad guys to jail. You never know how
people will react.

Gramps offered to drive me back to Missing Pieces, but
I needed time to walk and think. He drove off with the rest
of the fire department. I headed toward the corner without
looking back at the SBI agents swarming over Miss Mildred's house.

I heard footsteps coming up behind me on the shell and
gravel road. I glanced back, saw Kevin and started walking
faster.

He walked faster too. "I'm not the enemy, you know."

"No? I guess you were only on his side then."

"Chief Michaels isn't the enemy either. The enemy is whoever did this and set it up to look like Miss Mildred killed her sister."

I stopped. The sun was hot overhead even with the constant breeze rushing through the bushes. "You don't believe Miss Mildred killed her sister?"

"Of course not. I don't think the chief does either. But you were both bound to follow the rules. It's what happens in cases like this."

"Cases like *this?* How many ninety-two-year-old women are arrested for killing their sisters?"

"You'd be surprised. Maybe even more surprised if you knew how many of them actually did it."

I started walking again, maybe a *little* less angry. At least he seemed to be on my side. "Well, I don't believe Miss Mildred did anything wrong. But you're right. I know how the rules work. The chief was already questioning whether Miss Mildred should stay in her house by herself. Now it looks even worse. I don't want to think what a court-appointed doctor who isn't from Duck will think."

He nodded. "The chief will continue investigating. So will the SBI."

"Really? Once they establish that he found the murder weapon on her property and Miss Elizabeth's purse in her house, that will be the end of the investigation. Chief Michaels already pointed out to me that Miss Mildred wasn't that upset by her sister's death when we came to give her the news. Half the town was at the vigil when she said her sister probably didn't go to heaven because she was evil. I think you could say that's a slam dunk."

He didn't disagree. I kept wishing he would as we turned

to walk down Duck Road toward the shops on the board-walk. The road was crowded now with tourists driving in convertibles and SUVs. I wished it was winter, for once; have some peace to think.

"I looked up Wild Johnny Simpson in the hotel direc-tory last night." He changed the subject. "I found where he checked in on June 7, 1978. It doesn't show when he checked out."

"But it was around that time the old owner, Bunk Whit-ley, disappeared. Maybe Johnny was killed and the hotel closed so quickly, no one realized."

"Maybe. But someone had to put that key in the drawer. Whoever did it probably knew. I handed over the derringer to Agent Walker. I'm sure they'll check it against the bullet wound in Johnny's head."

We continued walking into the business district of Duck. I had to cross the crowded street to get back to Missing Pieces. I glanced at Kevin, wondering if all of this made more sense to him than to me. "You don't have to walk me all the way to the shop. I'm okay now. Unlikely to hold off the police, or the SBI, with hostages."

"I know. You were doing what you thought was right."

"Yeah. I'm lucky they didn't arrest me for it."

He laughed. "You're right. Of course, you're the mayor. It wouldn't look good for the town if that happened."

"True. But I won't push my luck again."

"Unless something else happens where you have to stand up for what you think is right. I might know you bet-ter than you know yourself."

"Quit profiling me!" There was an opening in the con-stant line of traffic going through town. I smiled and waved at Kevin, then darted across the street. I noticed that he waved back then set out toward the Blue Whale. I also noticed that he was wearing sandals. It made me smile again. Duck relaxation even got to hardened FBI types. Maybe someone could use that for a tourist slogan.

I unlocked Missing Pieces and turned on the lights. I was only there a few minutes before a crowd of shoppers began surging in. They were mostly looking for bargains and souvenirs. Nothing to threaten my treasures.

A few hours later, as I was ringing up some Duck T-shirts, Trudy came in from next door. She waited until I was finished with my customer to come behind the counter and take a seat. "I heard about Miss Mildred. It's awful, Dae. How can they arrest someone that old? I don't understand why they think she was involved in her sister's death."

I didn't want to go into the whole thing again. It was a little too fresh and painful to describe to her. "I'm hoping the police realize they've made a mistake and let her go back home."

"Someone said they saw you and your grandfather down there," Trudy whispered. "Did you see them take her away?"

I nodded. "I really don't want to talk about it right now. It wasn't exactly the bright spot of my day."

"I understand." She smiled a little and changed the subject. "I hear Shayla is dating that super-gorgeous new guy at the Blue Whale. I got that from her, so I'm *trusting* it's true."

"It's true. I went out with them last night."

A woman who looked as though she were carrying the weight of the world approached the counter. She had a little girl with her. The woman had a kid-size, blue party dress that had been part of a group of items I'd purchased from one of the local churches. It was left over from a Christmas bazaar. "How much for this one?" she asked.

I looked at the two of them and knew they couldn't afford it. No matter what the price was, there was no extra money for this dress. I also knew she wouldn't let me give it to her. It wasn't any psychic sense that made me understand. It was a few years of running a thrift store. Those who didn't need what I had to sell typically came in with a certain look of confidence, even arrogance, on their faces. People like this woman, however, had hopelessness written in their eyes. As mayor, I was well aware that among the well-to-do tourists and comfortable year-round residents, there were people in need living in Duck. I wished I could do more for them.

"I'm afraid that dress isn't for sale," I told her.

She looked at the little girl and tried to smile. "Oh. Thanks anyway."

"Some items I can only barter for. It's kind of a state law for thrift shops." Would she believe it?

She blinked twice and glanced at the girl again. "I don't think I have anything to barter for it. What did you have in mind?"

I wasn't quite sure. It had seemed like a good idea when I'd said it. The girl would get the dress and I would get . . . that's about where my thoughts ended. Now that I'd made up the bartering fantasy, I wasn't sure where to go with it.

"I need someone to go through all those children's clothes back there. I've accumulated too much recently. I need to get rid of some of them. But I don't know much about children's clothes. Maybe you could help me with that."

The woman grinned. "I'd be glad to. How long would you need me? I have to be at work at the restaurant by six, but I'm off tomorrow. Could I do it then?"

"That would be fine." I took out a piece of paper. "And your name?"

"Anne Maxwell. And this is Ginny. We live in Duck, down toward Southern Shores. Would it be all right if I bring her with me? I don't have a babysitter during the day."

"Sounds fine, Anne." I reached out my hand to her. "I'm Dae O'Donnell."

"The mayor? Or is that your mother?"

I laughed. "No, that's me. I guess I don't photograph very well."

"It was probably the black and white," she suggested. "Anyway, thank you for the opportunity. I'll see you tomorrow. Say good-bye, Ginny."

Ginny, probably five, waved her little hand and smiled to show her missing teeth. She had freckles on her cute little face, and her brown hair hung in baby curls on her shoulder.

I waved back, smiling, as they left the shop. "State law that makes you barter stuff, huh?" Trudy laughed.

"Did you see her little face? And how cute were her little hands?"

"Sounds like you'd like one of your own," Trudy observed. "I know I would. I don't know if it'll ever happen for me. But maybe for you. How many times has Tim proposed?"

"Too many. Please don't start sounding like Gramps." I tucked Anne's name into the drawer under the register. At least I wouldn't have to wonder *what if*, as I did with Brian McDonald, the purse snatcher. "Besides, we're independent women, right? We're business owners. Entrepreneurs. Men aren't necessary for women of the world like us."

"I don't know who you're talking about, Dae." Trudy got

to her feet and patted an invisible platinum blond hair back into place. "But I'd give up all of this for the right guy."

At that moment, Kevin walked into the store with an armload of Blue Whale T-shirts. Trudy and I stared at him for a long moment before we both started laughing. "Should I go out and come back in?" he asked.

"No." Trudy smiled at him. "I think you're perfect right where you are. You're not married, are you?"

"No." He looked at me as if expecting an explanation.

"Kevin, this is my friend Trudy Devereaux. She runs the Curves and Curls Beauty Spa next door. Trudy, this is Kevin Brickman."

"From the Blue Whale Inn, right?" She walked over to him and held out her hand. "Welcome to Duck, Kevin. I do men's cuts, manicures, and massages too. Stop in sometime."

She stood there for a long moment holding his hand and gazing into his eyes. Only a customer trying to get into the shop broke them apart. Trudy smiled apologetically, then went next door.

"Women are very friendly here." Kevin watched her go as he held the door for two more customers. "Busy day, huh?"

"Yeah. I didn't expect to see you again so soon."

"Is that a subtle way of telling me to go away? You *did* offer to let me put some stuff from the Blue Whale here."

I shook my head. I guessed I wasn't exactly one of those superfriendly women he was getting used to in Duck. "No. I was only surprised you weren't putting on roofing or something, that's all."

"I would be except that the Blue Whale is pretty much a crime scene and they don't want me to change anything right now. And it's almost dinner time, and I can't get in the kitchen even though nothing happened there. I never realized how annoying it is to have someone murdered in your home."

My stomach gurgled as I glanced up at the teapot clock. It was almost seven P.M. I hoped Kevin would be nice enough to ignore that abdominal rumble, but when I turned to face him again, I noticed he was laughing. "What?" I demanded. "I skipped lunch. Coffee only goes so far."

"Cranky *and* noisy. I guess you'd better buy me dinner."

"How do you figure that?"

"I came and rescued you by reminding you it was time to eat. I think that warrants dinner. Any suggestions where we should go?"

His enthusiasm was contagious. I'd had a good business day, and it wasn't unusual for Missing Pieces to be closed by now. The rush had kept me from worrying about Miss Mildred. "I'll tell you the truth, I don't eat out much. I probably couldn't recommend a good restaurant. I'm sure they're all fine, but I prefer my own cooking. You're welcome to come to supper."

"I'd like that. It must be nice to enjoy your own cooking. I don't know if Chef Boyardee in the microwave qualifies as cooking, but I'm not too crazy about it. I've spent most of my life eating in restaurants."

"I'll bet you've eaten in some exciting places while you were working for the FBI."

"Like every greasy spoon and two-bit diner across the country," he said. "Working for the FBI sounds a lot more glamorous than it really is."

We came to an arrangement for selling the Blue Whale T-shirts, and Kevin put his pamphlets on the corkboard near the door. I did a quick walk through the shop, checking to make sure nothing was missing, left behind, or about to be covered in Coke from a misplaced paper cup. "Still," I said, picking up the conversation when I was done with my inspection, "it must seem really tame to live in Duck after travelling so much."

"It's quiet," he agreed. "But that's what I was looking for."

I turned off the lights and locked the door behind us. Shadows were beginning to lengthen on the boardwalk, and the shops around Missing Pieces were closing too. The nightlife was beginning for our summer visitors, but for many of the people who lived here, the day was done and it was time to go home.

We walked down to the house, making small talk about the town and the difference there between summer and winter. "Actually, we call it off-season," I explained. "We don't like winter."

Kevin stepped away from the road as a car blew its horn, almost grazing his pant leg. "Whatever you call it, I'm looking forward to it. I didn't realize so many people would be here over the summer. Or in-season. Why don't you guys put in sidewalks?"

"Do you know how much they cost? It may look like we're rich, but we're not. We *are* working on sidewalks, though, and some other things."

When we got to the house, Mary Lou opened the front door as I reached for the handle. "Dae! Kevin! It's good to see you. Come in. We're getting supper ready."

This is different. Mary Lou was acting like Gramps's hostess. "Good to see you too. Where's my grandfather?"

"In the back. He's grilling. I'm in charge of salad. I hope you brought some dessert with you. We ran out of the apple pie I brought before we could eat supper." Mary Lou laughed and closed the door after us.

"I could go out and get something," Kevin offered.

"That's okay," I said. "I'm sure we can find something here."

"Dae, I want to talk to you about creating an ordinance to protect the sea turtles." Mary Lou put her arm around my shoulders as we walked into the kitchen. "People don't realize how fragile they are as a species. They go down there all times of the day and night, build sand castles. Really, we need an ordinance."

"Why is building sand castles bad for the turtles?" Kevin asked.

I knew what was going to happen, but I wanted to see Gramps without Mary Lou. As soon as Kevin asked, she switched to *his* side, explaining as she went. "Well, you see, the castles fall in on the baby turtles as they're trying to reach the sea. Sometimes it smothers them. Sometimes they get trapped there and a predator finds them."

I gave Kevin an apologetic look as I left the two of them in the kitchen. A few of Gramps's friends from his pinochle game were in the living room laughing at something on TV. I closed the back door as I went out and enjoyed the blessed silence for a minute. It had been a long, difficult day. I still felt that terrible guilt about not being able to help Miss Mildred. I knew I had to let it go, but it was hard.

"Are you going to stand up there on the porch all night," Gramps asked, "or are you going to come down and hand me those potatoes?"

I went down to help him. We had a few lights in the back, but they were mostly for show, party lights. They illuminated the swing and the pier going down to the sound but weren't there for practical considerations. "Lots of supper guests."

He laughed. "Nice, isn't it? Your grandmother loved to cook for big crowds. We were both sorry we couldn't have a large family. But we loved your mother. Lucky for us, we always had plenty of friends. Hand me that corn now."

The big grill, converted by Gramps from the old tank they'd used for heating oil when I was a child, was full of food. The smell was delicious, probably drifting out to neighbors, inviting them over. I expected to find several more people waiting for supper when I went back inside.

"What's with Mary Lou acting like she lives here?" I hoped that hadn't come out as bad as it sounded to me.

He glanced up from his basting. "Why? Have you got something against Mary Lou?"

"No. Not unless she's looking for somewhere else to live—like here. I don't think I could live with Mary Lou."

"In other words, I'm supposed to be alone the rest of my life?"

"Not alone." I scuffed my foot on the sandy grass. "You have *me*."

He stood up straight and hugged me (still holding the basting brush). "And someday, you'll meet someone and leave *me*. What will I do then?"

I hugged him back fiercely. "I'll never leave you. You know that. Me and you, right?"

"That's right, Dae. I'll never leave you either. But we could both do with some companionship from the opposite sex. This house was built for a big family. Don't forget, I came from six brothers and two sisters. I think we could both meet special people, and we could all live here. Unless, of course, you'd rather live at the Blue Whale."

I was totally amazed that he would even tease me about something like that. "You may think Kevin likes me that way, but believe me, he wants to be with Shayla."

"Maybe for now. But I'm a good judge of people after being sheriff for so long. Kevin Brickman is looking for stability in his life. He's not going to find that from Shayla."

"Lucky there are plenty of other women in town."

"Because you can do so much better?" He laughed. "Oh. That's right. I forgot about *Tim*."

I nudged him hard. "Despite what anyone thinks, Tim and I aren't going to end up together."

We heard the back door squeak open and both looked up at the porch. I was surprised to see Kevin's tall, broad-shouldered form silhouetted against the lights from the house. "Dae? Chief Michaels is here with Agent Walker. They need to speak with you about Miss Mildred."

Chapter 10

Kevin sounded so formal. I knew it wasn't good news. I could imagine him, back in his FBI days, using the same tone to tell someone their child had been kidnapped or something of equal horror. I glanced at Gramps. He nodded as I headed inside.

The number of people in the house had doubled since I'd gone out back. But the chief and Agent Walker stood out in the otherwise casual crowd. The chief's uniform looked a little wrinkled for him. Tough day, I guessed. Agent Walker was dressed in a dark suit and tie.

"Can we go in the next room and talk for a minute?" The chief raised his voice above the din.

"In here." I led the way into the dining room and was glad to notice Kevin accompanying us. I figured it would be good to have someone there who wasn't actively involved in what was going on. "What is it, Chief?"

He removed his uniform hat and spent a few seconds looking at the worn carpet before his eyes met mine. "Mayor, I thought you should know right away. They had to hospitalize Millie. She got crazy acting, then they found out she was dehydrated. The doctor said it seems like she hasn't been eating. She's still in police custody, you understand. But you could go visit her, if you like. I gave orders to the officer at the door that he was to let you in."

A few moments passed in uncomfortable silence as I fought to get my emotions under control. When I could finally speak, I said, "Thank you, Chief. I'd like to see her. What will happen now?"

Before he could answer, Agent Walker replied, "She'll be evaluated to see if she's fit to stand trial. Many times in these circumstances, we realize the person who's been charged with a crime isn't able to face a judge in a courtroom. We aren't without some semblance of mercy, Mayor O'Donnell, no matter what you think."

"You mean she wouldn't have to go to jail?" I felt a little ray of sunshine warm my heart.

"He means she'd be found guilty without a trial and sentenced to spend the rest of her life in an institution." Kevin's voice was dark when he spoke.

"Is that true?" I asked Chief Michaels.

"I'm afraid so."

"*No!* That's not fair! How much life do you think a ninety-two-year-old woman has left to live in the first place? Couldn't you let her live out her life with one of those electronic bracelets on her ankle? Whatever she's done, it may not be anything she'd do again."

"If we could do something like that, Mayor, you know we would," Agent Walker assured me. "But let's not forget that the evidence appears to support the theory that Mildred Mason murdered her sister, then tried to hide the evidence. Would you want her to live out the rest of her life as though nothing happened? What about justice for Elizabeth Simpson?"

There was no good or easy answer for that. My heart told me that Miss Mildred was not dangerous and surely hadn't killed her sister. The evidence seemed to be overwhelmingly against her, but it didn't seem real to me.

"I'm sorry, Mayor." The chief patted me awkwardly on the shoulder. "We'll do the best we can for her."

I felt numb. It was like watching this happen to someone in a dream. It couldn't be happening in real life. Years of growing up and being reminded to watch my manners forced a smile on my lips. "I know you will. You'll stay for supper, won't you? Gramps has a bunch of food on the grill."

The chief hitched up his pants and nodded. "You know, I'd like that. Where's Horace?"

"He's in back. Maybe you could help him bring all that food inside."

Agent Walker opened the dining room door, the noise from the other rooms spilling in. "I'll head on out and see you all tomorrow."

"Stay for supper," I extended the invitation. "Really, there's so much. We need all the mouths we can get. I'm sure you'd enjoy having a home-cooked meal after eating out so much while you've been here."

"Well, yes. I'd like that. Not to say anything bad about your local restaurants, but some home cooking sounds great. Thanks." He smiled for the first time, and I went out the door before the three men.

I let them go out and help Gramps with the grilled food while I went into the kitchen to help Mary Lou and several other female neighbors who'd turned up for the meal.

They'd brought banana pudding, slaw, peaches and a pie or two. I mashed a huge pot of potatoes (there would never be enough grilled potatoes for this crowd) and warmed up some leftover butter beans.

I didn't feel like eating. I wanted to be alone to think about everything that had happened and try to make some sense of it. I waited until Gramps came in with the grilled food before quietly escaping out the back door. It wasn't too hard not to be noticed. There had to be at least thirty people there.

It was cool and dark in the backyard. I walked out to the end of the pier and sat on the old fishing bench. I couldn't count the number of times I'd come out here for solace after my mother died. It had become my thinking place.

I looked out at the stars over the Currituck Sound, the light gleaming off the water. I could see the Bodie Island Lighthouse, warning ships at sea of the dangers along the Outer Banks. The light came and went as it swept from shore to shore. It had stood there for more than one hundred years. It had inspired me my whole life. I hoped it would work for me now.

I felt the vibration of footsteps on the pier behind me before I heard them. I thought it might be Gramps, until Kevin said, "I noticed you walked out without a plate. I loaded up a bunch of food for you. You'll have to eat it to keep me from cleaning both our plates."

"Thanks." I was touched by his thoughtfulness. I stood up and took a plate from him, then scooted over so he could sit down too. "I don't know if I can eat anything after finding out about Miss Mildred."

"It won't do you any good to starve. You have to keep up your strength so you can help her."

I looked at him, barely able to make out his features in

the dim light. His words made so much sense. Why hadn't I seen it before? "You're absolutely right, Kevin! I *can* help her. All I have to do is find evidence that contradicts the evidence they found at her house. It had to have been planted there. I *know* she didn't kill Miss Elizabeth. And isn't all of that evidence circumstantial anyway? She didn't confess. No one saw her do it. Just because the purse and the murder weapon were at her house doesn't mean she's guilty."

"I meant so you could go see her at the hospital." He put down what looked like a piece of chicken. "The chief and Agent Walker know what they're doing, Dae. I know you don't like what's happening to your friend, but I'm afraid anyone could make this case against her. The purse and the weapon that killed Miss Elizabeth are a *big* deal, even without a confession. Believe me, they've convicted people with less."

But his dark, sensible words meant nothing to my sudden sense of euphoria. "I'm sure that's true. But I think we should be able to prove it wasn't her. All we have to do is find out who the real killer is."

"Wait a minute. *We?* I'm not in that game anymore. And I can't tell you how much I hated civilians who thought they could interfere in the process. Bad things happen to those people. Ask your grandfather. He'll tell you. The real killer could try to kill you."

"And that would reveal what we need to know." I put my plate down on the pier between us. "I can probably do this without you, Kevin. But think how much safer I'd be if you helped me. Not to mention that you know the ins and outs of this sort of thing. I could pay you."

"You don't have enough money to pay me to investigate Miss Elizabeth's death." His words sounded like a blunt refusal. Then he added, "But I suppose if you're determined to do this, we could trade labor."

"What kind of labor?"

"Did you notice how bad the paint looks on the outside of the Blue Whale?"

I thought about it all night after everyone had gone home. It all made perfect sense to me. The next morning I was feeling full of myself. I had a plan and I was working it. It was going to set Miss Mildred free. I would have to trade a few hours of painting time at the Blue Whale, but I had to admit that having Kevin onboard made me feel a lot more optimistic.

I got up, took a shower and put on a blue sundress dotted with daisies. I clipped my hair back out of my face and dabbed on a little pink lipstick. Gramps had agreed to open Missing Pieces for me while I went to see Miss Mildred in the hospital.

I was worried the status of everything could change if she was found incompetent. I wanted to see her while I could. Her recollection of events wasn't always crystal clear. I was hoping the hospital stay, some decent food and fluids had left her a bit more lucid with regard to Miss Elizabeth's purse and how it got into her house.

Kevin had kindly agreed to have breakfast with Chief Michaels and Agent Walker to find out whatever he could about the investigation. He thought it would be a good idea to learn a bit more about the alleged murder weapon, the mysterious shovel Chief Michaels had found in Miss Mildred's shed. Though the chief had said the shovel was small, I was hoping it was still too big for someone Miss Mildred's size and age to have possibly used. Nevertheless, there was also the discovery of the purse in her kitchen to contend with. Hedging my bets on who could come up with the most useful information seemed like the best way to handle the situation.

It was too long a drive to the hospital in Kill Devil Hills for me to take the golf cart. I managed to hitch a ride with Tim. He was supposed to relieve the officer who'd been on duty at the hospital last night. I hoped he (and everyone else) didn't read more into the ride than there was. And I *really* hoped being alone with him for thirty minutes wouldn't encourage him to propose again.

I was surprised to learn that Shayla had gone out with him the night before. "Yeah." Tim backed out of the drive into traffic. "She liked the way I handled myself when we found Wild Johnny Simpson at the Blue Whale. Chicks dig a uniform, you know."

"That's—nice." I wasn't sure what to say.

"I can't wait forever for you, Dae. A man has needs. I want to settle down, raise a family. Shayla wants that too."

I wondered if there was some other person named Shayla living in Duck. The Shayla I knew had *never* liked Tim, wasn't planning on settling down and surely didn't want to have a family. "I thought Shayla was interested in Kevin."

"Apparently, he dumped her. Stood her up when they were supposed to meet at the Curbside last night."

Last night? Had Kevin forgotten? Or was Shayla being too hopeful? "I guess that was good for you then, Tim. I don't blame you for not waiting for me. If you and Shayla are good together, you should go for it."

He grinned at me. "Thanks, Dae. I appreciate that coming from an ex-girlfriend. I hope you realize this means my last marriage proposal is null and void."

"I completely understand. I appreciate you keeping me informed." I looked out the window at the passing scenery and smiled. I could only hope it would be this easy.

"I know you're feeling a twinge or two of heartache right now," he continued. "You'll get over it. I know you're going to find the right person for you someday."

To stem the tide of this conversation, I decided to change the subject. No reason not to pump him for information since Kevin was trying to squeeze something out of the chief and Agent Walker. "I suppose you had to turn over all the evidence to the SBI."

"No. They're assisting us, but we're the top dogs on this case. The chief wouldn't have it any other way."

"I've been wondering about the murder weapon."

"I can't tell you anything about that shovel, Dae. Don't even ask me."

"Of course. I'll bet it has to be small and light for you to think Miss Mildred could use it against her sister."

"You could say it's not your average garden shovel," he agreed. "I can't say anything else about it. The hair and blood we found on it went to the lab for identification. If it comes back a match to Miss Elizabeth's, that's all she wrote for Miss Mildred."

So they *weren't* completely sure yet. It seemed unlikely Miss Mildred would have a shovel of any kind that had hair and blood on it, but as long as the proof wasn't positive, we still had a chance. "I'm going to ask Miss Mildred about Wild Johnny Simpson while I'm at the hospital today," I told him. "You never know. She might've killed him too."

His eyes almost bulged out. "You think so? That would be something."

"I guess you never know. Someone killed him, right?"

"Someone sure did. Mind if I step in while you're talking to her? It could go a long way toward a promotion if I found out who killed Johnny."

"I don't mind, but you know you can't get promoted until the chief retires. There's nowhere else to go."

"I can rack up a whole lot of points until then," he reasoned. "Then when the chief retires, people won't try to look outside Duck for his replacement."

"That's true. And you've got a long time to do it. The chief isn't that old."

"True. And his family doesn't die young, that's for sure. His father is really old and still living."

I was sure I remembered Gramps talking about Chief Michaels's father. They'd worked together in the sheriff's office years ago. But I was also sure his father had died before Gramps retired. "I don't think the chief's father is old or living, Tim."

"Yes, he is. I drove the chief up to Manteo the other day to see him in a rest home. He's not in the best shape, but he's definitely not dead."

I didn't say anything else about it since we'd arrived at the hospital. It was probably a communication glitch between Tim and the chief. Not really worth arguing with him.

Miss Mildred's room was on the second floor. Tim walked up with me and tapped Officer Scott Randall on the shoulder, startling him out of his sound sleep. I supposed there wasn't much to keep you awake when you were watching an old woman who probably couldn't get out of bed.

"Tim!" Scott stood up and nodded to me. "Mayor O'Donnell. The night was uneventful. No one tried to get in or out of the suspect's room."

"Good." Tim nodded. "I'll take over now. Get some breakfast. Report to the chief when you get back to Duck."

"Yes, sir!" Scott smiled at me, a shy, sweet smile, then headed for the elevator. He was a quiet young man with dreamy eyes. He'd been a police officer for only a few months. He didn't seem suited to it. I didn't expect him to stay.

I knocked softly at the door, then pushed it open a little when there was no response. "Hello? It's Dae, Miss Mildred. I'm here to see you. I've brought you a few things."

"Dae?" a faint voice responded. "Come in. Don't dawdle there by the door all day."

Miss Mildred seemed so much smaller, more fragile, in the big hospital bed. All the color had washed out of her dear old face, leaving only gray lines. Her blue eyes were sunken and had none of their usual fire. I bit my lip to keep from crying at the sight of her hooked up to tubes and machines.

"How are you doing?" I knew it was a bad beginning, but I was stumped for something witty to say given the circumstances.

"How do you think I'm doing? I'm in a hospital and people think I killed my sister, which I assure you is *completely* wrong. The only good thing I can tell you is that I slept all night. I don't know if that was due to the drugs they gave me or if it was because Lizzie couldn't find me here."

I put the assorted magazines, lip balm, flowers and hand lotion on the bedside table. "At least you got some sleep. They told me you weren't eating or drinking at home either. You made yourself sick."

She made a *humphing* noise in her throat. "People get sick when they've lost the only person left in the world who matters to them. Now that Lizzie's gone, it's just me, Dae. You don't know what that feels like yet. I know you think you do because you lost your mama, but believe me, this is much worse."

"I believe you." I drew up a chair, and noticed Tim hovering at the edge of the room, inside the doorway. "Do you think you could answer a few questions for me?"

"What kind of questions?" she barked. "I've been asked so many questions. I wish people would just let me die."

I sat down and covered one of her hands with mine. It was so cold. "You don't really mean that. I know Miss Elizabeth is gone, but you still have friends."

She sniffed and turned her face away from me. "Friends? No one who cares. It was only me and Lizzie. Now it's just me. How do I go on like that, Dae? There's nothing left for me but rattling around in that big old house."

I tried to divert her by bringing out the goodies I'd brought with me and offering to have Trudy come and do her hair. I knew what it was like to feel as though there was nothing left that mattered. There was nothing anyone could say to make it better.

Eventually I brought out the chocolate pudding cups that had been near the bottom of the bag. We sat eating them with plastic spoons for several minutes, not really talking, enjoying our pudding. When we were finished, Miss Mildred handed me her empty cup and smiled. "You've always been a good girl, Dae. Everyone is proud of you. You make a very good mayor too, especially being a woman and all."

I thanked her, setting all the goodies aside and not minding that I was a good mayor considering I was a woman. It was time to say what I'd come to say. I took a deep breath and plunged into it. "Miss Mildred, did you kill your sister?"

"Don't be stupid, Dae. I understand what they think. I don't care. I know I didn't kill Lizzie. They can think what they will."

"It's not that simple. You could go to jail or a hospital for the rest of your life unless we can prove you didn't kill Miss Elizabeth."

"I don't know that I care. But if I did, what would I have to do to prove I didn't kill Lizzie?"

"You can tell me again how you came to have her purse."

"Lizzie brought it to me after she died. She said she needed me to keep it safe. You know how she felt about losing her purse. It was a big worry for her. I told her I would. She left."

"Did she walk out the door?"

"Of course. How else would she get out?" Miss Mildred looked at me like I was the one who was crazy.

"If she was really a ghost, she could go through the door," I explained.

"No self-respecting ghost in Duck would be such a show-off."

I heard Tim snicker behind me. Miss Mildred told him he'd always been a problem child who had a hard time keeping his attention on anything. I brought her back to my questions by asking, "What did Miss Elizabeth look like? Was she pale? Covered in sand?"

"Don't be vulgar," she snapped. "My sister would never come to call on me in that manner. She didn't have a hair out of place. She looked as neat as a pin in her black dress with the pink hearts. You know, I gave her that dress for her birthday three years ago."

Only Miss Mildred could conjure up the image of neat ghosts. I felt sure if I were ever lucky enough to see my mother again, she'd be untidy. She had never been a neat person.

"What about Wild Johnny Simpson?" Tim stepped forward out of the shadows created by the light coming in through the narrow window. "Did you see him when he was here thirty years ago?"

Miss Mildred looked flustered. "To my knowledge, Johnny never came back after he left Lizzie. That was right after Gary Bentley steered the ferry into shore and wrecked it back in 1945. About the time the war was over."

Leave it to someone from Duck to notice that a ferry wrecked before thinking about World War II. I gave Tim a stern frown, but he kept questioning. "Johnny was here at the Blue Whale right before it closed. You didn't know anything about it?"

"Even if he had been, why would I know? You'd have to ask Lizzie about that." Miss Mildred turned her head and closed her eyes. "I'm tired now. Please leave, both of you."

To add to her plea for solitude, a nurse came in and shooed us out. I told Miss Mildred I'd try to come back again. When I got Tim out in the hall, I gave him a hard time. "What were you doing in there? She's very fragile. She can't take that kind of agitation."

He shrugged. "I was asking questions about the murder investigation. You were tiptoeing around it like a little cat. We need to get the truth from her."

"You think she killed her sister *and* Wild Johnny?" I thought I said it with sufficient scorn to make him back off. I was wrong.

"I think it's possible. You sounded like you did too in the car. Let's face it, thirty years ago, Miss Mildred was still teaching school. She was capable of killing the man who'd rejected her for her sister. It happens."

"Never mind." I held out my hand, not explaining that I wasn't serious earlier about Miss Mildred killing Wild Johnny. "I need the keys for the squad car."

"I can't do that, Dae. Only officers of the law can drive that car. I guess you'll have to stay here with me during my shift." He grinned and sat down in the chair by Miss Mildred's door.

"You forget, Officer Mabry. I'm not only the mayor of Duck, I'm also a fully deputized auxiliary police officer. Hand over the keys. Someone will be here to relieve you later."

He fished the keys out of his pocket and reluctantly handed them to me. "I'm glad I'm not in love with you anymore. Shayla isn't half as contrary."

I smiled. I had no words for his defection to my friend. I knew it wouldn't last. That was probably the worst part about his infatuation with me. He kept dating other women and then using me as a fallback when he broke up with them. It wasn't very endearing.

Traffic was building on Duck Road by the time I got back home. The weather was a little overcast, but it wouldn't be summer if we didn't have a lot of rain.

I'd thought about Miss Mildred the whole way back, but I didn't have any new ideas. I felt certain she *believed* she'd seen her sister's ghost. I believed her, but it was unlikely Agent Walker would share that belief.

What else could've happened? I knew she didn't kill Miss Elizabeth. Whoever killed her knew the sisters enough to torment Miss Mildred and throw her to the police as a suspect. With her health and mental state being so delicate,

Miss Mildred couldn't possibly stand up to that storm. She was already bowed and broken from the winds of fate blowing across her.

I wanted to tell Kevin what had happened, but he wasn't answering his cell phone. I had to relieve Gramps at Missing Pieces, so I couldn't make the detour to the Blue Whale. It would have to wait until later.

Missing Pieces was packed when I got there. There was a bus full of tourists on the boardwalk, creating a stir in the shops that fronted the sound. Gramps told me he'd already sold a few pieces. "Nothing important," he said. "Don't get that thundercloud look on your face. I know what to sell and what not to sell."

"It's not that," I told him, stepping behind the counter. "I'm not happy at all with my interview with Miss Mildred."

"Interview, huh? I thought you were going for a visit."

I told him about my plan to find out who really killed Miss Elizabeth and set Miss Mildred free. "I asked Kevin to help me since he has so much experience doing this kind of thing."

"Why Kevin and not me?"

"Because, as much as I love you, anything you find you'd be likely to give to Chief Michaels and Agent Walker. You were the Dare County sheriff for too long."

"And you think Kevin won't do the same thing?" He looked skeptical. "Once a lawman, always a lawman. He can't help it anymore than I could."

"I think he can. I think there's something in his past that made him give it up."

"Since when do you get impressions from people besides finding what they've lost?"

Before I could answer that, a young man came into the shop with a box. He glanced around, then came to the counter. "I'm looking for the owner. I heard she's interested in unusual items. I have something I'd like to sell her. I found it at the old Blue Whale Inn."

Chapter 11

"I'm Dae O'Donnell. I own Missing Pieces." I put out my hand to him as I felt the familiar sense of slow motion that meant this was an important find. "This is my grandfather, Horace O'Donnell. I'll be happy to take a look at what you've got."

That's true and not true, really. I hate when things come in that I think might be stolen. There have been plenty of times I wished I could've kept things that I knew I shouldn't keep. But I adhere to a code of ethics, and I never accept things that don't belong to the person selling them. Unfortunately, this felt like one of those times. Too bad for this young man that the former sheriff was also there to view his discovery.

"I'm Austin Bray, Betsy Bray's son." He shook my hand too quickly for me to get an impression. "This was something some friends and I found a few years back. It used to be popular to hang out down at the Blue Whale because everyone said it was haunted. We were all hoping to see something, you know?"

I knew that part was true. In high school, my friends and I had done the same thing. It was interesting and creepy at the same time. I asked, "Did you ever see anything?"

"I don't know. One time I thought I saw a man in the fog. He was kind of strange looking and his eyes glowed. My friends told me it was a dog, but it spooked me and I never went back again."

"Exactly when was it you found this treasure, Austin?" Gramps asked in his old sheriff voice.

"Let's see. I'm in my first year of college and that was my sophomore year in high school, so I guess about three years. I saw the thing about the dead guy they found at the inn and decided to bring this here. I don't want to get in any trouble."

Bad place to bring it. "Maybe you should've taken it to the police station."

"I didn't steal it, if that's what you mean. I found it outside on the ground. I kept it in my closet all this time. You can ask my mom. She was threatening to throw it away now that I've moved most of my stuff out of the house. I started thinking it might be a bad thing for me to have."

"That could be a piece of police evidence," Gramps agreed. "I don't know if we should even look at it."

But I couldn't resist. Before he could make me turn the whole thing over to Chief Michaels, I grabbed it from Austin. It was a beautifully hand-carved box, carefully detailed with seashells, gulls and an image of one of the area lighthouses. Though some sand was lodged in the crevices of the design, I could see the workmanship was exquisite.

"It's gorgeous!" I studied it despite Gramps's dark look.

When I went to open it, I found that it was locked up tight, but a flash of brilliance made me open the cash register and retrieve the tiny key I'd found at the inn and forgotten to give Kevin.

The key turned stiffly in the lock. The lid was old and hard to lift, but when I did, music began to play. "It's absolutely wonderful!"

Austin looked uncomfortable. "How did you get that key? I tried to open it a few times, but it wouldn't budge. What song is that playing?"

"I found the key like you found the box," I mentioned. "I don't recognize the song either."

"I do," Gramps said. "'Five foot two, eyes of blue, has anybody seen my gal?' It was popular back in the day."

I turned the box over, then looked at the inside again. It was lined with mother-of-pearl. A small inscription carved into it—*"To Lizzie from Johnny. You'll always be my girl."*

"What do you think?" Austin eagerly asked. "Worth at least something, right?"

"I'm sorry, son." Gramps took the music box from me. "I'm afraid this is part of the police investigation into the murder at the inn. If that turns out not to be the case, you might get it back. I'll leave word with your mother, if that's the case."

"I'm not going to jail or anything, am I?" He said as he began writing down his name, address and phone number on a piece of paper Gramps had handed him.

"I don't think so," Gramps said without much reassurance. "But next time, don't go removing things off of private property without permission."

Austin seemed a little skittish at this point. I smiled to reassure him. "If it turns out that you get to keep the box, I'd like to buy it from you."

I copied his address and phone number since I knew the original would go to the police. Gramps looked at him sternly before he left. I wished I could clean up the music box and listen to it play for a while.

But Gramps wrapped it up in some newspaper and set it to the side. "Maybe it shows that Johnny was here to see Lizzie. Maybe he thought they could make up after all those years. I guess we'll never know."

"But surely it doesn't prove Miss Elizabeth killed Johnny either," I argued. "It seems more like something he didn't have a chance to give her."

"You have a good heart, darlin'." He kissed my forehead. "But sometimes good people do bad things. It's the nature of man. Or woman. I'm going to take this down to Chief Michaels. I'll make sure he knows you'd like it back."

The overcast skies gave a gloomy feel to the rest of the day. Of course, it didn't help that I spent much of my time thinking about Miss Mildred being tested to see if she was competent to stand trial for something she didn't do. I didn't care what Gramps said about good people going bad. That wasn't what had happened here.

Once it started raining at about three P.M., foot traffic disappeared from the boardwalk. Shayla, Trudy and I had coffee before I went back to Missing Pieces. Anne Maxwell and her daughter were waiting for me. We stepped in out of the rain, and I showed her the racks of clothes I needed her to go through. I left her alone with them while I showed Ginny the toys in back where she could play.

Kevin came in around five, his Windbreaker soaked. The wind and rain accompanied him in the front door, creating a puddle on the floor, but I was still glad to see him. "Not much going on out here," he observed. "Too bad it's so wet. We can't do any painting today either."

I was virtually stuffed full of information and bursting to share what I'd learned since I'd seen him last. We sat on the tall stools behind the counter and watched the seagulls playing tag in the rain while I told him about my visit to Miss Mildred and the discovery of the music box.

"I heard from the chief that they released Brian Mc-Donald around lunchtime," he told me. "They knew he didn't steal Miss Elizabeth's purse, and he had an alibi for the medical examiner's time of death. It was from his girl-friend, so it wouldn't have stood up if they'd found him with the purse. The chief told him to get out of town."

"He's not prosecuting him for stealing all those purses?"

"I guess not. You didn't press charges. None of the other women did either."

"What about Miss Mildred?"

He nodded. "I think they had a judge and the DA up there talking to her today. Luke Helms was there with her. They'll probably bring in a psychiatrist and a few other doctors to make the final assessment. But from what you've told me, they'll find her incompetent and she'll be institutionalized. The only good thing about that is that it spares her jail time."

"Because she won't back down from saying she saw Miss Elizabeth's ghost, right?"

"Yeah. Even in the Outer Banks, it's one thing to believe in folklore but another thing when a ghost turns up with evidence that places you at a murder scene."

"Have you heard anything about the testing they're doing on the murder weapon?"

"The chief gave me back the derringer we found at the inn. It wasn't the weapon used to kill Johnny. I haven't heard anything about the weapon they think killed Miss

Elizabeth. But ballistics is faster than DNA. It'll probably be a while before we know for sure about that."

"The only thing I could squeeze out of Tim was that the shovel they think was the murder weapon was not a regular garden shovel." It wasn't much, but I wanted to add what I could to our investigation.

The news we shared did nothing to alleviate the dark day. We sat for a long time not talking as the evening came down prematurely on Duck. Anne and Ginny finished up the clothes. They waved as they walked out the door. I took a look at the job Anne had done and admired her work. If I could ever afford to hire someone, I'd certainly give her a call. In the meantime, at least both of them had some new-to-them clothes to wear.

I closed the shop about five. It was early, but no one had come in for hours. The rain was still a steady downpour. My mind kept working on helping Miss Mildred, but there didn't seem to be anything I could do.

Between that, the rain and no customers, I was completely depressed. Even Kevin's offer to cook dinner in exchange for eating at my house the night before didn't pick my mood up. But knowing Gramps would be out that night playing pinochle, I agreed to go to the inn with him. Better to be depressed with someone else than by yourself.

Shayla and Trudy stopped us as we walked toward town hall so I could check my messages. We stood under the bright blue canopy on the boardwalk, which thankfully kept most of the rain off of us. "Don't you two look chummy?" Trudy giggled and nudged Shayla.

"A little *too* chummy," Shayla said, giving me an evil look. "Where are you two going?"

"Dinner at the Blue Whale," Kevin explained. "You're both welcome to join us. I make a very good lasagna. My grandmother on my mother's side was from Italy. She taught me how to cook when I was a little kid. There's plenty for everyone."

Shayla muttered something under her breath about Kevin being too full of himself to think there was enough of him to go around. Trudy giggled again. Both women agreed they wanted lasagna for supper in the worst way.

"I have to check my messages," I told them. "Then I can go."

"We'll meet you there," Shayla said. "You can find the way without us, right?"

"Sure." I wondered what she was up to. Didn't she and Tim have something going on now? She acted like she was still interested in Kevin and I was getting in her way.

"We'll wait." Kevin smiled. "Maybe the rain will ease up."

"Shayla has the coolest idea," Trudy told us. "She wants to do a séance for Miss Elizabeth and maybe Wild Johnny too. The Blue Whale would be the perfect place for it. It's kind of spooky anyway."

We all looked at Kevin to see what he thought. He shrugged. "Why not? Although I'm not crazy about people thinking the Blue Whale is spooky. It might hurt business once I'm open."

Shayla linked her arm through his as we walked into town hall. "*Whatever!* You don't understand the tourist climate down here, sweetie. If people thought your place was haunted, you'd have a crowd there every night waiting for a place to eat and stay. People *love* ghosts."

I said hello to Nancy, who was still at her desk, and then heard someone clear his throat. At the sound, Shayla moved away from Kevin. "Tim! I didn't know you'd be here," she simpered. "I was just thinking about you, honey."

Tim nodded to me. "Dae. Could I have a word with you? Official police business."

"Sure. Come in my office." I glanced at the four people left in the lobby. "We'll just be a minute."

Once the door closed behind us, Tim said, "The chief wanted me to remind you about the ribbon cutting tomorrow at the new restaurant across the street. It's at ten thirty."

"I know. I have it on my calendar. You brought me in here to remind me about the ribbon cutting?"

He looked down at the floor. "They talked to Miss Mildred today. I heard her crying from out in the hall. She's losing it, Dae. They're going to put her away. I don't think there's anything any of us can do."

I put my hand on his arm. "I guess we'll do the best we can. Thanks for telling me."

We went back into the lobby where Shayla had convinced Nancy to join us for what had become lasagna *and* a séance at the Blue Whale. Nancy handed me my messages as she put on her bright yellow rain gear. It didn't take much to convince Tim that he should come along. Within moments, we were back out in the rain and headed for the Blue Whale.

After the short, wet walk to the ocean side of Duck, we all worked together in the big hotel kitchen. Kevin put Tim and me in front of a table-sized wooden chopping block with instructions to cut vegetables. Nancy and Trudy grated fresh cheese while Kevin and Shayla made the sauce. The sauce making seemed to be more fun than the jobs the rest of us were doing. Shayla kept laughing and saying, "Oh, Kevin! You're *crazy*!"

"I hope he remembers that Shayla is *my* girlfriend," Tim growled as he chopped carrots.

"If *she* remembers, you won't have any problem," I advised him.

Kevin uncorked a couple of bottles of muscadine wine and told us all about the Mother Vine in Manteo that he visited when he first came to the Outer Banks. "Did you know it's been there for four hundred years?"

"We've lived here all our lives," Tim told him. "I think we know about the Mother Vine."

"I haven't lived here all *my* life," Shayla said. "Tell me about the Mother Vine."

Kevin turned on some late-eighties rock music and poured us all some of the sweet red wine. He talked about the early settlers and growing grapes as though he'd memorized the information from a tour. Nancy and Trudy giggled as they grated. Tim kept setting up pieces of Boston bibb lettuce and chopping them into shreds.

The lasagna noodles were finally in the pan with the appropriate sauce, cheese and vegetables. The kitchen smelled like garlic and herbs. I looked around the room, which was almost as big as the whole downstairs of my house. I could see where Kevin had done renovations to the walls and added a new stove and dishwasher. The room seemed ready for customers, if the Blue Whale ever opened. No telling how long it might be before the SBI was done looking at it. Gramps and I probably added to that by turning over the music box.

"It will be an hour until that's done," Kevin said. "What about this séance thing while we're waiting?"

"I think we could manage that." Shayla smiled up at him. She handed him her empty wineglass. "I could use a refill. Being a medium is thirsty work."

Kevin obliged and topped off our glasses too. "This way to the dining room."

The dining room was ready for visitors as well. It was beautiful with big rosewood tables, two large crystal chandeliers and green velvet drapes adorning the big windows that overlooked the beach. Plenty of local artwork hung on the walls, giving the room a nice, homey feel. Maybe that was because I knew some of the artists personally.

We picked out one of the big round tables, lit a tea candle in the middle of it and sat down. The room seemed very large and empty once we were all in our places. I had expected something different from Kevin. I'm not sure why. He was obviously very traditional, and this room suited him. If it had been mine, I would probably have painted the walls dark blue and tried to make it look like the bottom of the ocean. That was my nontraditional take on it.

"Okay. Everyone, hold hands," Shayla whispered, probably trying not to echo in the room. "It's very important to stay in your seat and not let go of the hands you're holding."

"Are you sure we should be doing this?" Trudy's voice had a small squeak in it. "I mean, what if these people want to be left alone?"

"What are the chances? They were both murdered," Nancy reminded her. "If someone kills me, I hope someone will have a séance. I'd want to tell who did it."

I agreed with her. It would be nice to know for sure whether it was possible to contact the dead and ask important questions. Or in my case, to apologize to my mother for being an idiot. But I guess having an argument with me wasn't enough angst to keep her hanging around. Murder, on the other hand, seemed likely to create ghosts.

"What do we do?" Tim asked. "What if we see something?"

"You let me do everything. Unless you see something. Then you ask questions." Shayla smiled at Kevin, who sat to the right of her. Tim sat on her left side. Leave it to her to hold hands with *both* men.

With everything set up, Shayla bowed her head and called on the spirits to come forth. We waited around her with quickened breaths, staring into the darkness of the old dining room.

I wondered how many ghosts could be hanging around the Blue Whale. It had been here forever. There could be some flappers, a few pirates and an innkeeper or two waiting to have a conversation with us.

"Miss Elizabeth Simpson!" Shayla called out the name, and I jumped in surprise. Nancy squeezed my hand as though she understood. "Mister Johnny Simpson! We call on both of you to come out and tell us your secrets."

I felt a cold draft go through the room. I glanced at Nancy to see if she felt it too, but her eyes were closed. Tim was looking around, squirming a little in his chair. Trudy was staring straight ahead as though she were afraid to look to either side.

Kevin was looking at Shayla when that chilly draft blew out the candle on the table. Trudy made a shrieking noise but didn't let go of my hand. The room was in complete darkness now. My heart thudded uncomfortably in my chest as I wondered if I would finally see a real spirit.

There was a sound. I couldn't identify what it was. It was like the wind sighing in the eaves when a storm comes up from the Atlantic. But something about it was unnatural. It was almost like a voice. I couldn't make out what it was saying, but I felt sure it was someone trying to tell us something.

"Is that it?" Tim asked.

"Shh!" Shayla responded. "Someone is near. You'll scare them away."

"Is it Johnny?" Trudy wanted to know. She craned her neck to look around the room.

"You have to be quiet!" Shayla said again. "What's wrong with you people?"

"I don't think I see a ghost, but I do smell lasagna that needs to come out of the oven," Kevin said. "Excuse me."

When he broke contact with the group, I felt the tension in the room ease away. It was like fog melting in the sun. Or in this case, faith in the face of so many nonbelievers. My chance to see a ghost slid away as everyone started moving back from the table.

An image formed in my mind and I realized I was still holding Nancy's hand. I could see something important she'd lost. It was a slip of daisy-covered Post-it that had fallen down between her desk and the old file cabinet beside it. She was worried about it. I sensed that the chief had asked her about it that afternoon and she'd lied to him. It was only a little lie. She didn't have any idea what had happened to the note.

I started to reassure her as we all got up and headed for the kitchen, then I decided against it. As much as I wanted her to feel better, I thought it might be for the best if I didn't tell her in front of everyone and embarrass her.

"Tim and Dae are in charge of salad," Kevin announced once we reached the kitchen. "The bowls are in that cabinet. I have the lasagna. Nancy, can you get the bread? Shayla and Trudy, you guys take up the slack. Whatever else we need, you're in charge."

No surprise, we decided not to eat in the dining room. The area in the bar was smaller but also less drafty and devoid of strange feelings. All the food was great—I was especially impressed by Kevin's lasagna. I complimented him on it, and he accepted with a grin. "It's the only dinner food I know how to make. Breakfast, I have covered. I make the best French toast in the world. I haven't worked on lunch yet, but I'm thinking I need more than grilled cheese sandwiches."

"I'm sure you can find someone to work here in the summer," I told him. "Winter help is a little harder to get. Only people who have been here awhile stay when it gets cold."

"But I'm sure Kevin will be able to find lots of year-round help once he opens." Trudy smiled and crinkled her pretty eyes at him. She didn't cause those frown lines for just anyone.

"Thanks," he said. "I hope all of you are suitably impressed enough to recommend me to the locals. I plan to pay a good salary too. With benefits."

Shayla leaned against him (she'd managed to sit between Kevin and Tim again). "Don't make it sound *too* appealing, sugar. I might give up my shop and come to work for you."

Tim leaned his elbows on the table beside his empty lasagna plate. "Just how is it an ex-FBI agent came up with enough money to buy the Blue Whale and do all these renovations and still have enough to hire help?"

If Kevin noticed Tim's irritated tone, he didn't let on. "Not everyone in the FBI comes from poor families. My parents were very well-off. They left me a nice nest egg. It was one of the reasons I decided to get out."

"But wasn't it exciting?" Shayla asked. "All that cloak-and-dagger, spy rings and late night meetings in smoky nightclubs. It sounds *sexy* to me, baby."

Kevin laughed. "As I was telling Dae, it gets old. I didn't want to spend my whole life chasing bad guys. It's a good game for someone right out of college. I like being an innkeeper. Bad paint and rotten wood are about as exciting as I want nowadays."

"Not to mention dead men in your upstairs," Nancy quipped. "Maybe you can leave the job, but it never really leaves you."

"You might be right," Kevin conceded. "I hope the dead man upstairs was the only thing left over from the previous owner. By the way, does anyone know anything about him? The previous owner, I mean. Bunk something, wasn't it?"

Tim laughed. "Of course. That's like asking if you can find your way from Corolla to Duck! Old Bunk Whitley is a legend in these parts. People say he bought the Blue Whale with smuggling money, like so many other people in this part of the world."

"But people also say the pirate gold he claimed to have found is what did him in too," I added. "Gramps swears the ghosts of the pirates came to get old Bunk. That's why they never found his body."

Kevin finished his wine and glanced around the room. "I hope we're not about to find another surprise. If old Bunk Whitley is stuck in some closet, I don't want to know about it. But it's a nice ghost story. Maybe I can use that in my brochure."

Trudy shuddered. "Isn't one dead body enough? And talk about legends! Everyone around here knows about Wild Johnny Simpson. How he broke Miss Elizabeth's heart. How he courted both sisters who were equally beautiful, but he only wanted Miss Elizabeth. How Miss Mildred never forgave her sister for taking him from her. Now *that's* the stuff of legends. Real legends, not some stupid pirate ghost."

At that moment, there was a loud thump that rattled the

windows in the bar. Kevin got to his feet and raced outside. We followed him and stood in the courtyard with the mermaid fountain, staring up at the roof, silhouetted against the dark sky.

"What is it?" Nancy whispered. "I don't see anything."

"Is it a pirate ghost come to get Trudy for being so ignorant?" Shayla demanded, nudging Trudy with her elbow.

"I wish it was something that interesting." Kevin ran his hand through his dark brown hair. "It's the roof. I was worried about some soft spots yesterday. See that hole up there? Unless we find Bunk Whitley's body in it, I'm going to have to put a new roof on over there."

Chapter 12

I went into work early the next morning. It was one of those cooler mornings when the fog swirls around the houses and lays across the sound like a blanket. Gramps offered to drive me to Missing Pieces on the golf cart, but I wanted to walk.

I had thought I'd be up all night thinking about everything that happened at the Blue Whale, but I fell asleep two minutes after I climbed into bed. That meant I needed some time to think before I opened the shop. I had promised Kevin I'd come back this afternoon to start painting, if the morning was dry. He planned to continue with his painting on the ground floor despite the new hole in the roof that needed patching.

I walked along Duck Road, glad for the early morning quiet. The bushes and shrubs dripped with the heavy fog. It was like being wrapped in gooey, wet cotton candy. I remember when I was a kid and hid outside under the bushes to keep from being seen. It's much harder as an adult to hide or even get away for a few minutes to think things through.

But what to think? If there was a ghost at the Blue Whale last night, he or she didn't give me any answers I could use to help Miss Mildred. We still had no clue who really killed Miss Elizabeth, let alone who killed Wild Johnny thirty years ago. I wondered, as I listened to some birds chirping from inside a thicket, if the two crimes were related. It seemed likely to me. What were the chances that we'd find Wild Johnny's body right after Miss Elizabeth was killed? On the other hand, no one could guess when Johnny's body *would* be found. The whole thing was giving me a headache.

The Duck Shoppes and the boardwalk were hazy in the fog, with seagulls folding their wings beneath the clapboard eaves, waiting for the sun. I headed to town hall first to surprise Nancy before she got there. I thought if I returned the note she'd lost to her desk, she'd think it had been misplaced. She could call the chief and tell him what he needed to know.

I slipped my key in the lock, glancing around now since I'd had my purse stolen. I was trying to be more aware of my surroundings, as Chief Michaels always advised. It appeared to be only the seagulls and me. None of the shops were open. I pushed open the door and closed it quickly, locking it behind me.

The Post-it wasn't hard to find. Of course it helped that I knew exactly where to look. I reached my fingers along the floor beside the file cabinet and snatched it out along with a few dust bunnies. With a flourish, I spread it out flat on Nancy's desk. She'd be surprised when she came in.

As I flattened the rounded edges and the part that

wouldn't stick anymore, I read the note. It was brief—
"I need to talk to you about Millie. Silas Butler. 252-
411-9750."

I stopped flattening for a moment and looked at the note
in disbelief. *Silas Butler?* Everyone knew about Silas Butler. He was Elizabeth and Mildred's younger brother. A
ne'er-do-well who was thrown out of the army. He'd come
home to Duck in disgrace only to take up gambling and any
other illegal activity he could find. He was legendary for
stealing a poor box from the Duck Presbyterian Church in
1964.

The unthinkable had happened after that. He was killed
in the 1970s running some kind of scheme or selling drugs.
I'd seen his grave marker in Duck Cemetery a hundred
times. My mother told me once that there was a song written about the Bad Butler.

This couldn't be the same person. There were probably
plenty of Silas Butlers in the world. *But how many who
wanted to talk to the chief about Millie?*

I glanced at the clock on the wall. It was one of those
standard round clocks, black and white with hands that
crawl from one number to the next when you're bored. I
had at least an hour before Nancy came in. I dialed the
number on the Post-it and waited for someone to pick up.

"Sea Oats Senior Care." The voice at the other end of the
line was cheerful for this hour of the morning.

At first I couldn't think what to say, and she repeated her
opening line. I gave myself a hard mental slap and said,
"I'm sorry. Where are you located?"

"We're in Kitty Hawk." She gave me the address. "Do
you need directions?"

"No, thanks. I was thinking about visiting Silas Butler
later today. I hope he's feeling all right."

"As far as I know. He's been popular here lately. Lots of visitors. That's a good thing, though."

I thanked her again and hung up. *Silas Butler*. It couldn't be coincidence. But *what* could it be?

I went and sat down in my office and considered the possibilities. Silas Butler was dead. Nancy probably wouldn't have realized the importance of this when she took the message because she had only lived in Duck for a few years. The Bad Butler was mostly forgotten now. Even we can't recall *all* our folklore. But Chief Michaels would know.

I turned on my computer and looked through the old files. Most of them had been slowly but surely put into the computer database. I typed in "Silas Butler" and his file came up. Silas had been shot and killed on Monday, June 8, 1978. The day after Wild Johnny Simpson's arrival at the Blue Whale!

I looked at the notes on his death. Silas was suspected of "illegal trafficking," which I'd learned from Gramps could mean anything from smuggled drugs to cigarettes. It was kind of a catch-all phrase used by the sheriff's department. I read further into the file:

Silas was shot and killed by a sheriff's deputy after failing to lay down his gun. Deputy Ronald Michaels was on desk duty for two weeks during an investigation. It was found that he had performed his duty adequately, and he was returned to his job without further issue. On August 19, 1978, he was given a commendation for his handling of the event.

The chief had shot and killed Silas Butler! No one had ever mentioned *that* part of the folklore. It never failed that in telling these tales, long-time Duck residents left out some facts and embellished others all in the name of making a better story.

I'd been only about five at the time Butler was killed, so naturally I couldn't recall anything about the death. But I had to wonder why Miss Elizabeth and Miss Mildred didn't hate the chief for his role in their brother's death. Finding that Post-it had led to more questions I couldn't answer.

I trusted Chief Michaels. But what did this Post-it mean? Was the public record wrong? Had Chief Michaels not actually killed Silas Butler all those years ago? Was it possible Bad Butler was still alive? And if so, why hadn't the chief said something about it? He wouldn't keep something like this to himself, would he? There had to be some mistake. Or I was misinterpreting what I'd read. One phone call could've cleared everything up. I didn't make that call.

I thought about it but argued that I would see the chief at the ribbon cutting for the new Mexican restaurant. I could ask him then. It couldn't be dead Silas Butler in Kitty Hawk at that nursing home anyway. It could wait.

But the morning dragged. I went and got coffee and talked to Phil for a while before I opened Missing Pieces. Of course it *would* be a slow day on the boardwalk. A lot of customers would've taken my mind off my worries. I watched the teapot clock in my shop crawl along until ten fifteen. I couldn't stand it anymore. I put out the "Closed" sign and locked the door.

Ribbon cuttings in Duck bring out the usual suspects. There's Barney from the jewelry store and Mark Samson from the Rib Shack. Both of them are members of the Duck Chamber of Commerce. Carter Hatley from Game World was president. He brought the big wooden scissors to cut the bright red ribbon. The ribbon is always provided by Betty's Boutique and Floral. Betty attends, enjoying the compliments on her elaborate ribbon design.

Once in a while, one of the other town council members

comes by to show support. Usually, this happens when there's food involved. But today, even though there was food, it was only me representing the town. No sign of the chief. I held the scissors and stood next to the red ribbon with everyone else behind me. The chamber of commerce secretary took a few pictures for the town's website and archives.

I don't think I've ever seen a newspaper or TV reporter at one of these events. But that's okay. It's a nice welcome to a new business. The owners all smile and shake my hand. I give them a small, gold plastic key that says "Duck" on it. It's exciting for everyone.

I saw Luke Helms in the sparse crowd right before the ribbon cutting. He came up to me after it was over and said, "I thought I might find you here. Do you have a minute to talk?"

"Of course. Do you want to go back to town hall?"

"No. This is fine. It's about Mrs. Mason."

I felt a terrible weight in my chest even as the sun finally broke through the heavy fog. It looked as if the day would clear up, probably be warm and sunny.

We walked over to the side of the road near a large purple horse decorated with sparkly stars. I wished I could jump up on it and ride to the hospital to rescue Miss Mildred. I knew it wouldn't happen, even if it were a real horse, but the urge to do *something* was overpowering.

"I'm afraid it's not going well for her. Yesterday, the judge found her incompetent to stand trial. I don't really know why. She's as sharp as a tack, except for this ghost thing. It's not something a judge wants to hear when he thinks you've killed your sister. It sounds like she invented a fantasy to block out what she did."

I knitted my fingers together, not sure what to say. "I

know you did what you could for her. I think she really *believes* the purse came from her sister. Someone is setting her up. They planted the purse and made it seem like it was Miss Elizabeth bringing it to her. Then they planted the shovel that killed her sister. It's a terrible thing."

Luke scratched his spiky, sandy-colored hair. "I wish I could do more. I'm not giving up yet. Not by a long shot. But she won't listen to reason, and I can't prove what you just said. It may be true, but without proof, she's a crazy old lady who killed her sister after years of feuding with her."

"Yeah. We all know about the feud. I suppose that didn't help either."

"I can tell you it didn't help when Chief Michaels testified about how calm she was when the two of you went to tell her Miss Elizabeth was dead. I know he's supposed to tell the truth, but it seemed to me that he went out of his way to make it sound worse than it was."

I thought about Silas Butler, but then shook my head. "If I can help in any way, please let me know. What happens now?"

"She'll be assigned to a mental hospital, probably on the mainland. Someone will be put in charge of her well-being. I suppose some family member will be given her power of attorney and they'll take care of her estate. She could be stripped of her rights in a legal procedure. But that will take some time."

"She has no family left. The sisters had no heirs. There aren't any cousins, nephews. At least not as far as I know." *Silas Butler* whispered in my brain.

"I guess a legal guardian will be appointed."

I put up my hand to shade my eyes from the sun behind his head. "Could that be *you?*"

"I don't know. I'll check on it and get back to you."

"Thank you so much, Luke." I put out my hand to shake his. "I really appreciate what you've done."

He shook my hand and smiled. "That's what I like about Duck. Everybody looks after everybody else. It means we all get in each other's business from time to time. But it's okay."

"That's true." We stood there smiling at each other for a few minutes. The rest of the small ribbon-cutting crowd wandered away. Part of me was thinking about Silas Butler and Miss Mildred. The other part was noticing how blue Luke's eyes were.

"Would you like to get some lunch?" he asked in an off-hand way, as though unsure of how I'd reply.

"Sure. Why not?"

I judged his age to be around forty, not too far ahead of me. He seemed to be in good shape. He must've been a very good lawyer to have retired so young. I could do worse for a lunch companion.

We agreed to try out the new restaurant. The enticing cooking aromas were already wafting out to the parking lot.

Inside was cool and colorful with Mexican music playing in the background. There weren't many people yet. I felt sure it would be popular later. We ordered our food, then sat back in the cool, dark booth to look at each other. Oh, the awkwardness of first encounters!

"How about those Braves?" Luke began the conversation after a long pause. "They're really moving this year."

I hated to admit I knew next to nothing about sports, so I nodded and agreed. I'd realized earlier in my career as mayor of Duck that this was all most people needed. "This is a nice place," I commented. "Especially since we don't have any other Mexican food down at this end."

He nodded, smiled and agreed, which told me he knew

next to nothing about local demographics. "I'm sorry I couldn't do more for Mrs. Mason. But I'll check on being the trustee for her estate."

"That would be wonderful."

The waiter brought some chips and salsa, and we spent the next few minutes munching. I could hear a TV somewhere in the restaurant, but I couldn't see it. That was okay with me. It was probably tuned into a sports event anyway.

"Can I ask you something?"

"Sure." I finished a chip and waited for the question.

"What makes you so certain that Mrs. Mason *didn't* kill her sister? Is that a Duck thing, all for one and one for all?"

I thought about it. "I've known her all my life. She taught most of the people who live here at some point in their school careers. She was widowed young like her sister. She never had any children of her own. She gives to every children's charity that exists, besides being an all-around good person."

He nodded. "I get that. But you know, sometimes good people do bad things. The case against her may be circumstantial, but it's strong. When I was working in the system, I would've considered this a slam dunk."

"Why did you offer to defend her?"

"Because she didn't have anyone else, and everyone is entitled to representation. That's what our government is based on. She seemed like a worthy cause to me."

"That's very good of you, Luke. Even if you don't think she's innocent."

He leaned his head closer to mine across the narrow table. "It's enough that *you* feel she's innocent, Dae."

I was very flattered by the way he said it. I glanced up as someone brushed by us and looked into Kevin's slightly sunburned face. I moved away from Luke suddenly, as though we'd been doing something wrong. Then felt silly for doing it. "Hi, Kevin. I'm surprised to see you here."

"I needed a break from roof repair." He nodded to Luke. "Hey there."

Luke nodded back in that way all men seem born to understand. "How's it going, Brickman?"

"Would you like to join us?" I ventured, since he seemed alone.

"No, thanks. I'm meeting someone. I'll talk to you later."

I watched him walk away and wondered if Shayla would be tripping in after him. Our food arrived after he was gone. Luke and I spent the next thirty minutes making small talk around burritos and enchiladas.

When all the food was gone and the conversation had simply died out, I smiled and said, "I guess I should get back to the shop. Lunch was great."

"It was. Let's do it again sometime. Where's your shop?"

I gave him the directions, which didn't take long. He picked up the check, and we said good-bye. I walked across Duck Road, wondering how someone who had seemed so interesting could end up being kind of boring. Maybe he was shy, although that didn't fit my ideas about lawyers.

At any rate, I didn't expect him to call or anything. We obviously weren't well matched. I stopped for an extra minute at town hall where Nancy was beaming. "It's been a very good day," she told me. "I had misplaced an important message for the chief, and somehow it found its way back to my desk. I think it was the janitor. Then they finally got the phone system working right. I even heard from my daughter. How was the ribbon cutting?"

"About like normal, maybe a few less people." I took my

messages from her, hoping there would be one from the chief explaining Silas Butler's message.

"And there was food too!" She pushed back her hair. "Someone needs to get after the other chamber members. What if a newspaper decided to cover a ribbon cutting? Say, about last night, did you hear or see anything out of the ordinary? 'Cause I have to tell you, I had a lot of wine, and I'm blaming it on a few things."

"Like what?"

"There was a sound. It was like someone was talking, in a breathy kind of way, you know? Then on the way home, I saw some shadows where there shouldn't have been shadows. Do you believe in ghosts, Dae?"

"I'd like to. I haven't ever seen one. But I did hear something last night at the Blue Whale. I'm not sure what it was, but I didn't have *that* much wine. I think someone was trying to tell us something."

Nancy's red lips formed an O. "That's what I was thinking too. I think Wild Johnny Simpson knows that some people think Miss Elizabeth killed him. He loved her even though he left. He doesn't want her blamed for his death."

"I guess that's possible."

"Any word on Miss Mildred?"

"Not really." I didn't want to repeat what Luke had told me. I didn't have the heart for it. There was no message from Chief Michaels in the small stack of notes she gave me. That made me feel even worse. Why hadn't the chief told me about Silas Butler? "I have to get back to the shop, Nancy. I'll see you later."

"All right, sweetie. You take care."

I followed the boardwalk back to Missing Pieces, hardly noticing the antics of the gulls over the water. I was surprised to find the "Open" sign out and the door unlocked.

Without thinking that someone might have broken in, I walked inside and looked around.

"I hope you don't mind." Gramps was down the aisle with the dinnerware. He wasn't alone. "Mary Lou wanted to come in and take a look around."

Mary Lou smiled and waved. "Hi, Dae. I can't believe I've never been in here. You have a *huge* collection. Mind if I look around with Horace?"

"That's fine." I gave Gramps the you-know-what-to-sell look and walked back outside. I was surprised to find Kevin about to walk in. "Done with lunch already? Shayla eats like a bird, but this is quick even for her."

He smiled. "What makes you think I had lunch with Shayla? I think she's dating your future husband right now."

"My future husband?" I searched my brain and remembered that he'd heard Tim propose to me at the Blue Whale. "That proposal was something he does from time to time. He started in high school and won't take no for an answer."

"Unless he's seeing someone else?"

"Exactly. Sorry for the Shayla crack. I know she likes you."

"I like her too, but not in the way you're thinking. I'm a humble innkeeper now. I don't think my life is exciting enough for her. Maybe she and Tim will work things out."

"That would be nice, but unlikely."

"Is that jealousy I hear? You don't want him, but you don't want anyone else to want him either?"

"No! That is definitely *not* it." I laughed, but wondered what brought him to the shop. Whatever it was, I was glad to see him. There was no one else I could talk to about Chief Michaels. Gramps would never take me seriously and worse, would feel the need to tell the chief. "You came to see me?"

"Yeah. Have you got a few minutes?"

We went to sit down on one of the boardwalk benches overlooking the water. It was a quiet day, probably a lot of visitors on the beaches since it wasn't so hot. The water lapped gently at the shore, and I spotted a bicycle tire someone had thrown out down there. I'd have to remember to mention it to the public works guys.

"I had lunch with an old friend of mine who's down here with the SBI," Kevin said. "He's working on both cases. They know it was a .22-caliber pistol that killed Wild Johnny. The bullet was still in his head. They're working on the DNA material they have, Johnny's, and the evidence they found with him. He had a calendar open on the desk. He met with Miss Elizabeth the day before he died."

I took in the information. "Or at least he was *supposed* to meet with her. We'll never know if he did or not."

"I'm afraid evidence doesn't work like that. The SBI will assume they met. A natural assumption after that would be that she went to the Blue Whale and shot him. Obviously, he trusted whoever killed him. He let her in his room and didn't look around to see what she was doing. Miss Elizabeth fits that profile."

"And she's not here to defend herself."

"Yeah. That makes her the perfect suspect. Everyone likes a closed case."

I took a deep breath. I hadn't known Kevin long, but I trusted him. I needed someone to hear what I suspected about Chief Michaels. "There's something else. I can't tell anyone else about this. I hope I can trust you with it."

"What is it?"

Strangely, I felt better that he didn't try to convince me to trust him. Maybe that doesn't make much sense, but I don't like people who try too hard. "It's about something that happened last night at the séance." I told him about Nancy and the note I found next to her desk. I explained about Silas Butler, minus the folklore, and kept to the facts from the sheriff's report. "I called the phone number this morning. It belongs to a nursing home in Kitty Hawk. Tim told me he took the chief out to a senior care center last week."

Kevin nodded as he stared off at the horizon. "So you think Chief Michaels is hiding the man he reportedly killed thirty years ago?"

"You see why I can't say anything to Gramps or anyone else from Duck. No one would take it seriously. But *something* is wrong. And it seems like a *big* coincidence to me that it's happening at the same time as all of this with Silas's sisters."

"I don't know the chief well, but I trust him," Kevin said. "There may be a reasonable explanation for it."

"I feel the same way, but I need to know what that explanation is. But what do I do now?"

"I guess you investigate. We'll drive down to Kitty Hawk and pay Silas Butler our respects."

"*We?* You mean you're willing to go with me?"

"A deal is a deal, although I haven't seen much painting going on." He grinned at me. "I'll trust that you're good for it. When can you go?"

We agreed to meet about five to drive to the nursing home. I also told him what Luke said about Miss Mildred being judged incompetent. "It might be for the best right now," he said. "As awful as it seems, at least she's safe where she is. Someone went to a lot of trouble to set her up so she could take the fall for her sister's murder. That same person might not like it if he or she feels their plan isn't working."

I hadn't considered that. "You mean they might try something else?"

"I don't know. I was in law enforcement a long time, Dae. I suspect everyone of everything."

I considered what Luke had asked me earlier about Miss Mildred. "Why are you helping me try to prove she's not guilty if you're so suspicious?"

"I don't know. Maybe I just need some cheap labor."

I was looking into his eyes when he said it, and I could see something there, something deeper than his joking words. "Thanks for listening to me about the chief. I'm glad you're on my side."

He smirked. "Looks like Luke is on your side too. How was lunch?"

"Different. Probably not something either of us would do again."

"I bet you'll be surprised." He got to his feet. "I'll pick you up over here at five. Do you have a tape recorder?"

I thought fast. "Nancy does. I'll borrow hers. Do you think I should bring a camera too?"

"Whatever we can do to prove Miss Mildred is innocent, Dae. Believe me, we have a long way to go."

Chapter 13

I ended up borrowing Nancy's MP3 player to record what was said at Sea Oats Senior Care. It was small and could hide easily in my pocket. I also borrowed her camera since the pictures my cell phone took were always blurry.

Nancy didn't comment on my spy-gear requests. She was still basking in praise from the chief after finding his message—the message I kept wishing he'd call and tell me about. I wondered if we'd meet him at the nursing home when we went to see Silas Butler. I hoped not.

When I got back to Missing Pieces, Gramps was manning the front; there was no sign of Mary Lou. I decided to ask him if he'd heard from the chief. "Was I supposed to?" he responded. "Has something else come up, Dae?"

I bit my lip to keep from telling him the truth. Gramps had been a sheriff's deputy back in 1978 too. I was sure he knew all about Bad Butler's demise. But if he didn't, and he got upset about Silas Butler still being alive and called the chief, we might never know what actually happened. "Not really," I finally lied. "I just thought he might call you before he told me anything."

"Don't worry so much." He hugged me. "Millie will be fine. You'll see."

Is he so confident because he knows about Silas Butler too? It seemed odd to me that he had never mentioned it if he knew Bad Butler was still alive. I couldn't be sure. It was beginning to look as though I was wrong about there being no secrets in Duck. "Sorry, I can't help it. I wish there was something I could do to help."

"I believe in the truth, Dae. You know that. It will come out, sooner or later. It always does."

"Like Bad Butler?" I asked quickly. "I was thinking about him the other day. It's funny how Miss Mildred and Miss Elizabeth didn't hate the chief for killing their only brother."

He sighed as he sat down behind the counter with me. "That was a long time ago. I think Millie and Lizzie were angry to begin with. But they got over it."

"I can't imagine getting over someone killing a person I loved."

His eyes narrowed. "Is there something specific you were thinking about Silas Butler? I don't recall ever mentioning that it was Ronnie who killed him."

"But it *was* him, wasn't it?" I shrugged. "I guess I heard someone say it."

"It was Ronnie who shot Silas. But Silas was in trouble for a long time before it happened. It could've been any of us that caught him in that situation. What are you thinking, Dae?"

I realized I was getting into hot water here. I had to think of a way out before I was parboiled. Gramps was too good at reading me. "I heard someone say that it runs in the family. They said Miss Mildred was like Silas."

"That was a damn stupid thing to say! Millie and Lizzie were nothing like Silas," he blustered. "Even later when he—"

"Yes?"

"Nothing." He shook his head. "I'm going to clean some fish for stew tonight. I'll see you later."

Was there a secret about Silas that Gramps and the chief knew? Were Miss Mildred and Miss Elizabeth involved too? It made me even more anxious to go to Kitty Hawk and talk to Silas.

The afternoon dragged by with only a few customers. This would've been a good day to be busy, but it never seemed to happen that way. Today, when I had somewhere I wanted to go, Missing Pieces felt like a weight holding me down. But then I looked around at all my treasures, the ones that would stay and the ones that would eventually leave me. This place was my second home. If I could be patient with slow sales, I could be patient until five P.M. when it was time to close.

I ended up closing a *little* early and ran home to change clothes before I had to meet Kevin. Most people, even in Kitty Hawk, knew I was the mayor of Duck. I wanted to look professional as I investigated my own chief of police. I checked in with Nancy for messages one last time, but there was nothing for me. I hoped I was doing the right thing. *Give me a call, Chief!*

I walked back into the Duck Shoppes parking lot at about five minutes before five. I saw Kevin leaning against his red Ford pickup and nervously twitched my knee-length white skirt with the embroidered hem. My matching white blouse was cool in the warm air and contrasted nicely with my light tan. I wondered if he'd notice.

He calmly assessed me from head to toe. "You look great! I don't think I've ever known a mayor I could say that about."

"Thanks." I felt a little awkward, not sure why. People compliment me on a regular basis. I'm not vain, but I think I'm kind of pretty. His words made me feel beautiful. "You look nice too. Not a bit like an ex-FBI agent."

He looked at his painfully plain gray suit and shrugged. "This is my *only* suit. I threw the rest of them away at the airport in DC."

We climbed into the pickup, and he headed toward Kitty Hawk. "I always thought FBI agents only wore plain brown suits," I said.

"I think you have FBI agents confused with police detectives. Our dress code wasn't that strict. Most of the time, I wore jeans and T-shirts while I was working."

"Undercover, right?"

"Right."

The conversation died there, and I tried to revive it with a mention of what we were doing. "I have a list of questions we can ask, if you think that would help."

"Such as?"

"Is he really Silas Butler? If he is, where has he been? Does anyone else know he isn't dead? Has he seen his sisters recently?"

"Those are right to the point. What makes you think he saw his sisters if no one else knows he's alive?"

"They never acted like they hated the chief for killing their brother. That strikes me as being a little odd. I asked Gramps about it, and I think he almost said too much.

Maybe they all *knew* he was still alive. If this man is *really* Bad Butler, of course."

He laughed. "Does everyone have a nickname like Wild Johnny and Bad Butler? I wonder what mine will be in a few years. Do you have a nickname, Dae?"

"I did once," I replied. "But that was a long time ago. I've changed."

"Really? Sounds bad. What was it?"

"It's not something I want to talk about." I carefully folded my list of questions and put them back in my purse.

"Were you Bad Dae O'Donnell at some point?" he joked. "It's hard for me to imagine you that way."

"We all have our dark days." I sat back against the seat. He wasn't getting an answer to that question from *me*.

"I'm sure Horace would be glad to tell me. Or maybe Tim." He glanced my way. "You might as well tell me."

"Not happening. Let's keep focused on what we're doing. I can't believe they didn't teach you that in the FBI academy."

"All right. I'll focus on our undead man for now. But you know I'll find out what your nickname was sometime. We live in Duck, right? Everyone knows everything."

We drove through the start of early evening traffic, bumper-to-bumper with RVs, open-top Jeeps and Cadillac convertibles. Many tourists would be headed home to shower and change for a night on the town. It was standard operating procedure for a visit to the Outer Banks.

"What did you think about the séance last night?" Kevin changed the subject (thankfully) as we stopped at another traffic light.

"It was all right. Nancy thought she heard someone speaking but couldn't make out what they were saying."

"What about you?"

"Old buildings make strange sounds. I heard something, but I don't know if it was a ghost or not."

"A skeptic?"

"Not at all." I folded my arms across my chest. "I'd love to see a ghost. I tried my best to talk to my mom after she died. It never happened. But that doesn't mean I don't believe. How about you?"

"I don't know. I've never seen a ghost either, but I've heard some weird stories from otherwise normal people. I had a partner in the FBI who swore his dead father was at the foot of his bed every night when he went to sleep. He wasn't the kind of guy you'd think would believe something like that either."

"Out here, people know that ghosts are real, like pirates. They're part of our heritage. It amazes me that a judge would rule Miss Mildred incompetent because she says she saw her dead sister."

"I'm sure it's because the judge thinks Miss Mildred *killed* her dead sister. Otherwise, it might be different."

"I guess you're right." I glanced at his profile as he drove. "What about you? Do you have someone you'd like to speak to on the other side?"

Was it my imagination or did his mouth tighten up a bit? "I don't think so," he answered. "I don't think there's anything to be gained by talking to someone dead."

Before I could respond, he turned the pickup into the Sea Oats Senior Care parking lot. I wanted to know what he was hiding. I'm pretty good at guessing when someone has a secret. There was a dead person Kevin wanted to see or talk to again. He just wasn't sure if it was possible.

"So we play this simple and laid back," I confirmed.

"Exactly."

The smell of baking pavement added to the diesel and

other exhaust coming from the overcrowded street. From somewhere close by, the scent of fried chicken added to the mix. People were coming and going out of the squat old building with the Sea Oats logo on it. The parking lot was half full, but I suspected most of the cars belonged to employees.

It was easy to get in the building. A smiling doctor held the door open, and we stepped inside the heavily shaded lobby. The antiseptic smell quickly destroyed any lingering odors from the street. It was like being wrapped in a Lysol bubble.

A heavy-set black woman dressed in a blue uniform smiled at us when we asked about Silas Butler. "You'll have to sign in first. Have you ever been here before? If not, I'll have someone take you down to the sunroom. Everyone usually gathers there after supper to watch TV and play games."

Kevin and I admitted we'd never been there as we signed in. Leticia (her name was on her shirt) *tsked.* "You know, that's part of the problem with these old folks. You come to a place like this, and your family writes you off. People need to *care* a little more. Is Silas your father?"

We glanced at each other, and I thought fast. "No. He's our uncle. We didn't even realize he was here until yesterday. Our mother died recently, and we found some information about him. It's terrible that she kept it from us all these years. I think it was the bad blood between Uncle Silas and our grandfather." I smiled in what I hoped was a pathetic way and leaned toward Kevin.

"That's awful. You know, families should stay close." Leticia sniffed a little, then pushed a buzzer for someone to take us to the sunroom.

"That was kind of elaborate," Kevin whispered as we

followed the attendant down the long hall from the lobby.
"I thought we were going to keep it simple."

"It's simple in *my* mind," I explained. "We're Miss Elizabeth's kids who didn't know her brother was still alive."

"Not that we know Silas *is* her brother yet. He might not be a relation at all."

We'd reached the sunroom, which was crowded with older folks playing Monopoly and Ping-Pong, and watching TV. A few gentlemen were sitting off to themselves, obviously engaged in a poker game for pennies.

"That's him over there." The attendant pointed to a skeleton-thin man hunched over a checkerboard, his blue Sun City T-shirt making a definite statement in the blue room.

We thanked the attendant and went to question our "uncle."

"Uncle Silas!" I made a show of calling him by name and hugging his wispy body. "I bet you thought everyone had forgotten you!"

Silas looked at me through his thick glasses as though I was a bug under a microscope. "Get out of here! You're not my niece. I don't even have a niece. If I did, she'd be a lot older, I can tell you that. Who are you two?"

"I'm Kevin Brickman, sir." Kevin extended his hand to the old man. "We wanted to ask you a few questions about Elizabeth and Mildred Butler. Can we have a few minutes?"

"Are you the stupid police? I know Lizzie is dead. You can't con me into anything. I don't have control of my money anymore, so don't waste my time."

Kevin nodded toward the bright orange chairs next to us, and we both sat down. Silas's checker partner wandered off, leaving us alone to talk. "So you *are* related to them," Kevin surmised. "That must've been quite a shock to hear your sister was murdered."

"You're Bad Butler, aren't you?" I asked. "You're supposed to be dead."

"You must be from Duck. Trust me, honey, not everyone is what they seem." He sat back in his chair and gazed at the ceiling. "Lizzie and Millie didn't know I was back. I left Duck a long time ago, thirty years. We had a falling out. I didn't think they wanted me in their lives anymore."

"I'm Dae O'Donnell. The mayor of Duck. You came back in time for one of them to die and the other to be charged with her murder," I said accusingly, though I wasn't exactly sure what I was accusing him of.

"I came back to the Outer Banks to die, little girl. I only have a few months. Lung cancer." He coughed long and hard, gasping for air. "I never believed those stupid cigarettes would kill me."

"What happened? I mean, I read the police report. It said Ronnie Michaels shot you. I've seen your grave in Duck Cemetery."

He grimaced. "Nothing to do with all you nosy busybodies in Duck. Why do you think I had to leave? Nobody can keep *anything* a secret."

"Anything like what?" I demanded. "What kind of secret makes a man fake his own death?"

"Never mind me," he wheezed, picking up an oxygen mask that was close at hand. "What are you doing to help Millie? You want to snoop around? Do something for her! She needs you. I don't. She shouldn't go to jail for what happened. She'd *never* hurt Lizzie."

"We're trying to help her," I assured him. "I could probably arrange for you to see her, if you like."

He pounded on his legs. "These things are useless now.

I don't get out much. Besides, she's better off without me. Always has been."

"Was Chief Michaels involved in faking your death?" I asked.

"Go away! Leave me alone. I'm dying already. Isn't that enough for you?"

"You left Duck at the same time Wild Johnny Simpson was killed." Kevin squeezed in one more shot. "You didn't have anything to do with that, did you?"

"Did I?" Silas squinted up at him through his thick glasses. "If I did, I don't remember. Maybe you should ask his ghost. You people still believe in ghosts, don't you? Good-bye, young man."

An attendant came to help Silas as he started coughing again. It was our signal to leave. The only question we had answered was that this was indeed Bad Butler.

Kevin and I walked out of the sunroom together. I was filled with too many questions. It was like eating too much at Thanksgiving—I was about to pop. There was a steady stream of visitors coming and going as we started down the hall. I recognized one of them and pulled Kevin to the side. *"Chief Michaels!"* I hissed as I turned us both around so the chief wouldn't see us.

We were still visible in the narrow space until Kevin put both his arms around me and hugged me close. "Stand still," he whispered so that his voice tickled my ear.

I stood there, not moving, knowing *why* it was happening, telling myself it didn't really *mean* anything.

He smelled good. Kind of like ocean air and paint thinner. I could imagine dancing with him under the stars on the beach. I could imagine talking with him all night and helping him look for treasure at the Blue Whale.

But I didn't have a good track record with men. There

was Tim and a few others I'd dated since high school but nothing that ever meant much. I'd come to accept that I was destined to be alone. It didn't bother me anymore. At least that's what I told myself.

I made myself stand on my tiptoes and peek across his shoulder. "He's gone. Fast thinking."

He held me an second or two longer than was necessary. I didn't let myself think about it. If he was interested in Shayla, he wouldn't be interested in me. Not like *that* anyway. "I don't get it," I said as we started back down the hall to the lobby. "Why would Chief Michaels keep this a secret?"

Kevin smiled at a young woman in a low-cut red dress as he held the door for her. Clearly, he wasn't all sweaty palmed or anything, like I was after standing close to him. Why was it that the men I liked never seemed to like me back? At least not in the same way. My high school yearbook was filled with boys who thought of me as their best *friend*.

"I think there may be more involved here than we realize, Dae. We should probably ask the chief about it."

"But how can we? If he wanted us to know, he would've told me. Or Gramps. He's known Silas was alive for a while but hasn't said anything. How can that be good?"

"There could be some things that would explain this," he said as we got out to the car. "I think we should give him a chance to defend himself. He's supposed to be innocent until proven guilty, right?"

"What kind of things? I've known him my *whole* life. How could he hide something like this?"

"Until you find out what's behind it, you're only speculating it's something bad," he reminded me.

"Gramps could be involved in it too." I sat down and

fastened my seat belt. All of the excitement I'd felt earlier about getting here and finding Silas had drained away. What difference did it make if Silas was still alive anyway? It wouldn't bring back Miss Elizabeth, and it wouldn't save Miss Mildred. I'd discovered a whole *new* problem with no answer. I still hadn't resolved the first problem.

He smiled at me as we stopped for a red light. "Would you like to stop somewhere for dinner? News of Bad Butler will wait another hour."

I smiled back. "Maybe. As long as the chief's car isn't in the parking lot."

"You're willing to condemn the chief kind of fast without any real proof," he argued. "You believe in Miss Mildred with *real* evidence against her."

"I think I have real evidence against the chief," I argued. "Silas Butler, a man he killed thirty years ago, is still alive. The chief has known about it for a while but hasn't said anything. Why wouldn't he tell someone?"

We turned into an interesting Asian restaurant I'd always wanted to try, but before we could get out of the truck, my cell phone went off. It was Gramps on the other end. He was more than a little upset.

"Dae, you won't believe what's happened. That new real estate boy who moved into town has put Millie's *and* Lizzie's properties up for sale."

Chapter 14

"Is this possible? Can he really do this?" I asked Gramps once we were standing in the kitchen at home. I'd wanted to ask in the truck on the way back, but I'd lost cell phone service when Kevin drove out of the restaurant parking lot. It figures. "Did they owe back taxes or something?"

"This isn't a tax auction," Gramps explained. "The property is being auctioned off by Chuck Sparks. I don't know how he got his hands on it."

Mary Lou brought the cheesy-potato casserole from the microwave with fish-shaped oven mitts on her hands. "It's a crime." She plunked down the white casserole dish on the table next to the fish stew. "Nobody can come in and take a house like that. It's down right thievery."

I didn't have to ask why she was here again tonight. Gramps had made that pretty clear. I was glad they had dinner ready since we'd rushed back from Kitty Hawk without eating. Mary Lou took out some of her prize-winning corn-bread and put that on the table beside the casserole. It smelled so good, my stomach growled.

"Somebody's hungry," Gramps observed with a laugh.

Hot color washed into my face. I guess he didn't care that we weren't alone. "Mary Lou's right." I tried to divert the subject. "No one can take the sisters' houses without notice or permission."

"The only way that could happen at this point would be if they had some relation who could step in and take control of their estates." Gramps poured tea. "Since neither of them had anyone except each other, I'll bet both houses were set up to go to the surviving sister."

I glanced at Kevin. "There's something you don't know." I told Gramps about Silas Butler.

"Silas." Gramps sat down, the color draining from his face, and gazed across the room. "So that's why you were asking so many questions earlier. Why didn't you tell me then?"

I waited for Kevin and Mary Lou to sit, then sat down myself before I answered. "I was afraid you'd tell the chief and Silas would be gone when we got there." I passed Kevin the stew. "Did you know he was still alive?"

He looked down at his plate, and I knew right away what the answer was. "We weren't supposed to talk about it. I still don't know if I should say anything. It could mean Silas's life."

"He's dying anyway, if that makes you feel any better," I explained, regretting my words after I'd said them. "I'm sorry. I didn't mean it that way. Chief Michaels has been visiting him for a couple of months. He never mentioned it?"

He looked stricken. "No. I don't believe it. Ronnie would've said something."

"I'm afraid it's true." Kevin took the potatoes I passed him. "And that brings up an interesting theory. If what you say is true about the sisters leaving each other their properties, when Miss Elizabeth died, her property would've gone to Miss Mildred. When Miss Mildred was declared incompetent, both their properties must have passed to Silas."

The four of us stared at each other across the cornbread, stew and potatoes. There was silence, except for the hooting of an old owl that lived in one of the trees out back and the ticking of the kitchen clock.

"Are you saying you think Ronnie is involved in taking Lizzie and Millie's properties?" Gramps glared at Kevin.

I jumped in on his behalf. "The chief knew Silas was alive and has been visiting him. He didn't say anything about it to anyone. Luke Helms told me at the ribbon cutting that the chief went out of his way to point out how unemotional Miss Mildred was when they had him testify. He also told the judge about the feud between the sisters."

Gramps slammed his fist on the table, making the silverware jump. "I don't believe it. I've known Ronnie all of his life. He wouldn't do such a thing. There has to be another explanation."

Mary Lou sipped her tea, then added, "I wouldn't put anything past anyone when it comes to money. What are those houses worth anyway? With the price of land around here, they could buy a turtle sanctuary with no problem."

I thought back to my encounter with Chuck Sparks and his mother's medallion. "If Chuck was right, we could be talking four or five million dollars for the two properties. When did you say the auction is being held?"

"The sign said Wednesday," Gramps said. "That doesn't give us much time to figure out what's going on."

"Some of that will be easy," Kevin responded. "The records for any land transfer have to be at the county court-house. I'm sure the real estate office has them too, but you couldn't make him give them up without a court order."

"I might be able to convince Chuck to help us," I said. "I *did* find his mother's medallion. Maybe I could guilt him into feeling like he owes me something."

It didn't sound like much of a plan, and I didn't feel any better. I didn't want to think about Chief Michaels helping himself to the sisters' properties, but I distinctly remembered Silas telling us that he wasn't in charge of his money anymore. Had the chief stepped in to help with that?

"If we find out someone"—I didn't mention the chief so Gramps wouldn't get riled again—"set this whole thing up, would that mean that person killed Miss Elizabeth and framed Miss Mildred?"

Gramps's angry expression told me he knew who I was talking about. Kevin agreed with me. "If we can prove someone stepped in to take the properties and sell them, we might be able to get the SBI to take another look."

I glanced at Mary Lou. Tears were running down her face. "I don't think I can handle all this. Excuse me." She got up from the table and went outside to the back porch.

I felt the same, but somebody had to save Miss Mildred. Being a rescuer herself, Mary Lou would realize that soon enough. I knew she was overwhelmed right now by everything that had happened. We all were.

"Tomorrow's Saturday," Kevin reminded us. "If we're going to prove anything in time to stop the sale of the houses, we better get moving."

Gramps said, "You remember I dated Olivia, the Register of Deeds? She has that nice white Cadillac convertible. I think I'll give her a call. I'm going to prove you're wrong about Ronnie."

"Okay. But, Gramps, you can't say *anything* about this to the chief until we know. If you're wrong and he's gone bad, he could make it impossible to stop the sale."

"I won't say anything to him, but not because he might do anything. I don't want to embarrass both of us by accusing him of something like this."

"I'll talk to my contact in the SBI and suggest an alternate scenario," Kevin said.

"I'm going to see what I can get out of Chuck Sparks." I got up from the table, not as hungry as I thought. The conversation had stifled even my taste for warm cornbread. "I guess we all have our jobs cut out for us."

Gramps went out to check on Mary Lou, and Kevin helped me clear the table. I tried to get him to take the rest of the food home with him, but he said he already had too much in the kitchen at the Blue Whale. "You know, if you want to back out of our deal to help me with this, I'll understand. It looks like it might be more complicated than either of us thought at the beginning."

"You can't get out of painting that easy." He grinned as he put the rest of the tea in the fridge. "It's okay, Dae. I'm not giving up on it yet. There's no such thing as an uncomplicated murder case. I knew what I was getting into before I agreed to help."

We went to sit outside on the front steps so we wouldn't bother Gramps and Mary Lou in back. "You know, everyone is speculating about why you left the FBI," I told him when the dark had closed around us and I couldn't make out his face. I'd wanted to ask him this for a while but had felt I didn't know him well enough. I was also worried it might be painful for him to explain.

"I know. Everyone in a small town like Duck feels like

they have to know everything about everyone. I knew it would be that way before I came. I can handle it."

As far as answers were concerned, that wasn't the one I was looking for. It would be rude to ask him outright why he'd left his career and moved to Duck. I tried another tack. "I know you said you didn't miss it."

"I didn't say that *exactly*," he corrected. "You don't do something like that for years without missing some parts of it."

Another vague answer that didn't satisfy my curiosity. "Well, I'm glad you're here to help with this, Kevin." Obviously he wasn't going to tell me about his past.

"Because otherwise you'd be having this conversation with Tim, right?"

"*No!* You couldn't pry Tim away from the chief with a big crowbar! I wouldn't ask him to help me with this. He'd be too distracted."

"But not because he might ask you to marry him again?"

What did I hear in his voice? Was Kevin trying to get information from me about the past as well? I could imagine only one reason he might be interested. My heart beat a little faster until I squashed the idea. He wasn't interested in me romantically. This was all leading somewhere else. I wasn't his type.

"No. He does that from time to time, like I told you. He was the first boy I ever kissed. Maybe I was the first girl he ever kissed. But until one of us settles on someone else, I think that's the way it'll be between us. You must've had someone like that when you were in school."

He laughed. "My dad sent me to a military academy when I was thirteen. It was all male at that time. I didn't kiss a girl until I was almost eighteen. And I never saw her again."

"I'm sure Shayla and Tim won't last long. She'll be interested in you again shortly. If not, there are plenty of unmarried women looking for new men. You'll end up with someone."

"Yeah. Someone who doesn't mind that I'm going to have to work on the Blue Whale for the rest of my life to keep it together long enough to pay off the mortgage. Someone who likes lasagna, even leftover lasagna, and who doesn't mind that Bunk Whitley is probably buried somewhere inside the inn."

We both laughed at that, then said good night. It was going to be a long day tomorrow trying to figure out what to do to help Miss Mildred. "I'll let you know what I find out from Chuck," I promised.

"I'll do the same when I know something," he said. "Be careful, Dae. There's a lot of money at stake, and someone may have already died for it. If that's true, whoever killed Miss Elizabeth won't hesitate to kill again."

"I don't think anyone would risk killing the granddaughter of the retired sheriff and the current mayor of Duck," I joked.

He took my hand and stood close to me on the stairs. "Don't underestimate your opponent. If you're going to investigate something like this, that's one of the first rules."

"All right. I'll be careful." My voice was a little fluttery when I answered. I hoped I wasn't about to make a fool of myself with Kevin.

"Good night then. I'll talk to you tomorrow."

I watched him walk down the dark path to his truck and drive away, staring until I couldn't see the taillights anymore. Kevin Brickman had a way about him. I liked it. I liked him. But I wasn't so sure anything more could come of those feelings.

Chuck Sparks had set up an office in a one-room space inside one of the rental buildings on Duck Road. There was a small sign on the door that read "Island Realty." In the background of the name was the logo of his mother's award medallion.

As I opened the door to his office, I hoped that the medallion would help remind him he owed me a favor. It was barely nine A.M., but frigid air-conditioning whooshed out at me. Some people don't acclimate well to warm weather. Either Chuck was one of those people, or his air conditioner was broken.

I recognized the teenage girl at the front of the room. She was a recent high school graduate. I remembered her receiving her diploma when I spoke at the graduation exercises in June. "Hi, Mandy! I see you found a job for the summer."

"Hello, Mayor O'Donnell! Yeah, I snagged this before anyone even knew about it. By the end of the summer, I should have some money put away for college. I got a nice grant, but this will be for living expenses, you know? Stuff I need like dorm furniture, cell phone bills, extra nail polish. That kind of stuff."

"That's wonderful! I'm very happy for you." I glanced at the empty desk behind her that was pushed up against the only window in the room. "Are you expecting Mr. Sparks today?"

"He should be here anytime." Just then, the door opened

behind me and her grin widened. "And here he is now! Good morning, Mr. Sparks. The mayor is here to see you, and you have several messages on your desk."

Chuck looked at me, then his eyes shifted away. "Mayor O'Donnell."

I took ten dollars out of my purse and handed it to Mandy. "Why don't you run over and get us some coffee?"

She glanced at Chuck. He nodded, and she left the office with the cash.

I shivered in the frosty atmosphere. "You know, it's not meant to be below zero inside when it's ninety outside. Maybe you should get a few fans."

"I *know* why you're here. I heard about what happened when they came to get the old lady." He put his briefcase down on his desk and turned back to me in an adversarial stance. "You might as well say what you have to say."

"Okay. I want to know who's selling the sisters' properties."

He fiddled with his palm tree tie. "I don't give out that kind of information. You can get what's registered easy enough. Or you can come to the auction Wednesday. Why are you *really* here?"

Shamelessly, I pointed to the logo on the front door. "If I hadn't found that medallion your mother lost, there would be a piece of your history gone forever. I know it didn't have much intrinsic value, but it was important to you. *This* is important to me."

He flopped down in the chair behind his desk with a gratifyingly unhappy look on his handsome, spray-tanned face. "I know I owe you, if that's the point you're making. I still don't understand how you managed to find that medallion. But you can't stop progress *or* keep me from selling those properties. It's the way things work."

I went to sit in the chair in front of him. "Have I told you how important this is to me, Chuck? I want whatever information you can give me about the sale. I'm not trying to stop anything. I want to know what's going on. What's the hurry? Miss Mildred has barely settled in her bed at the hospital."

He pyramided his hands on the desk in front of him. "I wouldn't tell anyone else this information. And if you try to use it against me, I'll deny it. You don't have a tape recorder, do you?"

"It's just me and you." That was the only promise I was willing to make. I was also willing to ignore his implied threats. "Why is this sale taking place so quickly?"

He pushed around some of the paperwork on his desk. "There's a developer interested in both of those properties. In fact, there are at least *three* developers interested in them. They have high-end clients who've been looking for larger pieces of property in Duck to build on. I told you land is at a premium here. It's very valuable and an auction is the best way to get the most money for the properties."

"I'm not sure that explains why you're doing it so quickly."

He sat back in his chair and stared at me. "My client is in need of some capital right now. The sooner, the better, to settle some outstanding debts. I think you can imagine something like that, Mayor."

Really, I couldn't. I'd never even had a credit card. The idea of a debt so great it had to be taken care of in a few days or you'd face the consequences was beyond my understanding. "Who's your client?" I held my breath when I asked the question, fearful that somehow Chief Michaels had received power of attorney from Silas Butler and needed to settle gambling debts. Or something equally as sinister. I could suddenly imagine him running away from members of the mob who wanted their money back.

"OBX Land Trust, LLC."

"Who is that?" I'd never heard the name before.

"As I said, it's my client who has ownership of these properties."

"And is related to Silas Butler in what way?"

"I don't know who that is, Mayor. I haven't dealt with anyone by that name."

I felt sure he was lying, but there was no way for me to prove it. Mandy returned with the coffee, the hot liquid causing clouds of condensation in the cold office air. I had little more information than I'd had when I first walked in. I hoped Gramps could get more.

Chuck got to his feet, apparently sensing I'd run out of steam. "Anything else I can do for you, Mayor, please let me know."

He put out his hand and I shook it, wishing I could get some sense of what he really knew about the sale of the sisters' houses. A chill trembled through me. I could see he'd lost his cigarette lighter. I wasn't about to tell him where I saw it. "I hope there's nothing wrong with this sale, Chuck. It would be a shame to waste all your money setting up a business in Duck, then lose it over something stupid."

"There's nothing wrong with this sale. It's straightforward. I hope you'll come to see that in time."

I left after that, with a smile for Mandy. It was good to be back outside, even if it was humid and hot already. I wasn't prepared to spend much time in winter temperatures in the middle of July. I crossed Duck Road and walked up to the Duck Shoppes, stopping at town hall before I went to Missing Pieces.

Nancy was there, of course. She wasn't supposed to be

since it was the weekend and town hall wasn't officially open. Sometimes it seemed like she never went home. She offered me coffee and donuts she'd purchased from the Duck High School cheerleaders' fundraiser. "What are you doing in here, Dae? Do you need something specific?"

"No. Just thought I'd check in."

"I actually have two messages for you, both from Mary Lou Harcourt. She's holding a turtle rescue day she'd like you to come to. And people are *still* building sand castles, endangering the turtles trying to reach the water."

I took out my calendar and marked the turtle rescue event in it. "Wednesday morning, ten A.M." I thought about the auction the same morning and wrote that down too, not that I was likely to forget it. "Thanks, Nancy. I think I'll go in the office for a few minutes."

"Okay, sweetie. Shall I hold any calls, especially turtle-rescue calls?" She smiled knowingly.

"Thanks. I won't be here long. If Mary Lou comes in later, you can send her down to Missing Pieces."

I closed the door to my office behind me. Nancy was probably wondering why since I usually left it open. I thought about looking up the property owner for the sisters' houses on GIS—Geographical Information Survey. It marks the person who pays taxes on the property as well as the owner. Unfortunately, GIS had not kept up with recent events. Miss Mildred and Miss Elizabeth were still listed as both owners and taxpayers. It was a dead end.

Not that it wasn't possible to use the information I got from Chuck. If Gramps didn't come back with more than Chuck had, we might still be able to find out who was behind the sale. OBX Land Trust had to belong to someone. I typed the name into Google but nothing came back. If the group had been active in the Outer Banks buying other properties, it seemed like they'd have a listing. Unless they'd put the company together just for this sale.

There was a knock on the door, and I absently called out, "Come in." I looked up and saw Chief Michaels closing the door behind him. I had a brief moment of panic at the idea of being alone with him, then dismissed it. Whatever was going on with him right now, he was still the same man I'd known all my life. Maybe there was some way to help him.

"Mayor." He nodded. "I'd hoped to have a few words with you."

I wondered if Gramps had spoken to him. I felt like I was blindfolded and not sure which direction to go. But I smiled and gestured toward one of the chairs in front of my desk. "Of course, Chief. What can I do for you?"

He settled himself into a chair and pulled off his hat. His blue uniform was starched and pressed as always. His shoes were as shiny as the medals on his chest. I remembered him receiving several of them. One was for saving a little girl during a house fire. He'd risked his life to pull her out. The town had thrown a huge appreciation party for him right in the middle of Duck Road. That was before the park was finished.

"I think you may have the wrong idea about what I was doing yesterday at the senior center in Kitty Hawk."

I didn't want to, but I felt a little nervous. Chief Michaels looked pretty intimidating in his uniform, and of course, there was a large gun on his hip. Before the last few days, I wouldn't have believed the chief would be capable of hurting me. Now I was a little less certain. What if he was being pressured by tremendous outside forces? The way Chuck had described things, the seller of the properties was a desperate man with terrible financial burdens. Maybe I didn't know Chief Michaels as well as I thought.

"I really don't have any ideas about why you were there," I lied. It seemed the wisest course of action. "Is there something I should know?"

"I know you've been looking into what happened to Lizzie," he said. "Tim told me you don't believe Millie killed her sister. I don't want to believe it either, but sometimes bad things happen. You have to accept that we've done the best we could by Millie. I wish it could be different, but the evidence is stacked up against her. The evidence *never* lies."

"What evidence is there besides her seeing Miss Elizabeth bring her purse to her?"

"That speaks to her frame of mind, Mayor. She lost it when she realized what she'd done. Agent Walker and I believe the DNA tests will confirm that the blood and hair on the shovel we found in Millie's garden shed will match Lizzie's. Millie's fingerprints were all over Lizzie's purse. How much more do you want? We would've tried to put the purse snatcher away just finding the purse at his motel room."

That was a dizzying amount of information. I didn't want to hear it. He was right about that. But I also still felt that all this so-called evidence added up to someone trying to point the finger at Miss Mildred. "She's being framed for this, Chief. I don't know why you can't see that."

"Who would possibly think of doing something like that, Mayor? With all due respect, you should leave this kind of thing to the professionals."

"The professionals are wrong this time, Chief. I'm sorry, but I'm not giving up on Miss Mildred that easy. I'm certainly not going to let someone sell her land out from under her as they set her up to take the blame for Miss Elizabeth's death."

He glared at me. He'd done that before, but this time I felt the impact more deeply. "I'd hoped to explain the situation to you, but I can see you're as stubborn as your grandfather. When he got the bone between his teeth, he never let go. That's what made him such a darn fine sheriff. Just remember, you *aren't* a law enforcement official."

Was that a threat? My hands shook as I played with my stapler. "I appreciate that. And I know you've done all you could for Miss Mildred. If there's a personal issue I can help you with, I hope you know Gramps and I will always be there for you. You're part of the family, Chief."

He smiled, or what passed as smiling for him. "Thank you, Mayor. But I'm fine. I only wanted you to know that there's nothing illegal going on now. Everything is well in hand."

I nodded, and my voice almost broke when I said, "What about Silas Butler, Chief? How long have you known he was alive and living in Kitty Hawk?"

Chapter 15

Chief Michaels got up and walked to the door. I thought he was going to leave rather than answer my question. He stopped for a moment with his hand on the door handle. When he turned back, the grimace on his face made me aware of his anger.

He came back to my desk and leaned on his hands, glaring down at me. "Are you questioning *my* integrity, Dae O'Donnell? I've been in law enforcement since you were in diapers. Are you saying *I* did something wrong?"

I really wanted to back down. I wanted to hold up my hands and assure him that I would never question *anything* he did. I could give him my big mayoral smile and pretend I wasn't serious. Anything to get him to leave.

But I couldn't do it. "I guess I'm asking if you're part of this whole auction thing for the sisters' properties. I'm sorry, Chief. I don't want to ask that question, but I'm not the *only* one asking." I was, but he didn't have to know.

He paused for a long moment, then looked out the window at the sound with his hands held behind his back, legs spread, like an old-time sea captain. "You do things for a long time on autopilot. I guess because you know your way around so well. Maybe *too* well."

He sat back down and faced me. "I've only known about Silas for a few months. Of course I went to visit him when I found out. I never expected to see him again."

"What happened? Why isn't he buried in Duck Cemetery?"

"He turned state's witness against Bunk Whitley. It was the only way we could get at him. Old Bunk was the real problem back then. He was into everything from gambling to prostitution. Silas worked for Bunk."

"And you agreed to pretend he was dead so Bunk wouldn't kill him." That made so much more sense than thinking the chief had gone rogue.

"We did. Horace knew about it too. He was there with me that night. We took Silas across to the mainland and were supposed to keep him at a motel until the trial. But Bunk was too clever for us. He skipped out and was never heard from around these parts again. Silas was too scared to come back, though. He left the island. He told me he only came back to die because it didn't matter anymore. Then Miss Elizabeth was killed."

"Their properties came to him, didn't they?"

He nodded. "Silas told me about it right after we picked up Millie."

"But there are no other relatives, so he gave it to Chuck Sparks to sell."

"Not exactly. There's another relative, Mayor. Silas has

a grandson. He's the one selling the properties. I assume he has power of attorney over his grandfather's affairs. I knew it was coming. That's why I went down there yesterday, to ask him if there wasn't some way to stop it."

"What did he say?"

"He said he wouldn't if he could. He's dying. He might only have a month or so to live. He doesn't care if Bunk is still alive and can come after him. He thinks what's happening with his sisters' property doesn't matter either since Millie was arrested."

"What about this grandson? Does he live in Kitty Hawk?"

"No. He lives on the mainland. You know him. It's Jerry Richards."

"The TV guy?" I could hardly believe it. "He's the one who has to sell the properties right away because he owes people money?"

"What did you think, Dae? Did you think it was me?"

I hated to admit it, but I nodded, keeping my gaze on his. "I'm afraid so. Sorry, Chief."

He got up and paced the office for a few minutes, occasionally looking back at me. "I know Horace didn't think it was me. I know he knows me better."

"I'm sure you're right. He didn't say much when I told him, but I'm sure he didn't really think it was you. I didn't want to, but it looked that way from where I was standing."

"Well, I'm glad we got that settled then."

"Have you considered that Jerry Richards may have killed Miss Elizabeth and framed Miss Mildred for the murder?" I asked, excited about the possibility. "He obviously had a reason to do it as soon as he realized both of the properties would come to him if anything happened to his aunts. Chuck told me the properties together could go for more than five million dollars. With that amount, Richards could probably pay off all his debts and still have a lot left over."

"Of *course* I considered that! I'm not a complete fool. But Richards has an alibi for the time the ME thinks Lizzie was killed. He was still on the mainland, taping a news segment to be used later. I don't think it was him, and neither does Agent Walker. We also checked out Sparks's alibi since he's new around here. He was at a big sales bash in Corolla."

"But you can both wrap your minds around *Miss Mildred* killing her sister." I hoped my tone conveyed enough sarcasm. "Really, Chief, just because everything is laid out all nice and neat doesn't make it the truth."

"I've given you the information I know about. All of the *real* evidence is against Millie. I don't like it anymore than you do, Dae. And I wish I could point a finger at Jerry Richards or *anyone* else for what happened here. But I can't, and you should let it go too."

"Just one last thing," I said. "Did Miss Mildred and Miss Elizabeth know their brother was still alive?"

He frowned. "Yes. He wouldn't leave unless they knew. It was hard at the beginning. They didn't speak to me for a long time. Part of the charade. Eventually, most people forgot."

"Thanks, Chief. I appreciate you giving me this information. Forgive me if I can't let this go that easy."

The chair legs scraped on the wood floor as he pushed back from the desk. "I guess you have to do what you think is right. But be careful you don't get in trouble. Brickman may have been FBI, but don't think he knows it all."

He left the office, and I sagged over my desk, my cheek against the cool wood. That wasn't something I *ever* wanted to do again. But at least it had cleared the air, and I felt certain the chief wasn't involved. Now I had to find out who was.

If Jerry Richards and Chuck Sparks had been ruled out as suspects, who was left? Someone else had to benefit, but who could that be?

I told Nancy I'd see her later and almost ran out of town hall. I sat for a long time on the bench overlooking Currituck Sound, trying to piece everything together. From where I was sitting, I could see the door to Missing Pieces, and when a prospective shopper finally decided to visit, I reluctantly went to answer the call.

The rest of the morning flew by as a few more shoppers followed the first. I sold one Blue Whale T-shirt for Kevin and put his money in an envelope for later. I noticed one of the shoppers seemed to be searching for something special. She picked up my Roosevelt jelly jar right away, then put it down only to circle back to it again.

She finally brought it up to the front, her cinnamon-colored brows knit together, very red lips determined in her pink face. "This one doesn't have a price on it. I realize that means it's more expensive, but I'm prepared to haggle."

That was a little different than what I'd come to expect. Usually, my special shoppers paid whatever I asked for the treasure, no questions. We eyed each other like opponents before a prize fight. I came out swinging first, with a price in mind.

Her blue eyes widened comically. "That's outrageous! I'll give you half that."

I could see she *really* wanted it. More important, she knew what it was. "You won't get a jelly jar actually used by Mrs. Roosevelt while she was staying here in Duck for any less than I'm asking."

"I've seen one or two for *half* of what you're asking."

Hmm. She wasn't very good at haggling. "I'll tell you what. You can have the jelly jar and the butter keeper that goes with it for my original price."

"Deal!" She put out her heavily ringed hand to shake mine and we sealed the agreement. "Wait until the girls back home see this! Of course, I'll have to add it to my will."

Will! Why hadn't I thought of it before? Miss Elizabeth had a last will and testament, but Miss Mildred wasn't dead. The only legal document that could give someone the power to sell her property would be a power of attorney. If Miss Mildred knew Silas was still alive, she probably had put that in his name in the event of Elizabeth's death. That meant Jerry Richards could sell the property *if* he had access to that document. He'd be fine as long as no one questioned it.

The customer wrote me a check, and I wrapped her items carefully. We parted ways congenially, both of us satisfied with the transaction. Two more customers came in behind her and bought some souvenir items. Mary Lou followed after them with some Turtle Rescue Day flyers to put up in the shop window.

"I hope you'll be there, Dae, and that you'll pass the word." She took my tape dispenser and hung up several flyers in the windows and around the store. "This is an important opportunity for fund-raising and education. Thousands of baby sea turtles are lost every year, you know. We have to protect them."

I'd heard it so many times already, it had lost some value for me. I knew the turtles were important, but Mary Lou was a little too focused on the subject. "I'll try my best to be there," I promised. As mayor, it was the least I could do.

"I'm so disappointed, really. You know, Millie promised part of her beachfront would be made into a turtle sanctu-

ary when she passed. I wish I could hold her to that promise now."

"She hasn't passed yet," I replied, thinking about the
auction coming up Wednesday. If what Mary Lou said was
true, it seemed even more possible there was a missing
document that could shut down the whole property sale. A
written promise to donate land to the Turtle Rescue League
was enough to take to court.

"No, but she might as well have. I haven't heard anything from her lawyer about the land. Her promise might as
well not exist." Her mouth made a disapproving frown that
marred her otherwise smooth complexion. She was really a
very pretty woman still, and I guess Gramps saw that, as
well as her ability to play a mean game of pinochle.

"I'm sure she meant well," I said soothingly. "Who's her
lawyer?"

"Oh, I don't know that she had one. I suppose if she did
it would've been old Bunk Whitley. But I don't think he's
living, so I don't know. I'd love to stay and chat, Dae, but I
have to get around town with these flyers. I'll see you
Wednesday, if not before."

It was nearly noon when I looked at the teapot clock.
Mary Lou left only moments before Kevin got there. Gramps
followed him in the door. "We need to talk," Gramps said
with a serious frown on his face.

"Let me close up and we can go eat lunch." I shut off the
lights and put up the "Closed" sign. "I'm starving. And I
have plenty to tell you both."

Hoping not to run into Shayla or Trudy, I chose to
have lunch at Wild Stallions on the boardwalk. Normally, I
wouldn't care if they were around, but time was running
short on solutions for Miss Mildred. I didn't want to have
to catch them up on everything.

We went into the dark bar and grill. Cody and Reece took our orders right away. We talked about Cody's new son for a few minutes. He was a big boy, eight pounds and four ounces. His name was Zak. Cody planned to name a burger after him.

"So what do you have for us?" I asked Gramps when Cody and Reece were gone.

"I went to see Olivia this morning. We had a nice breakfast at that new pancake house they built in Manteo. Anyway, she knew about OBX Land Trust, LLC. Turns out the owner is Silas' grandson. You won't believe who that is."

"Jerry Richards." Kevin and I said at the same time. Gramps sat back with a scowl after we spoiled his news.

I told him about my encounter with Chuck that morning. "This has to be at the heart of why Miss Elizabeth was killed. But Chief Michaels said Jerry has an alibi for the night she died."

"What else did the chief have to say?" Kevin asked.

"I hope you didn't try to confront him, Dae," Gramps added.

"It kind of slipped out. I really didn't plan to upset him." I explained everything the chief had said to me.

"Richards showed up at the courthouse while my SBI friend was there," Kevin said. "He overheard him asking about a power of attorney document for Miss Mildred. He wanted to know if she'd ever had one filed with the county. Without one stating her intentions, he can take her estate. He's technically next of kin."

"That's funny because I was thinking the same thing this morning," I said. "What did they tell him?"

"They couldn't find one for her. There was a will for Miss Elizabeth. My friend checked on it. It left everything to Miss Mildred, like everyone speculated. There's no help there."

"Maybe Miss Mildred's will is at her house, if she has one." I looked up and thanked Cody as he brought our lunch to the table.

Before Kevin had a chance to tell us anything more, Luke Helms joined us. He slid in the booth beside Kevin with an easygoing nod, wondering if he could buy us lunch. "I've had a strange morning, and I'm hoping you guys can help me out. It's about Mrs. Harcourt and some kind of turtle-saving effort."

"I heard about that," I said. "She put up flyers in my shop. What does she want you to do?"

"She wants me to have Mrs. Mason sign a legal document that leaves everything to the turtle charity." Luke thanked Cody, who'd brought over a Coke for him. "I talked to Mrs. Mason about it after the incompetency ruling. She said she has a power of attorney document, but she said she doesn't know where it is."

"What about her lawyer?" I asked. When Luke raised his ginger-colored eyebrows, I clarified, "The lawyer who drew up the will."

"That would probably be Bunk Whitley." Gramps nodded. "Old Bunk was the only lawyer in Duck for a long time."

"Not him again," Kevin muttered. "Don't tell me he not only vanished mysteriously but took everyone's legal documents with him."

Luke sipped his Coke. "I don't know anything about Bunk Whitley, but there should be a copy of the power of attorney filed at the courthouse."

Gramps shook his head. "That horse don't run. Jerry Richards was already there looking for it. Apparently Bunk did his usual slipshod job and forgot to file it."

"But even if it wasn't filed officially, wouldn't it still

be legal if there's a copy of it at Miss Mildred's house?" I asked.

"It could be." Luke ordered a burger and sat back. "I guess I came to the right place. You know everything that's going on, Dae."

"That's why we made her the mayor." Gramps laughed. "It was either that or the editor of the *Duck Gazette*, but that closed down ten years ago. Not enough local news to fill a newsletter much less a newspaper."

Kevin was quiet even before his sandwich got to the table. I wondered if he didn't want to include Luke in the discussion about what he'd found. I didn't press the issue in case that was true. I ate my sandwich and fries, and listened to Gramps and Luke talk about a small brush fire they'd put out in Southern Shores last week. I could always ask Kevin later what he'd found, if anything.

As the meal was winding down, Gramps nudged me and said to Luke, "You should take Dae up to see Millie. She could find the power of attorney without us ransacking the house. It would save us all some time."

Having grown up with everyone in town asking me to help them find their lost things, I wasn't exactly shy about my abilities. But the look on Luke's face, as Gramps explained what I could do and how I could do it, was strong disbelief.

"You're kidding, right?" Luke looked at all of us with a grin on his face, waiting for the punch line. "Come on, Kevin, you aren't from here, and the FBI doesn't fool around. You don't believe Dae can find things with her mind, do you?"

Kevin polished off his drink and nodded. "She already proved it to me." He told him about the hidden key. "You can't argue with that kind of success."

Luke stared at me for a long moment. "No one can really do something like that," he argued. "Not Dae. Not *anyone*."

"Try something," Gramps said, encouraging him. "Go ahead. It's okay. Dae has found things for most of the people who live here. I'm sure she could find something you've lost."

"How does it work?" Luke smiled and whistled the opening to the *Twilight Zone* theme. "Do I wait for her to go into a trance or something? Does she have to be possessed?"

"*She's* sitting right here and doesn't appreciate being treated like she's invisible," I told him. "There's nothing to it. Give me your hands and think about something important you've lost."

He started to reach his hands toward me, then pulled them back and looked at his watch. "You know, I have to run. Maybe next time we can scrounge up a Ouija board or something." He grinned and threw down some money for lunch. "I'll see you later."

"Well, that was unpleasant," Gramps said when Luke was gone. "I don't understand what his problem is. If she couldn't do it, nothing would happen. If she could, he would've found what he's lost."

"*She's* still here," I repeated. "Why is everyone talking about me like I'm not here?"

"Not me," Kevin chimed in. "I was waiting for Luke to take off before I told you what else I found out today."

I leaned forward a little to whisper, "Don't you trust him?"

He leaned forward too until our faces were close together. "I *never* trust lawyers."

"If you two are done flirting"—Gramps smiled, then cleared his throat—"I'd like to hear what Kevin found out this morning before someone else joins us for lunch."

I ignored the flirting part of his remark and hoped that

Kevin would too. I sipped some water and waited to hear what he didn't want to say in front of Luke.

"There were bloody gloves in Miss Elizabeth's purse. I guess something like gardening gloves. The police and SBI think they go with the garden shovel. They think Miss Mildred was trying to hide them before she had her breakdown. They say she couldn't deal with it. They believe the blood on those gloves belonged to Miss Elizabeth. The chief was right when he told you the case was all but closed."

It wasn't as if I didn't know about the gloves in the purse. I'd seen them before anyone. But the whole idea bothered me. It all fit together so neatly, crushing Miss Mildred with its perfection. One part bothered me more than the rest. I explained my doubts to Gramps and Kevin. "All of that makes sense, I guess, except for the part about the gloves. You know yourself, Gramps, Miss Mildred has hands like sandpaper. She's *never* worn garden gloves."

"Maybe not," Kevin said. "But that's a small detail compared to the whole picture. I'm sure you would've picked her up on the strength of this evidence too, Horace. I know I would've considered myself lucky to get all of this together."

"I agree." Gramps stroked his white beard. "But Dae makes a good point. If you would've told me there was a pair of white church gloves in that purse, I would've gone along with that. But Millie has the roughest hands in the county and proud of it."

"I think what Kevin is saying is that it's not enough to force Chief Michaels or the SBI into looking at this crime from another angle." I glanced at Kevin. "Right?"

"Yeah. The SBI is looking at Wild Johnny's death now. They're done with Miss Elizabeth."

Gramps laughed. "You know, I was the sheriff for a long

time in this county. When it doesn't involve you *personally*, you can think whatever is necessary to get a conviction. Knowing Millie the way I do, I can't believe anyone would think she could kill Lizzie."

"And yet the chief seems to think so," I reminded him.

"He's doing his job, Dae," Gramps argued. "You don't know what that's like."

"Except it sounds like the chief might be doing his job a little *too* well," Kevin said. "He certainly helped put her away."

"I don't think he's involved in setting up Miss Mildred. Other than keeping Silas up-to-date on what's been going on, he's stuck to doing his job, like Gramps said," I replied. "I think the murder is tied to whoever wants those properties. Either Jerry Richards's alibi is bogus, or Chuck Sparks killed Miss Elizabeth. Either one of them could have set up Miss Mildred."

"What about the power of attorney?" Kevin asked. "I know Luke didn't seem crazy about the idea, but he doesn't know what you can do, Dae. Maybe you should go and see Miss Mildred before it's too late. If there is a document, maybe you can sense its location from her."

"I think that's the best idea," Gramps agreed. "Why don't you and Kevin go do that, and I'll watch the shop?"

I knew a done deal when I heard one. I hoped Kevin didn't. He seemed oblivious to it and agreed right away. "It shouldn't be that hard to get in to see her." He took out his cell phone. "Let me see what I can do."

It turned out that Kevin couldn't do anything, but when I called Luke, he agreed to set it up for me. He apologized for leaving so quickly and said he hoped I didn't take offense.

I assured him it was fine and that I hadn't noticed anything unusual about the way he'd left. After I ended the call,

I noticed Kevin and Gramps staring at me. "What? Were you listening in?"

"What do you think?" Gramps smirked. "Is there a little romance in the air between you and Luke?"

"I don't think this is a good time to discuss that," I told him and turned to Kevin. "I'm ready if you are."

"I need a few minutes. In fact, maybe you can help me. I'm looking for the Duck Museum of History. Somebody told me they stored the old records from the *Duck Gazette* there. I'm looking for some information about Bunk Whitley."

"Sure. I know right where that is. We can stop there on the way out of Duck. I've been meaning to see Max Caudle for a while."

I started to give Gramps a key to the shop. He reminded me that he didn't need one and pulled his copy out. "I thought it would be good to have for an emergency."

"Like sneaking in there with your girlfriend?"

"I don't ask you when you sneak out. I don't think it's polite for you to ask me when I sneak in." He laughed and hugged me. "Besides, Mary Lou wanted to take a look around. She thought you might have something in that hodgepodge of stuff that you could donate for the raffle on Wednesday."

My eyes narrowed. "You know the rules."

"I know. I won't let her take any of your special items."

With that in place, I walked out with Kevin into the watery afternoon sunshine. Despite the overcast skies, it was sweltering. I could never understand how it could be so hot when there was a constant breeze blowing across the island. As soon as we stepped out of the air-conditioning, my clothes felt limp on me.

"You and your grandfather have a great relationship,"

Kevin said as he opened the truck door. "It must be fantastic having someone like that in your life."

"I wouldn't know what to do without him," I replied. "He's always been there for me. Even when he was the sheriff, he always found time for me."

Kevin started the truck and headed down Duck Road toward Southern Shores. "You know, Dae, I'm all for a good investigation, but you should be prepared in case that's all this is. Your friend might be guilty, no matter how much you want her to be innocent."

"I know," I said as the first fat raindrop hit the windshield.

The Duck Museum of History was a plain little building that had been donated to the Duck Historical Society a few years back. It was actually an old store that had once sold gas, chips, Pepsis and sunglasses. Max Caudle was the museum director. He'd held that position since I was in school, probably because no one else wanted it.

Outside the blue, three-room building, a large statue of a duck stood beside a statue of a horse. The display also included two rusted cannons legend said had washed up on Duck's shore back in the 1700s. Several cannonballs were stuck in concrete around them.

Inside, the old museum was cool and musty smelling. The light was too dim to really see everything the historical society had managed to piece together down through the years. I was proud of this little place anyway. It represented the heritage of everyone who had been born here. From pirates to wild horses, all of it was part of our past.

"Mayor O'Donnell!" Max greeted us at the door. "It's so good to see you."

Max was a short, stout man with curly brown hair and

ruddy skin. He always looked as though he'd been out in the sun too long, despite the bookish quality the glasses perched on the end of his nose gave him. His face matched his always-present red suspenders. I didn't think I'd ever seen him wear anything except sandals on his feet.

"Please, Max, call me Dae. Otherwise I have to start calling you Mr. Caudle again like when I was in school." I smiled at him, then turned to Kevin. "This is Kevin Brickman. He's new to Duck."

"That's right." Max stepped up to shake Kevin's hand. "The man who bought the old Blue Whale. Nice to meet you. If you find anything old you don't want over there, be sure to send it my way."

Kevin smiled. "I'm looking for Bunk Whitley right now. I was hoping you could help me."

"Haven't run across him yet, eh?" Max laughed at his own joke. "I have the old *Gazette* microfiche in back if you'd like to look through that. It's kind of funny. We have a lock of Blackbeard's hair and the masthead from a clipper that went down off the coast in 1809. But I haven't seen hide nor hair of old Bunk. There's a lot he could answer for if someone found him."

Max took us in the back to what had probably been a storeroom at one time. There was a very small table with the microfiche machine on it. Yellowed copies of the *Gazette* decorated the walls. "Let me get you another chair," he offered. "We don't usually have so many people in here at one time!"

Kevin sat down at the machine, and I took the side chair. Max went to find cold tea and maybe a leftover cookie or two. His wife, Agnes, ran the Beach Bakery and was always generous with samples.

I sat there and watched as the old pages flipped by on the

screen. They were hard to read in some places. I squinted to recognize an old photo of Gramps taken after he'd caught a thief who'd held up stores in several Outer Banks towns.

"Pay dirt," Kevin said after about twenty minutes. "Look at this. I think we found old Bunk."

It was Bunk Whitley. At least the caption under the picture said so. I wouldn't have recognized him from some of the other pictures I'd seen of him. In this photo, he looked to be in his late twenties. Two beautiful young women in bathing suits were standing on either side of him. I squinted at the writing and read out loud, "Bunk Whitley, owner of the Blue Whale Inn, had a difficult choice to make for the crown of Miss Duck. Pictured with him are Miss Elizabeth Butler (left) and Miss Mildred Butler, both of Duck. Miss Elizabeth Butler won the crown of Miss Duck."

Chapter 16

"So Bunk Whitley was the mysterious pageant judge that fateful day in Duck." I told Kevin the old story that had cost such long-lasting pain between the two sisters.

"Well it sounds like Miss Mildred had something to complain about. Between that and Wild Johnny Simpson, it's surprising the sisters spoke at all." He read the rest of the *Gazette* page on the microfiche. "That's all that's here about him."

Kevin kept moving forward with an eye for articles about Bunk. The newspaper was liberally sprinkled with them. Bunk was a member of every group in town. He attended all of the charity and society events in Duck and was apparently known for being a hearty diner. He seemed to be at the openings of every restaurant in the area.

"I think I wouldn't have had a chance if he'd been here to run for mayor."

Kevin agreed. "He was definitely the Duck man about town. Maybe that's why the Blue Whale is in such bad repair now. He never stayed home to keep up with maintenance."

"How are things coming along?" Max came back into the little room and looked around. "You know, it's a small place, and I couldn't help overhearing your conversation about Bunk. He was a larger-than-life type of personality. He dominated the town for a few years. Never married. No one to inherit the old inn, which is why it sat around empty for so long. People said he never got over losing Miss Elizabeth to Wild Johnny Simpson."

"Sounds like that could be a motive for murder." Kevin smiled at me.

"Oh, you don't know the half of it," Max told us. "I've heard when Johnny came back to beg his bride's forgiveness, it was like the Fourth of July around here. Fireworks! Bunk was courting Miss Elizabeth at the time, and suddenly, Johnny shows up. Bunk didn't like it."

"How long ago was that, Max?" I asked him.

"About the same time Bunk went missing. No one ever knew what happened to him. There was a massive manhunt. Dae, your grandfather would know more about it. I don't know if anyone ever saw Johnny again after that either. Miss Elizabeth was still a handsome woman, even in her sixties. You can probably find some pictures there. The *Gazette* loved the drama."

Kevin finally found that timeframe, back in the late 1970s. Max was right. There were plenty of pictures of Miss Elizabeth with Bunk. "I don't see any pictures of Johnny here."

"Wild Johnny didn't like the limelight like Bunk. Some people said he stayed to himself because of things he'd done after he left Duck. I think the *Gazette* photographer liked Bunk better."

I sat down and stared at the old newspapers on the walls. It was hard enough to think through what could've happened to Miss Elizabeth. A thirty-year-old murder was too much of a strain. "You said you knew Bunk, Max. Do you think he could've killed Johnny and then left town to keep anyone from finding out?"

Max shrugged, dislodging the red suspenders on his shoulders. "It doesn't seem like him. There would've been so much drama in a good murder trial. I think he'd have preferred it. But who knows how a man will react until he's faced with those circumstances? One thing's for sure—if Bunk ran away because he killed Wild Johnny, he wasted his time. He could've lived with Miss Elizabeth for the last thirty years. Maybe if he had, she'd still be alive."

The sad tale of Bunk, Miss Elizabeth and Wild Johnny left me feeling blue as we said good-bye to Max and headed toward Elizabeth City in the rain. A heavy fog had moved in over the sound, obscuring the bridge linking the Outer Banks and the mainland. The only way to know the truck was still traveling on the bridge was the sure sound of the tires on the concrete.

Elizabeth City was a long drive from Duck but not as long as the drive to Greenville, where Luke said Miss Mildred would be transferred eventually. The rain and fog weren't as dismal as my thoughts on that matter. I'd begun to feel helpless against the weight of the world crushing down on Miss Mildred.

"There's no way to know if Bunk had anything to do with Johnny's death," Kevin said. "Since no one knows what happened to him, there's not much chance they can link any

DNA evidence they find to him. This is one case there may not be an answer for."

"And I know how much lawmen hate when that happens," I bit back. "Tying up all the loose ends nice and neat, even if they don't really go together, is what it's all about."

I felt him glance at me but didn't look back at him, keeping my eyes on the bridge rail as we went by. "Dae, I'm sorry about Miss Mildred. But evidence is evidence. You can't fault the investigation."

"No. Just the results. I *know* she didn't kill her sister. Gramps and Chief Michaels know it too. They'd rather believe their guts and DNA than their hearts."

He didn't say anything else for a long time. I didn't blame him. I wasn't the best traveling companion. Maybe I should've warned him and he could've stayed in Duck. After all, we weren't really even friends yet. More like acquaintances caught in a bizarre set of circumstances. We might have lived in Duck for years without spending this much time together. Probably not, but it was possible.

When the front tires hit the pavement off the bridge and we slowed to a stop for the red light, the sun began poking through the clouds. Rays of light shimmered down between the raindrops, and I suddenly knew, without exception, that everything was going to be all right. I can't explain it, but I *felt* it. I knew Miss Mildred would somehow be cleared of Miss Elizabeth's terrible murder. We would catch whoever was responsible for what happened to her.

"I'm sorry I snapped at you." I smiled at Kevin before the red light changed.

"That's okay. I know she means a lot to you. Maybe if you can get something about the power of attorney from her, another piece of the puzzle will turn up with it. All we need is a little of that hard evidence you hate so much, except in our favor."

"I guess I wouldn't hate it so much then." I laughed. "I just don't like it when it goes against me."

"I don't think anyone ever does."

By the time we arrived in Elizabeth City, the rain was completely gone. It was hot, the sun steaming the water from the streets. It might still be raining off the coast at home. It wasn't unusual for the weather to vary significantly along the hundred-mile stretch of the Outer Banks.

The small facility where Miss Mildred was being kept was painted a sterile white. A sign, barely visible from the road, led us into a parking lot where the armed attendant took down our names and the license plate number of the truck. "It's a good thing you had GPS," I told Kevin as he looked for a parking place. "I don't know if we could've found this without it."

"People don't like to advertise this kind of place. Not that the people here will be the worst of the worst. I don't think they'd send someone like Miss Mildred to a place like that. But you have to be aware the people here are prisoners like those in Raleigh. Some of them have done terrible things."

It was a sobering thought. I looked at the whitewashed walls and thought about being unable to go outside or make personal decisions for myself. Miss Mildred might not have a lot of time left to live her life. She deserved better than this. I knew it was up to us to provide the evidence she needed.

They checked our IDs again as we started inside the building. I had to leave my purse at the front desk. The smell of antiseptic filled the air. But there were no open hallways here as there were at Sea Oats Senior Care. The few people standing around were uniformed guards with handguns and large batons in their belts. I'd been with Gramps to the county jail in Manteo many times growing up, but I'd never felt the oppression I did here. Maybe it was simply an adult point of view. When I'd gone with Gramps to the county jail, I was a child.

"Mr. Brickman, Ms. O'Donnell." A grim-faced woman in a bad green sweater shook both of our hands, then led us through the security door that buzzed open. A dark maze of hallways leading in various directions lay before us. "I heard the rain has stopped."

I stared at her for a moment, not really believing she was making small talk in this terrible place. "Yes," I finally managed to say. "The sun is shining."

"Well, we needed the rain."

It's amazing how people can find the most mundane things to talk about when they don't know each other. I knew I was supposed to stick out my hand and introduce myself as the mayor of Duck, big smile plastered on my face, but I couldn't. I couldn't ignore or put aside why we were there.

I glanced at Kevin, and he didn't seem able to put it aside either. On impulse, I grabbed his hand as we walked what seemed like forever to find Miss Mildred. He smiled at me and squeezed my hand back. I thought it made us both feel better, and for once, I wasn't wondering why.

"Here she is." The woman in the bad green sweater unlocked the plain white door with a card key and held it open for us. "Mrs. Mason, you have visitors."

I looked at the woman as I walked past her, my hand accidentally covering hers as I caught the door. The contact lasted long enough for me to get a small image from her. "We all call her Miss Mildred. She doesn't believe she's old enough to be called Mrs. Mason, you know. And you left your umbrella at the restaurant where you had lunch. It's not in the car."

Kevin stifled a laugh as the woman choked out questions, wondering how I knew. I shivered as I broke contact and left her thoughts.

The tiny room contained only a hospital-type bed, a metal chair and a small desk. There was a TV hanging from the ceiling and metal mesh covering the only window. It was difficult to make out anything outside through the metal.

"Dae? Is that you?" Miss Mildred rose slowly from the metal chair. "Child, I never thought I'd see you again." She put her thin arms around me and squeezed with all her might. I could hear her crying quietly as I hugged her back. She'd lost so much weight in the short time she'd been gone. There was hardly anything left of her.

"It's me, Miss Mildred," I assured her, tears sliding down my face. "And look, I brought a friend. This is Kevin."

She tossed her white hair, which looked as if it hadn't been brushed that day. "Oh, I *know* him. He was crazy enough to buy that old white elephant we call the Blue Whale. I guess somebody knew what they were doing when they sold *that* property."

Once the woman in the bad green sweater had gotten over me telling her where her lost umbrella was, she went to find two more chairs for me and Kevin. I'd hoped she planned to leave the room and give us some privacy, but she pulled in another chair and sat by the door. It wasn't that I was nervous about what I was going to do with Miss Mildred. I only hoped the woman could handle it.

"Miss Mildred," I began, scooting my chair next to hers and taking her hands. "We want to help you. There are so many things going on."

Her pale blue eyes welled with tears again. "Don't I know it! They think I killed Lizzie. It's crazy of course, but they think *I'm* crazy because I saw her ghost. I can't tell you how many people I know in Duck who have seen ghosts. I never thought they were crazy."

"I know. I feel the same," I reassured her. At this point, I was getting nothing from her. It was like looking into a black hole. "We're trying to prove you didn't kill your sister. Can you think of anyone who might have wanted to hurt her?"

She made a *humphing* sound. "You mean besides *me?* You know there have been plenty of times that I wanted to kill her. But I didn't. It's one thing to get angry and say things, but you don't mean them. I can't believe Lizzie is dead."

She broke down again, crying for a few minutes. Kevin passed me some tissues, which I handed to Miss Mildred. Finally, she calmed down. "Miss Mildred, right now, we're trying to keep them from selling your house so you have someplace to come home to."

"*Them?* Who's trying to sell my house, Dae?"

"I don't know a good way to tell you this, but your brother, Silas, is still alive."

"Silas? I knew that. Who'd have thought he'd come back after all these years? Why didn't he phone or come over? How is he?"

"He's sick. He might not live long." I'd caught a glimpse of something tangible when she mentioned her brother, but it had no form, no focus. "He's at an assisted living center in Kitty Hawk."

"He's the one who wants to sell my house? *Our* house, really, since that's where we grew up. Daddy left it to me when he died with express commands to let Lizzie or Silas live there later if they needed to. We'll bring him home. No reason for him to live in a place like that. I'll tend to him."

I didn't remind her that she was in no position to bring anyone home. I tried to keep her focused on what was happening. "It seems Silas has given his grandson power of attorney to take care of his finances. His grandson is selling your house."

"You mean my house *and* Lizzie's house." Her lips grew thin and mutinous. "I was Lizzie's only heir in her will. That makes double properties for that young hyena to sell. Silas always was a little soft in the head. Does this young devil live in Kitty Hawk too?"

"No. It's Jerry Richards from the TV station. You know him."

"I certainly do. And I have a few things that need to be said to him. Dae, help me out of this chair and fetch my clothes. He can't sell our houses. It's simply not done."

Out of the corner of my eye, I saw the woman with the bad green sweater start to her feet. I didn't want any kind of confrontation to erupt. I knew Miss Mildred liked to have her way. "I'm afraid we can't do that right now." I tried to calm her down. "But there's something we can do to stop the sale."

Miss Mildred looked at the attendant by the door and seemed to rethink her position. "What can we do, Dae? How can I save Daddy's property?"

"Do you have a power of attorney document?"

"Of course. Lizzie and I had ours made at the same time by that ne'er-do-well, Bunk Whitley."

"He never filed anything with the courthouse for either of you. Do you have a copy?"

"That man! He was good to look at, but he was a burden. That's why I didn't marry him after my husband died and

I let him court Lizzie instead. But I kept a copy of everything. I have a copy of Lizzie's will too."

I could feel excitement straining inside me. I glanced at Kevin and smiled. "Where do you keep it?"

She paused and looked at me. "You know, I'm not really sure. It was behind the piano for the longest time. It fell off the top one day, and I couldn't get that nice man from the church to come and help me move it for several weeks. I'm trying to remember where I put it after that. You know, I left both properties to the town in the event Lizzie and I both died. I thought my house might be a nice park, especially since I left five hundred yards on the beach to the Turtle Rescue League to start a sanctuary."

That was news. I didn't expect those properties to be left to Duck. There might be someway we could use that information to stop the sale, *if* we could find the power of attorney. "Think about it, Miss Mildred. We've done this plenty of times before. You think about it and I'll find it."

She smiled at me and took her hand away to pat my cheek. "You've always been such a good girl, Dae. I've been very proud to watch you grow up."

Miss Mildred put her hand back in mine, and we both closed our eyes. I was beginning to get a clear picture of something in the house. It looked like a large jar, the decorative kind, painted in a blue and white Chinese motif. It seemed to be on a shelf, but it was difficult to say which room it was in. I concentrated harder, trying to pinpoint the area.

There was a loud rap at the door, startling everyone in the quiet room. The woman with the bad green sweater jumped up and opened the door. Another attendant, along with Jerry Richards and a man in a dark suit who had to be a lawyer, stood in the doorway.

"I have a legal document that says these people can't talk to my great aunt," Jerry said. "Serve it, Mr. Hudson. I want all of you out of here. Don't try to see her again. It's not good for her, and you aren't family."

How had I never noticed the nasty little wrinkles on Jerry's face? He looked like a large, ugly ferret, already counting the money he'd make from the sale of his great aunts' properties. I knew I wouldn't know the difference between a real legal document that forbade me from seeing Miss Mildred and something Jerry had made up. I looked at Kevin to help me out.

He got to his feet and held his hand out to the lawyer in the doorway. "I'm Kevin Brickman, Ms. O'Donnell's attorney. I'd like to see that document."

He was so *smooth*, so believable. It was as if he'd been planning for this moment all morning. It reminded me of all the old police detective shows I'd ever watched on TV. Apparently, things like this really did happen.

Mr. Hudson shook Kevin's hand with deliberation, then took a document from his briefcase. "I believe you'll find everything in order."

Kevin glanced at the document and nodded to me. I trusted his judgment—he'd certainly seen more warrants and court orders than I ever had. Since becoming mayor, I'd seen and signed a lot of resolutions and proclamations, but they weren't the same thing.

"I'm afraid I'll have to leave, Miss Mildred." I leaned close to her and kissed her cheek whispering, "Don't fret. I'll be back, and I'll get you out of this place. I promise."

I thought she might cry again, but she held on to her dignity. "I know you will, child. I'll wait for you." Then she turned her pointed gaze to Jerry. "So you're the young mischief maker who thinks he can sell my house, my *father's* house, out from under me. You've got a lot to learn, young man. Wait until I tell your grandfather."

Jerry smirked, not at all concerned by her threat. "You take care of yourself, Aunt. I'll take care of everything else."

Kevin and I left the room. Jerry and his lawyer stayed behind. I could hear his explicit instructions to both attendants all the way down the hall. I was never to be let in to see Miss Mildred again. I was a troublemaker who only wanted to make her unhappy.

"Did you see anything?" Kevin whispered, close at my side.

"Yes. I think I can find it. I wish I'd had a few more minutes to clarify which room it's in—Miss Mildred has a lot of bric-a-brac. But I'll have to search until I find it."

"I'll help you. I'm sure we can get all the help you need."

We went back out to the truck and got inside. I grinned at Kevin as he fastened his seat belt. "That was awesome how you stepped in. You almost had *me* believing you were a lawyer. I bet you used to do things like that all the time."

He started the truck. "All the time."

"And you don't miss that?"

"Not at all. This is almost too much excitement for me."

"You're teasing, right? You really wanted to help, didn't you?"

"As much as you want to paint, which by the way, we'll have to get to sooner or later. What do you make of the relationship between Bunk Whitley and the two sisters? It sounds like he was courting them both."

"He was a man about town." I settled back for the trip home. It was hard not to be anxious about finding the power of attorney, but the truck could only go so fast. As Gramps was fond of saying, we'd get there when we got there. "And don't make it sound like it's my fault we haven't painted. *You* haven't painted either."

"But that could change if the rain ever stops. I hope you're prepared for that."

"Do you think Bunk killed Johnny, like Max suggested, then skipped town?"

"It wouldn't surprise me. If so, it turned out to be a good plan. Since it took thirty years for someone to buy the Blue Whale and find Johnny, it seems likely that Bunk, or whoever killed him, will get off without consequences."

"Or someone else will get the blame."

"There may still be a way to pin this on Bunk. If they can't match DNA, they might be able to match fingerprints. It occurs to me that they may be able to get a look at his fingerprints from his military records."

"But would fingerprints be enough to convince a jury he was responsible for Johnny's death? Because it seems to me Bunk's fingerprints would be all over the inn."

He smiled at me as we approached the bridge to the Outer Banks. "You know, you're pretty good at this. I'm surprised you didn't follow in your grandfather's footsteps."

"Me, in law enforcement? Can you imagine me shooting someone?"

"Sometimes people go their whole career and never shoot anyone. Did your grandfather ever shoot anyone?"

"Yes. I remember him talking about it when I was in high school. It was very traumatic for him. But I guess you're right. As far as I know, that's the only time." I looked at his profile as he concentrated on the bridge. "How about you? Ever shoot anyone?"

I saw the change in his face right away. It was a terrible sight. He didn't look at me. His eyes didn't move from the road, but I could feel the regret coming from him. "Too many times." His voice was bleak and hollow. "I knew it was time to leave when it began to keep me up at night. You can't do that job and worry about it."

The clouds and rain had moved away from the sound, making it easier to see where we were going. Hoping to dispel the tension my question had caused, I rambled on without stop, telling funny stories about the bridge and the Outer Banks. By the time we got to the island, that awful feeling was gone. I knew I would never bring up that subject again. Kevin was entitled to the secrets in his past.

I called Gramps when we got to Southern Shores and told him about our plan to search Miss Mildred's house. He agreed to meet us there and bring Mary Lou with him. "Don't tell her what I said about the turtle sanctuary, will you? I don't want to go through that with her yet. If we can't find the will, there's nothing there for the turtles anyway."

"I won't mention it. But she's not obsessed with the turtles, Dae. She's only interested in their welfare," Gramps explained.

"All right. I'll take your word for that, but let's not push it right now, huh?"

He agreed, and Kevin maneuvered through the heavy traffic that always comes out after the rain. Not that there's much room to maneuver. It's a two-lane road, and traffic usually moves slowly, thanks to the many summer tourists who generally don't know where they're going.

"What is it with Mary Lou and those turtles?" Kevin asked as we got behind a pink convertible full of middle-aged women in bathing suits and hats.

"I don't know. I guess everybody needs a hobby. Mary Lou makes quilts in the winter, but once it gets warm, she's all about the turtles. She's been cited a couple of times for running kids off from the turtle area. A turtle sanctuary would be good for her and the community."

We finally reached the turnoff for Miss Mildred's house. I thought about her plan to donate the land to the town. I supposed the town council would probably decide to sell at least part of the land so we could use the cash to finish the park and a few other projects. But the town might be able to use Miss Mildred's house, which would be adjacent to the turtle sanctuary, for something else.

But not yet. I pulled my thoughts back from where they were going. Miss Mildred was coming home. Someday her land might belong to the town, but not yet.

The lazy red roses nodded in the sun beside her drive as we pulled in behind Gramps's golf cart. We were barely out of the truck before Gramps and Mary Lou walked out of the house. I could tell from their faces that something was wrong.

"Someone broke in," Gramps said. "It's a mess in there, Dae. I don't know if we can find anything. I need to call Chief Michaels."

He took out his cell phone, but I stopped him. "Don't call him yet. Let me take a look around and at least try to find the power of attorney papers. Once the police take over, I won't have a chance."

He frowned. "I know you and the chief are having some issues. But he's been my friend all of my life. I don't believe he's done anything wrong, and I think he'd help you if he knew what was going on."

"*Please.* Just a few minutes. Then you can call him. You know if anybody can find this document, it's me."

He agreed, and the three of us went into the house. Mary

Lou had left us to it, going down to the beachfront to scope out the best place for a turtle sanctuary sign.

Gramps was right. The house was completely torn apart. Someone had been here looking for something, probably the same thing we were looking for. "I'll bet Jerry Richards heard what we were saying and called ahead." I carefully picked my way through ripped upholstery and shattered china.

"What a mess," Kevin said. "This is definitely a search, not a random break-in. Whoever came through here destroyed things they could have pawned or sold. No one would do that unless they had something specific in mind."

"I hope we can find the power of attorney in all this," Gramps said. "What kind of container did you say you saw it in, Dae?"

I lifted an empty, broken blue and white Chinese vase from the floor. It had been on a shelf near the piano. As soon as I'd spotted it, I knew it was where Miss Mildred had stored the documents she'd retrieved from behind the piano. "It was here. I think Jerry beat us to it."

Chapter 17

"We're down for the count," Gramps said. "I'll call Ronnie now. He should know about this."

A weird idea popped into my head. "What if we act like we found the power of attorney?"

"What would that accomplish?" Kevin asked.

"I don't know," I admitted. "Maybe if Jerry thought we could stop the auction, he'd make some move that would incriminate him. That could work, right, Gramps?"

"Maybe," Gramps said. "I suppose it could buy you some time. But you'll have to be careful, Dae, or the whole thing will backfire on you."

"What kind of backfire?" Since I assumed I'd be taking all of the risk, I thought I should know.

"Lawsuits. Maybe fraud charges," Kevin counted out for me. "If you could keep from putting anything in writing and be *really* careful how you word it, you might be able to get away with it."

"Right now I only need to get away with something for a couple of days," I reminded him. "I guess either they take the bait or not."

"You could be in danger," Gramps pointed out. "If Jerry was willing to hire someone to kill Lizzie, or whatever happened, he won't think twice about getting rid of a small-town mayor."

I hadn't thought of that. It was a valid point. Who knew what Jerry was capable of if he were desperate enough? I'd be taking on the risk that he might send someone after me. I pushed aside my reservations. "Okay. Let's do it. Where do you think we should start?"

Gramps laughed. "Probably with Mary Lou. Besides loving turtles, she has an uncommon love for gossip. She makes a good lemon meringue pie too. And she likes to cuddle."

"That's about all I need to know on that subject." I stopped him. "Let's get going. Before Wednesday, we could have this spread all over the Outer Banks."

And it was easy. By seven p.m. Monday night, I had heard a short piece on the radio about finding new evidence in the murder case of Mrs. Elizabeth Simpson. I saw pictures of me flash twice on the TV at eight. The reference was vague, but the idea was that I had new information that might stop the auction of the properties and possibly point out who killed Miss Elizabeth.

There were five of us at my house for supper on Monday night when we heard the updated news story. Tim was kind of the odd man out since Kevin and I were there with Gramps and Mary Lou. Gramps had cautioned me against saying anything to anyone else. He didn't even tell Mary Lou the truth, and I followed his lead.

"Wow!" Tim looked at me. "So what's this new information in the murder case? Dish it out, girl."

"You've been hanging around with Shayla for too long." I laughed at his words. "But there's nothing I can really say about what I know. The DA told me to keep my mouth shut."

Tim was impressed but disappointed. "I suppose *Kevin* knows all about it."

"Not exactly. He knows as much as you do." I lied, but it was for the sake of expediency. If Tim knew Kevin knew, he'd pout and complain, maybe even tell other people, which would mess up our plan.

The doorbell rang, and since Gramps was dishing out blueberry cobbler, I went to answer it. Chuck Sparks stood on the stairs, glaring at me. "What kind of new information do you have, Mayor? I think I deserve to know."

I sighed. Another person who felt entitled. But it was a good thing. If Chuck knew about it, then Jerry knew about it. It was what I'd wanted, but it was eight P.M. now and I was beginning to worry. There might be no peace until this blew over. "Would you like to come in, Chuck?"

He nodded and stalked inside. "If there's something else going on, you can trust me to keep a secret."

"Really? Why would I trust you with information that could keep you from selling those properties?"

His eyes narrowed. "That's not fair. This is my first big sale. We've gone through a lot to plan for this. Do you know what a case of champagne costs?"

I'd had about enough of his whining. "Does it matter to

you at all that the woman they have in custody for killing her sister isn't guilty? Or that this house has been in her family for several generations and she doesn't want to lose it?"

He looked abashed for a second or two. Then his real-estate-agent killer-shark instincts kicked in again. "It's not for us to decide who's guilty and who's not. The fact of the matter is that the property belongs to Jerry's grandfather now and Jerry has his power of attorney to do what's best with all of the family property."

I stepped closer to him. We were about the same height. "Did it ever occur to *you* that someone else might have a legal document that trumps Jerry's power of attorney? Silas Butler isn't the only one who wanted someone to take care of his property."

"There's no power of attorney or any other legal document listed at the Dare County Courthouse for *either* of the sisters." He sniffed in a righteous way. "Jerry told me so."

"I'm sorry, Chuck." I managed a small smile. "Jerry's wrong. He's about to find that out. Maybe you should break the bad news to him before I give it to the media."

He stared at me as though trying to decide if I were telling the truth. "I don't want to tell you what to do, Mayor, but I'd be careful if I were you. Jerry isn't a good man to cross."

"Is that a threat?" Kevin asked from the doorway.

Chuck backed down right away. He thrust his hands into his pockets. "I'm just saying."

"Thanks for the warning." I opened the front door. "Good night, Chuck."

"It won't get any easier," Kevin warned when Chuck was gone. "At least not for the next couple days. You should probably plan to be with someone all the time."

Tim came up behind him, a wide grin plastered on his face. "I could spend the night, if that would help."

Chuck was the last disturbance at the house before everyone, including Tim, went home. Once the coffee and the blueberry cobbler were gone, the conversation had more lulls than talk. It had been another long day, and Tuesday didn't promise to be any better.

I stayed up late watching a romantic spy film on TV, thinking they might make a movie out of my part in this whole affair with Miss Mildred. Tuesday morning dawned warm and clear with no portent of the day's activities to come.

I got up, showered, and dressed in black shorts and a black tank top. I'd decided to avoid bright colors for a while, reasoning that they might make me an easier target.

Gramps had left me a note on the table saying that he'd gone to help Mary Lou get ready for Turtle Rescue Day. He reminded me to be careful and said he'd see me later.

I was too nervous to eat. I crammed a Pop-Tart into my purse and started out the door. I paused a moment, hand on the doorknob, wondering what was on the other side. I don't usually get feelings of dread over my decisions, but I had a moment of deep anxiety about what I'd causally offered to do. Making myself a target for killers had *seemed* like a good idea at the time. Now, I wasn't so sure.

But then I took hold of myself and stuck a small can of Gramps's pepper spray next to the Pop-Tart package in my purse. He kept a case of the stuff in the garage. I had never used it before, although he'd taught me how when I was a teenager and insisted I carry it on dates.

Feeling better, I opened the front door and almost walked into Kevin. His fist was outstretched to knock on the door.

"Good morning!" I was surprised and pleased to see him there. "Gramps is gone for the day." It was the first thing that entered my mind. After I'd said it, I regretted it. I probably sounded kind of lame to him.

"Good morning. I'm not here to see your grandfather. I'm here to collect my painting assistant."

"I can give you a couple of hours this evening after I close Missing Pieces," I offered. "I have to lead tai chi at the park this morning before I open. It's a mayor thing."

"That's okay. Later is good. I'll walk over to the park with you."

I locked the door behind me, realizing with a smile why he was really here. "You're my bodyguard, right? You said someone should be with me."

He laughed as we walked down the drive to Duck Road. "I didn't mean to cause that problem with Tim last night. Did you have trouble getting him to go home?"

"Not at all," I assured him. "Tim offers to spend the night all the time. It goes along with proposing. He and Shayla must've broken up again."

"Short relationship."

"Yeah. Anyway, I appreciate you worrying about me. But do you really think anyone will try to take me out right here on Duck Road?"

"Miss Elizabeth was right in the heart of Duck when they took her out."

I thought about that as we walked in the early morning sunshine. A few cars passed us, but traffic was still light. "That's kind of ominous, don't you think?"

"It's the truth," he said. "You shouldn't take this lightly."

"All right. I guess I appreciate your help, then."

He nodded, and we continued down the road. A few people passed and blew their horns, waving as they went by. Friends, or friends of friends, all citizens of Duck. I'd never felt uneasy here until Miss Elizabeth's murder. It struck me that Duck was changing with the increase in tourists and the march of time. The town had changed many times before. Why had I thought it would always remain the way I wanted it to be?

Much to my surprise, the park was packed when we arrived. Normally, only ten or fifteen people come out to do tai chi. I'm not the instructor, Andy Martin is, but I show up a couple times a month to boost morale. A few town council members do the same thing. It's like making an appearance at the VFW dance or the community auction.

But this was *much* more. There were at least three TV station vans and twenty extra cars. Our small parking lot was almost full. "I think there might be some extra people doing tai chi this morning."

"Do they usually televise Duck residents doing tai chi?" Kevin asked.

"Not usually." I glanced at him. "I guess this is where the fat hits the fire, as Gramps always says."

"Just remember to be vague about what you know. Let them word it."

"I'm the mayor. They taught us that in mayor school."

"You went to school to be a mayor?" Kevin raised his eyebrows in surprise.

"Sure." I fastened on my big smile and pointed to my face. "Always smile. They taught me that too. Here goes."

Jerry Richards led the pack of reporters coming my way. I felt like I was in one of those battles you see on TV where the good guys are hopelessly outnumbered. There we were, rushing at each other across the park. Their weapons were microphones and cameras. Mine seemed to be my big mayoral smile and, hopefully, sparkling wit.

We confronted each other, the reporters surrounding me as we met. I was amazed that Jerry had the nerve to confront me so openly. He had to be very sure that I wouldn't out him on the sale of the properties. I had to bite my tongue not to say what I wanted.

"Mayor O'Donnell," he addressed me first, "what's the big secret regarding the death of Elizabeth Simpson?"

"I'm not at liberty to say. I'll have a statement ready for you when I am." I tried glaring at him, hoping he'd back off. No such luck.

"Isn't it true that you've been working with the police to try and clear Mildred Mason of the charges against her?"

It had to be a *slow* news day. There were reporters here from Virginia Beach and Raleigh. Surely they had a news story more interesting than me to report on. I was glad Kevin had been enclosed in the circle of reporters too. I wasn't nervous exactly, although I wasn't used to this much attention. I could see the people standing in the park waiting to do tai chi. Andy Martin had a disapproving frown on his face. Apparently he didn't like reporters interrupting his class.

"I can't comment on that at this time." I smiled and waved to Andy to let him know I was on my way.

Suddenly Jerry lunged closer to me. I jumped back in reflex, not liking the feral gleam in his eyes. "Maybe you'd like to tell me what kind of mumbo jumbo you were doing with my great aunt yesterday," he muttered so the other reporters couldn't hear what he was saying.

I didn't plan to answer that. I wanted to set him back by accusing him of trying to steal Miss Mildred's house. But before I could form the words, Jerry was pushed up and away from me. In an instant, Kevin had him down on the ground, holding Jerry's arms behind his back while the cameraman filmed the whole thing. It was like a scene out of TV movie in which the FBI agent finally apprehends the bad guy.

I tried nonverbally to remind him that he wasn't an FBI agent anymore and that Jerry wasn't a perp, but that wasn't working so I yelled, *"Kevin!"*

"I hope you're getting this," Jerry yelled to his cameraman. "I'm going to sue for assault. You can't manhandle the press."

"I'm the mayor's bodyguard," Kevin growled. "I can do whatever is necessary to assure her safety. You look like a threat to me."

I could see this wasn't going to end well. Kevin was trying to help but possibly overdoing it, although I'm not sure why Jerry invaded my personal space. That had never happened before. I took a step toward them with the overeager eyes of the rest of the press following me. "Kevin, let him go. Jerry, don't threaten me. Not unless you want everyone here to know about you selling Miss Mildred's house out from under her. It makes you a good murder suspect, don't you think?"

Kevin let him go with a reluctance I could feel. Jerry straightened his blue suit and picked up his microphone, though he held it at his side. "I have an alibi for the Simpson murder," he hissed.

"So who'd you hire to do it?" Kevin demanded in a low whisper.

That made Jerry back off. "I don't know what you're talking about."

"Of course not," I said sarcastically. "But I'm wondering

who you had ransack Miss Mildred's house. Because I think you're responsible for *that* too."

"You're crazy. But you won't stop me. Everything I'm doing is totally legal. If you don't think so, ask the sheriff or the clerk of court. They can tell you." He signaled to his cameraman, and the two of them stalked away, leaving the rest of the press confused and wondering what had happened. Mostly wondering what they'd missed.

"What's up with you and Jerry?" Tom Murray from the Virginia Beach newspaper asked. "Is that guy *really* your bodyguard? Has someone threatened you, Mayor O'Donnell?"

"I'm sorry. I have nothing else to say at this time. I'll have our town clerk get in touch with each of you when I release my statement. Thank you for visiting Duck today. I hope you'll stay and take in the sights."

Kevin and I hustled out of the crowd and headed across the park where Andy was already starting his tai chi class. "Thanks, I think," I said to Kevin as we walked across the dew-covered grass.

"I thought he was getting too close." He shrugged. "We don't know what that guy is capable of yet. Sorry if I scared you."

"I think you scared him a lot more. I should take you along to all my press functions. Not that most of them are that dramatic. But you could liven them up."

"Better to act when you're not sure."

"I agree." I put my hand on his arm, enjoying the little tingle that accompanied the contact. "Thank you for protecting me."

"My pleasure."

I spent the next twenty minutes with Andy's tai chi class. Except that once I got there, they didn't want to do tai chi anymore. They wanted to ask me questions about what had happened with the press. Then they wanted to ask me questions about Miss Mildred. By the time I was done answering questions, Tai Chi Time on the Green was over.

"Sorry." I smiled at Andy. "If I'd known this would happen, I would've called and canceled."

"That's okay." He stood close to me, staring at Kevin, who was a few yards away, waiting and watching. "Is that guy *really* your bodyguard? Did the town pay him to be here?"

I reassured him that *no one* had paid for Kevin to be here. I knew there would still be questions about it at the next town council meeting. That's the way it goes when you're a public figure who could be spending the town's tax money.

With all the excitement behind us (I hoped), Kevin and I walked back to the Coffee House where word of the encounter had already made the Duck grapevine. People stood back when they saw Kevin, even moving out of line to let us order first. Seriously, I could get used to *that* kind of respect!

"Don't you run the Blue Whale?" Mr. Finklestein, one of our New Jersey immigrants, asked Kevin while Phil made our coffee.

"I do." Kevin shook his hand. "Or I will, when I finally get it open."

"Good deal! You do what needs to be done, young man! That's the way to live!"

Our presence silenced the chatter that usually drowned out the sound of the espresso machine. Everyone seemed to be watching us to see what would happen next. I decided getting first place in the coffee line wasn't all it was cracked up to be. I could almost hear the sighs of relief when we walked out the door.

"Where to now?" Kevin asked, sipping his triple-shot latte.

"I'm going to open Missing Pieces, as usual. I think I should be safe there. You must need to go back to the Blue Whale."

"Actually, there's not much I can do there anyway. I'll hang out at your shop for a while."

I didn't want to hurt his feelings or sound ungrateful, but I also didn't want him glowering at my customers. "No, really, I'll be fine. Maybe we could meet later for dinner or something."

I guess he understood because he agreed to meet me for lunch. That was some reprieve anyway. He cautioned me about wandering around the boardwalk alone, and we parted ways close to town hall.

I checked in with Nancy, who was frantically trying to find volunteers to help set up Turtle Rescue Day. "Mary Lou called in here a while ago. Some of her volunteers are out sick, but they have a lot to do to get ready for tomorrow. I hate to ask, Dae, but could you go over there? They need people to take supplies out to the beach. You know most of those turtle rescue people don't drive anymore and don't walk so good either."

"Sure. I'll put a sign up at the shop letting everyone know I'll be opening late. I'll go through my cell phone directory and see if I can round up some more volunteers too."

"Thanks, sweetie. I appreciate your help." She turned back to start typing again. "No messages yet. Check back later."

I took out my cell phone and called as many potential volunteers as I could think of while I walked to Missing Pieces and put out my "Back at One" sign. Some of them said they'd go down to the beach and help out. Some were working and couldn't leave. I talked to Cailey Fargo at the fire department.

She promised to send everyone available over to the turtle rescue site. That's one thing I love about Duck—we all pull together.

I was on my way home to pull out Gramps's old Jeep when Tim almost ran into me. He swerved his shiny police car in my general direction, pulled up short in front of me, flashing his blue lights. "What do you think you're doing out here alone?"

I shaded my eyes from the sun with my hand so I could look up at him. "I think I'm on my way back to my house. The turtle rescue people need vehicles to transport stuff."

"I understood that *someone* was supposed to stay with you at all times." He glanced around, sniffed and hitched up his belt. "Where's Brickman?"

"At the Blue Whale painting, I hope. The way we've had rain lately, he better get some painting done before another storm hits. Why?"

"I guess I'll be going with you, then. We'll take my car. Your grandfather's old Jeep doesn't run half the time anyway. It's because you never use it. Cars aren't meant to sit in garages for months without being started."

Great. Another guardian. "I'm sure it'll be fine, Tim. I'm not going that far. Don't you have a patrol or something? I'm sure the town council doesn't want to pay you to chauffer me around."

"As it happens, I'm going off duty for a short while. Besides, I think it would be considered a town courtesy to give the mayor a ride to an emergency."

There was no way to talk him out of it. I got in the car without further fuss. If I continued to argue with him, the morning would be gone and I wouldn't be any closer to the turtle rescue area.

I waved to Shayla, who was riding her bike toward the

Duck Shoppes as we went by. She waved back, then stared for a minute. Later, she'd want to know what was going on.

The road down to the area where Turtle Rescue Day would be held was made of hard-packed sand. Most of the time, vehicles weren't allowed to drive down here. Signs had already been posted to inform visitors they would have to park along Duck Road tomorrow. But today, to expedite the trip back and forth to fetch supplies, Carter Hatley was waving people in and out of the narrow road that went straight into the Atlantic.

"You better get down there, Mayor," he leaned in the car window to say. "Mary Lou is having a cow. She needs somebody to get all of this organized."

I smiled, and we drove down to the beach. Obviously, the problem wasn't lack of help. There were at least a hundred people walking around not doing much of anything. Mary Lou was running back and forth across the beach trying to get things moving. A few men were carrying banners and signs, but they didn't seem to know where to put them.

"Oh thank heaven you're here, Dae!" Mary Lou actually half collapsed against me, her arms dramatically stretched out. "I don't know what to do. Everything is such a mess. We won't be ready tomorrow, and we'll lose all of our donations. You know how we depend on that for the rest of the year. The baby turtles will be abandoned."

Even for Mary Lou it was heavy drama. I thought she might cry, but she pulled herself together and looked me in the eye. "Now that you're here, we can get some things done. You take that side, and I'll take this side. Here's a clipboard. It should be self-explanatory."

She marched off with more confidence than I was feeling. My side consisted of a large group of men and women in bathing suits. Some were holding signs, and others were holding shovels. Buckets, gloves and other paraphernalia littered the flat sand. It was low tide, not a deadly sand castle in sight.

I looked at the clipboard and saw that my side was supposed to be putting up barricades that would close off the beach and also protect the turtle nesting area. It seemed simple enough. "Okay. I think all of those big orange cones are supposed to go across there." I pointed to the far left side. "Half of you start on that. The rest of you, grab some shovels and we'll get those posts in."

I picked up one of the lightweight, stainless steel shovels as I walked by the stack. There were piles of blue plastic gloves, always donated by the hospital. Tim stayed by the police car, choosing to watch instead of participate. Mary Lou was headed off in the opposite direction with her small army following as fast as they could.

"Excuse me." A burly man in a Myrtle Beach T-shirt stopped me. "I have a load of collapsible picnic tables with umbrellas that are supposed to be delivered here. I can't get them down the road with all the other vehicles in the way."

"All right." I waved to Tim. Apparently, he was going to come in handy anyway. "This man will help you take care of that. Thanks."

"Hey! I'm supposed to get a check when I drop these off. Have you got the check?"

I admitted I didn't have the check and asked him to wait while I ran to get Mary Lou. He informed me quite clearly that he wasn't going anywhere without his check. I didn't bother replying, hoping Mary Lou had this in hand.

But when I reached her, she fell apart again. I was surprised at her emotional state. True, she was near fanatic about protecting the turtles, but aside from that, she was usually calm and capable. I guessed her agitation was due to the fact that this event was so important.

"I don't have my wallet." She covered her face with her sandy hands. "How could I be so *stupid*? Now he won't deliver the tables."

"Never mind, we'll work it out. Where's your wallet?"

"I think I left it at home. Would you mind getting it, Dae? It's in the kitchen, I think. The key to the house is under the mat if the door is locked."

"Not a problem. Tim can drive me there and back right away. I'll have the driver wait. It'll be fine." I started to walk away, and she called me back.

"There are some baskets on the porch. Could you bring those back with you too? They're for the relay race tomorrow. Everyone has to crawl like a turtle. That should be funny, huh?"

Chapter 18

Mary Lou's back door was unlocked. I didn't say anything. I didn't have to. Tim shook his head when he saw me push it open. "You know, the chief and I tell people to lock their doors. We walk around town and find doors open like this all the time. How do people expect us to protect them when they don't protect themselves?"

"I suppose most people aren't worried about it. We only have one or two break-ins a month. I'd probably forget to lock the door all the time at home. Gramps remembers it religiously."

"That's what comes from living in a small town." He shrugged as we walked into the house. "People expect crime to be low. Maybe Miss Elizabeth's death will wake a few people up around here."

"I wouldn't count on it." I saw the baskets on the side of the porch. They were heaped up on top of each other near the inside door. "Could you get those while I go in and get Mary Lou's checkbook?"

"Sure. I'm going to talk to her about this, Dae. We should really have a fine of some sort for leaving your house open. It's an invitation to crime."

"I'll let you be the one to go on record with that at the next town council meeting. You don't run for public office. I bet that whoever goes along with that idea won't be reelected."

I knew I wouldn't vote for it. And not because people wouldn't like another fine. It was more because *I* wouldn't like it. We have plenty of fines already.

The door that led into the kitchen was open too. Mary Lou had a nice modest-size clapboard house. The outside was a weathered slate color. The inside, from what I could see, was mostly yellow. In the kitchen, a small wood table with two chairs was nestled between a dish cabinet and a stove. A toaster oven sat in the middle of the stove, mute testimony to the stove's disuse. There were plenty of pictures of her only son, Derek, and his two children. Derek lived in California. As far as I knew, he hadn't been back to visit in many years.

The house looked a little sad and lonely, not neat and orderly like Miss Mildred's house. There were boxes, crates and turtle rescue signs everywhere. Every other free space was taken up with sewing projects. Heaps of material waiting to be cut into quilt squares dominated her living room.

I looked quickly through the kitchen and living room but didn't see any sign of her purse. I glanced out the door and saw Tim still moving baskets. How hard could it be to find a purse? I went back over the same territory with more determination. Still nothing.

I made my way into Mary Lou's bedroom, wishing I

didn't have to. It felt a lot like spying on her, but I guessed if she wasn't worried about it, I wouldn't be either.

The bedroom was a mess, with clothes strewn everywhere. I pushed a few shirts off of her beautiful antique vanity but still no sign of the purse. I turned on the overhead light and glanced in the bathroom. Nothing in there either.

I was about to call Carter Hatley's cell phone (I knew Mary Lou didn't have a cell phone) when I glimpsed what looked like a purse next to an open ironing board near the bed. I shifted some of the clothes away from it and success! I carefully searched for her checkbook in the surprisingly neat confines of her purse and fished it out with all the excitement of catching a two-hundred-pound tuna.

I didn't want to be in her house without her for any longer than was necessary. As I turned to run back out the door, my gaze fell on a black dress. Suddenly, I felt the slow-motion sensation I usually felt when I found something important.

The dress was draped across the ironing board, four or five other dresses with it. Immediately the thought hit me: *She has a dress just like Miss Elizabeth's*. I put the checkbook on the bed and picked up the dress.

I was right. The same classic style: black dress with pink hearts, just like the one Miss Elizabeth had been wearing when I found her. It appeared to be made out of the same cotton material and even had the same fluted neckline and puffed sleeves.

For a few minutes, I stood there looking at it. A thousand thoughts raced through my brain, but I rejected all of them. This had to be some kind of terrible coincidence. It had nothing to do with what happened to Miss Elizabeth. A lot of local women might have a dress like this one if one of the local boutiques had sold it a few years back. It didn't mean *anything*.

As I was telling myself this, the stack of clothes I'd shoved out of the way fell to the floor. Despite the heat outside and decided lack of air-conditioning inside, I felt a chill rush over me. It raised goose bumps on my arms and sent a prickle across the back of my neck.

Under the pile of clothes was a gray wig, too similar to the way Miss Elizabeth wore her hair for there to be any mistake about it. Despite my reluctance to touch it, I picked it up and studied it.

I don't know what possessed me, but I put it on loosely over my hair and held the black dress up against me. I looked at myself in the full-length mirror that hung on the closet door and almost jumped out of my skin.

"Holy Mary Mother of God!" Tim backed out of the room as quickly as he'd come in.

I couldn't find my voice as I stared at myself in the mirror. I didn't move, didn't turn away from the ghastly reflection.

"What the hell is going on, Dae?" He strode back in with a determined look on his face. "Where did you get that? Is that someone's idea of a sick joke? I've heard of people doing things like this for Halloween, but it isn't *funny*."

I moved, finally feeling free of the spell that had come over me. I took off the wig and held the dress back to look at it. "It was here. There has to be some *reasonable* explanation for it."

"What do you mean? It doesn't *have* to make any sense. Put it down and let's get out of here. Did you find the checkbook?"

I nodded. "Why would Mary Lou have this getup?"

"Who cares? Let's get out of here, huh? You're starting to creep me out."

"I don't think we were supposed to see this, Tim."

"Don't even say it, Dae. It's only a dress. There are probably hundreds of them, *thousands* of them. And lots of older women wear wigs, right? They cover hair loss and stuff with them."

"Mary Lou dyes her hair Gentle Sable Brown. I was at Curves and Curls when she was having it done. *Nobody* wears a gray wig to cover that."

"I don't care." He snatched the wig from me and threw it on the bed. "We don't have any business being in here, looking at her private things. Put the dress down and let's get back to the beach. They're going to wonder what's taking us so long."

"Tim, think about this for a moment," I urged. "Someone brought Miss Elizabeth's purse to Miss Mildred. That person made her think it was her dead sister. We've kind of *assumed* she saw Miss Elizabeth's ghost and that maybe someone from OBX Land Trust made her think that. But what if it *wasn't* them? What if it was Mary Lou?"

"Now *you* stop and think! Why would Mary Lou do such a thing? Are you really saying you think she had something to do with Miss Elizabeth's death? That's crazy talk. Your blood sugar must be low or high, whichever it is that makes people do crazy things. Mary Lou *didn't* hurt Miss Elizabeth. She sure didn't dress up like a ghost to take her purse back to Miss Mildred. Get a grip, Dae, and let's get out of here."

I bit my lip, but I couldn't leave. "We can't ignore this. We have to tell someone."

"I'm a sworn officer of the law." His face contorted with anger. "I can't go in people's houses, pick up their things and accuse them of murder. It wouldn't stand up in court, for one thing, and I'd lose my job for another. We have to go."

"You can't do it, but *I* can." I picked up the wig again. "We have to know what happened. Can't you see that? We have to confront her with it."

"Then what? She falls all over herself to tell us the truth? If what you're suggesting is true, Dae, Mary Lou went out of her way to throw the blame on someone else. I'm not saying she's hard, but someone like that has it thought out. You know what I mean? We'll have to talk to the chief, get a search warrant and then confront her at the station. That's the way it's gotta be done. Nice and legal."

"I'm taking it with me." I heaped some clothes over the spot where I'd found the dress. "If we leave it here and she destroys it, we'll never know what happened. There has to be another way."

I thought Tim might try to stop me, but he stepped aside. "I'm not saying Mary Lou had anything to do with this, but you do what you think is right. You *always* do. Hell, I think she might be *related* to me. That's a whole nightmare if she is convicted of a crime. The chief might never trust me again. They say it's genetic."

"We can't stand here discussing it." I found an empty shopping bag and stuffed the dress and wig into it. "I'll think of something. You can pretend you didn't know anything about it. I don't think the chief will think any less of you if you're related to Mary Lou. Besides, there might be some other explanation for why it's here."

"You mean besides Mary Lou killing Miss Elizabeth, then trying to blame it on Miss Mildred?" He shuddered. "We need to get out of here *now*. I don't think that breakfast burrito is sitting right with me."

I swept up the checkbook as I walked out of the house, determined not to doubt myself. Taking the dress and the wig was the right thing to do, but I needed to figure out what my next step should be. Mary Lou was as much a part of my life as the two sisters. She was even dating Gramps. But something was wrong. I didn't believe I'd found the dress and wig for nothing. I had to think of a way to get Mary Lou to tell me why she had them. I could only hope Tim was right and there was a good explanation besides the one that had crept into my brain.

We got back in the police car, and Tim cautioned me about what I could say. "If you say *anything* about finding that dress and wig, no one will be able to use it in a court of law."

"I don't plan on saying anything. What would be the point?"

He nodded. "Exactly. It's obviously a mistake. Maybe the dress and wig don't go together. Maybe she had the same dress as Miss Elizabeth. And she had an old person wig from before. Maybe Halloween or something."

I looked at him as he started the engine. "You don't really believe that, do you?"

"I don't know what to believe. And neither do you. You should put that dress back in Mary Lou's house, and we should forget we saw it."

"And let Miss Mildred take the blame for killing her sister?"

"Let it go, Dae." That was his last word on the subject before he raced out of the drive. We didn't speak again until we reached the turtle rescue area and Carter waved us through.

I saw Gramps getting out of his golf cart, Kevin in tow. I took the shopping bag that held the dress and wig and stashed it under the seat in the golf cart. I glanced around to see if Tim was watching. He was talking to Chief Michaels.

They both turned and stared at me, but by that time, the bag was out of sight.

"Are you in trouble?" Gramps asked with a nod toward the two police officers.

"I can't explain right now," I answered quickly when I saw them walking toward us. "I have to take this checkbook to Mary Lou."

"I can take care of that if you need to do something else," he volunteered.

I looked at his dear face and kissed his cheek. "I'm sorry if I hurt you. I mean, if I *ever* hurt you. I would never do it without really believing I didn't have any choice."

He frowned and glanced over my shoulder toward Chief Michaels. "Dae, you're worrying me. Is there something I should know?"

"Not now. Not here. I'll tell you later." I handed him the checkbook, relieved that I wouldn't have to face Mary Lou. I wasn't sure my face wouldn't give me away. I didn't want her to get in trouble, but I wouldn't let Miss Mildred spend the rest of her life in an institution because of something someone else did.

I didn't want it to be Mary Lou. It would've been a lot more convenient for Chuck Sparks or Jerry Richards to be the one who'd killed Miss Elizabeth. They were greedy, grasping people who didn't care who they hurt in their quest for money. I would've gladly handed over evidence to Chief Michaels that proved they were the ones responsible.

"Mayor." Chief Michaels addressed me with a general nod in my direction.

"Chief. I see they volunteered you too." I could see Kevin kind of nonchalantly standing in earshot of us.

"Tim tells me you have something to say."

I glanced at Tim, who was standing behind the chief. "No. Not really."

"Is something wrong? Tim says you went to Mary Lou's house and picked up some items."

I wished my eyes were laser beams that could burn a hole in Tim's forehead. The man couldn't keep his mouth shut, especially around the chief. He didn't want *me* to say anything, but he thought it was okay for *him* to say something. I didn't know what he expected me to do.

"She sent me there to pick up her checkbook. Tim brought some baskets out here too." I wasn't going to say anything about the dress and wig. At least not until I could figure out what to do with them. I really felt that sharing this information with the chief wasn't the way to go.

It was the chief's turn to glare at Tim. "Would one of you mind telling me what in blazes is going on? Tim says you found something over at Mary Lou's house, but he won't tell me what it is. You're telling me it's a checkbook and some baskets. Is that about right?"

I shoved my hands in my pockets. "That's about right."

The chief exhaled loudly and his nostrils flared. "I don't understand you young people. I swear I don't."

"I'm sorry. I'm not trying to be difficult." I gave him my best mayoral smile and walked away. It was hard since I was nervous about the bag under the seat in the golf cart. I was afraid I might look at it as I walked by. Or was I trying too hard *not* to look at it?

Neither one of them followed me or rummaged around in the golf cart, so I thought I was safe. Confused and uncertain, but safe. I glanced over my shoulder briefly to see Chief Michaels yelling at Tim, and even making strangling motions with his hands.

"So what did you *really* find?"

I jumped when I heard Kevin's voice from behind me. I'd forgotten about him in my eagerness to get away. "You startled me."

"Sorry. What did you find in Mary Lou's house?"

I didn't tell the chief. I didn't plan to tell Kevin. I wasn't sure who to trust with the information. "If you were eavesdropping carefully, you know I got the checkbook and Tim got the baskets. That's all. End of story."

"I saw you give your grandfather the checkbook. And I saw Tim take the baskets to one of the volunteers. That leaves whatever you put in the golf cart. I think it was too big to be a check and too small to be a basket. Is there some reason you don't want to tell me?"

"Yes." I started walking down the beach. All around us, volunteers were feverishly trying to get things set up for the next day. I thought about Chuck Sparks and Jerry Richards trying to get ready for the auction tomorrow. Was what I found at Mary Lou's house enough to prevent the auction from happening?

"All right." He stayed beside me as I walked, the wild Atlantic breeze tousling his hair. "This must be *really* bad."

I didn't respond, trying to weigh what might happen if I told him about the dress and wig. He could demand that I tell the chief, as Tim wanted me to do. He could decide to confront Mary Lou. I didn't like that scenario any better.

"Am I on the suspect list?"

I stopped walking. No one was close to where we were standing, and I thought the noise from the ocean and the gulls would mask anything I said. "I found something at Mary Lou's house that might implicate her in Miss Elizabeth's murder. But I don't want to tell the chief because we didn't have a search warrant and Tim says it's crazy anyway. And I don't want to confront Mary Lou and embarrass everyone. Gramps would never forgive me."

He moved closer. "What did you find?"

I told him about the dress and wig. "I know it's important. You'd think after all these years Tim would trust me enough to believe I find things. Everyone knows I find things. I didn't want to find this. But I did, and I don't know what to do."

We sat down on a large gray rock that was underwater during high tide. There were still a few starfish clinging to the bottom where the rock was wet. Tiny crabs scuttled away when we sat down. The sun had warmed the stone, and the cool water reaching the shore felt good on my toes as I dipped them, and my sandals, into the surf.

"What do you *want* to do with the information?" he asked.

"I don't know. I feel sure this is why Miss Mildred thought she saw her sister's ghost. I know it doesn't make any sense, but we know someone set her up."

"And you think Mary Lou was the one?"

"I don't *want* to think it." I glanced at him, narrowing my eyes as I faced the sun. "What do you think?"

He considered it. "I think unless she confesses, it would be hard to make a case out of this. Was there any animosity between Mary Lou and Miss Elizabeth?"

"Not as far as I know. Mary Lou helped out at her house a lot. They seemed to be friends. I can't imagine her hurting Miss Elizabeth. But there's something else too." I nodded to one of the workers a few yards away. "Those blue gloves over there are like the kind that were in Miss Elizabeth's purse. And those little stainless steel shovels they all use could be the same kind that killed her."

"Of course, those shovels and gloves are sold everywhere on the island," he reminded me. "That wouldn't be enough to reopen the investigation."

"What would be?"

"New DNA evidence. Or a confession."

"I don't know how to get new DNA evidence." I thought about what I was saying with my head and not my heart. If Mary Lou was guilty of killing Miss Elizabeth, even if it was an accident, she needed to explain herself and rescue Miss Mildred. "But I might know how to get a confession."

"What do you have in mind?"

It was well past midnight, not a time I'm used to being out and about. Traffic on Duck Road had slowed to only a few cars. There was the faint sound of music coming from some of the bars and restaurants. A few crickets chirped, and the breezes rushed through the bushes around me. I looked at the dark shadow of Mary Lou's house and felt a terrible chill.

What if I was wrong? What if Mary Lou had nothing to do with what happened to Miss Elizabeth and I was only too eager to pin it on anyone to save Miss Mildred? What if I ended up convincing Mary Lou that she'd done something wrong when she hadn't?

"What are you doing out there, Mayor?"

The voice was coming from the earpiece I was wearing. It was Agent Walker, who was waiting in a surveillance van not even half a block away. Kevin had convinced me (though I'm not sure how) that we needed help. He'd told Agent Walker my plan to get a confession from Mary Lou, and surprisingly, he'd agreed.

"You have to go into the house," he said. "I don't think you can scare a confession out of her from the backyard."

I didn't want to respond to his prodding. I had a bad case of cold feet. Making Mary Lou believe I was Miss Elizabeth's ghost had *seemed* like a good idea when I suggested it on the beach yesterday. But that was before I actually had to do it. "Maybe we should wait," I whispered.

"The auction is only a few hours away," he reminded me. "This was your idea. Are you saying now you don't think Mary Lou had anything to do with what happened to Mrs. Simpson?"

I had been amazed that Kevin and Agent Walker thought scaring Mary Lou into a confession was a good idea. I was still amazed that they even considered she could be involved. Agent Walker had confessed, when Kevin and I told him a few hours ago, that he'd felt through the whole investigation that something wasn't right.

Of course, I felt completely guilty that I hadn't told the chief and asked for *his* help. Tim's reaction had surprised me yesterday. I was afraid the chief would feel the same way, and the truth, whatever it was, would never come out. More than a small part of me wished I *had* told the chief and he'd talked me out of the whole thing.

I wasn't too pleased to be standing in Mary Lou's backyard in the middle of the night. I was wearing the black dress with the little pink hearts—sort of. I'd had to cut out the back to fit into it (who knew Mary Lou was so much smaller than me?) and then pin it on over my bathing suit to keep it from falling off. I'd put on some white makeup from last Halloween and arranged the gray wig on my head so she couldn't see my hair.

I'd felt the first twinge of doubt when I looked at myself in the mirror at my house. Would this getup scare Mary Lou to death? Would she admit to killing someone because she was terrified? The whole thing had suddenly seemed like a bad idea.

I would've backed out. Really, I didn't have the backbone that Agent Walker assured me I had. I didn't want to hurt anyone. And I didn't like to think how Gramps was going to feel when he found out I'd done this. Whether Mary Lou was guilty or not, I *knew* he'd find out.

"Are you ready to move in? We can't sit here all night. We only have this van for a few hours," Agent Walker's voice prodded from my ear.

"I'm going. I can't talk anymore."

It was really Kevin who'd convinced me (again) to go through with it. When he pinned the small microphone and receiver on my dress, he looked into my eyes and told me, emphatically, "You can do this, Dae. You might be the only one who can."

That, and that funny fluttery feeling I got around him, sent me out the van door and into the warm, humid night. But that was as far as it had gotten me. Now, I was standing under the bushes, watching Mary Lou's house, wondering again whether I was doing the right thing.

Then I thought about Miss Mildred and Miss Elizabeth and Wild Johnny Simpson. All of their lives had been built on mistakes and misunderstandings. I had to make sure this wasn't one of them. I couldn't allow myself to be scared. I had to find out the truth.

I walked up to the old house, jumping a little when an owl hooted and flew down close at me to take a look. "I'm too big to be a mouse," I whispered.

"What was that?" Agent Walker asked from the van.

"Nothing. Just talking to the owl."

He didn't remark on that. I moved steadily across the

sandy ground, carefully skirting the rose bushes and gravel that might give me away. I half hoped the back door might be locked. There wouldn't be anything to do about that but go home. Too bad. Nice try.

But the back door was unlocked, even slightly open. I crept across the dark porch, trying not to step on buckets and shovels left there from the turtle rescue project.

I pushed open the door to the house and walked into the kitchen. I navigated carefully around the table and chairs, glanced at a nightlight glowing from the bathroom. The house was *so* quiet. No sound from the friendly owl outside, not even traffic sounds from the road.

I wondered, as I approached her bedroom door, if Mary Lou had noticed that the dress and wig were gone. Even with the mess, she might've been able to tell the difference. If she'd noticed, would she have thought of me and Tim?

I could hear her snoring softly from the bed. I wasn't sure what I was going to say. I had a silly image of myself holding a flashlight under my chin, like we used to do when we told ghost stories around the campfire. I walked closer, wondering if I should make some scary sound, booing or something, then I tripped over a pile of clothes in the middle of the bedroom floor.

That was enough to startle Mary Lou out of her sound sleep. I stood completely still, not even daring to breathe, as she turned on a flashlight and pinned me with the beam. "I knew it was you, Lizzie. Come for me, have you? Well, you can't make me feel any worse than I have for the past two weeks since I accidentally killed you. Go ahead. Take your revenge."

Chapter 19

"Get her to talk about it, Dae," Agent Walker said in my ear. "We need as much as we can get."

Wasn't it enough already? Mary Lou had confessed to killing Miss Elizabeth. How much more was there? I didn't move, couldn't speak. I stood still, the flashlight beam shining in my face.

"Aren't you going to say anything, Lizzie?" Mary Lou asked. She had slipped her legs out of bed. I could she was wearing the same short brown pants she'd been wearing at the beach. "I don't blame you for being angry. I made a bad mistake. I'm sorry I tried to blame it on Millie. It was wrong. I don't know what I was thinking."

I realized at that moment that I couldn't go on with the charade. We knew now that Miss Mildred wasn't responsible for killing her sister. Surely Mary Lou deserved a lawyer now before she said anything else. It was an accident. Agent Walker didn't need to know more.

I started to walk out of the bedroom. Mary Lou followed me. "Where are you going, Lizzie? Please take me with you. I don't want to live with all this guilt. Someone else will take care of the turtles. Let me go with you, please."

"Keep her talking," Agent Walker advised in my ear.

I walked out of the house into the dark yard, hoping she'd stay inside and have a cup of coffee or something. I couldn't warn her off any more than I could get her to confess anything else. It was over, as far as I was concerned. We had what we needed to set things right.

"Lizzie! Why won't you talk to me? Where are you going?" Mary Lou stayed one step behind me.

Between Agent Walker's proddings and Mary Lou's plaintive calls, my ears were ringing. I kept hoping she'd give up or I'd find a big bush to hide behind. I couldn't believe she'd confessed to killing Miss Elizabeth. I'd suspected her and helped catch her, but knowing for certain was different. It was like trading one friend, one piece of my life, for another.

I wished Agent Walker would stop talking. I wanted time to absorb all of this and grieve for another loss.

"Lead her back to the van." Kevin's voice replaced Agent Walker's in my ear. "Let us take it from here, Dae. You've done what you could."

I wanted to scream at Mary Lou to run away and hide. Agent Walker had his information. We could save Miss Mildred with it. I knew Mary Lou would have to be punished. At least my rational mind knew it. With all my heart, I wished she'd get in her car and drive far away. But I kept walking, and she kept following across the sandy ground and down the road.

We finally reached the van where Kevin and Agent Walker waited. I didn't know if I'd ever been so exhausted. I felt like I could fall on the ground and sleep for days. I thought it was probably a reaction to being so nervous and finding out I was right about Mary Lou.

I heard the van door slide open, then saw a glint of something metallic in the dim light from the interior. Without thinking, I threw myself in front of Mary Lou. She cowered on the ground before me, whimpering, probably thinking I meant to kill her. "Don't hurt her! It was an accident. She deserves to be judged by a jury," I yelled out.

"Dae?" Mary Lou looked up at me. "Is that *you?*"

"I'm Agent Walker with the State Bureau of Investigation." He stepped beside her as several lights flashed on from outside the van. "We need to have a serious conversation, Mrs. Harcourt. Why don't you come with me and tell me what happened to Mrs. Simpson?"

"It was the turtles," she blurted out with a sob. "They *need* me. I couldn't leave them during nesting season. Look at the damage done by the storm."

Agent Walker helped her up. I realized the glint of metal I'd seen was his badge and not his gun, as I'd feared. I fell down on the soft ground, my legs giving out. I didn't know what to think, but I was glad it was over. I couldn't have walked another step if I'd tried.

"Are you okay?" Kevin asked, crouching beside me.

"No. Not really. I know this had to be done. I'm glad for Miss Mildred. But I hate that it had to come to this. I've known her all my life. This is terrible."

"Tell me how it happened, Mrs. Harcourt," Agent Walker coaxed, explaining her legal rights. "I promise it will make you feel better when it's all out."

"I couldn't feel any worse, son," she admitted. "When I

saw Lizzie's ghost standing next to the bed, I wasn't a bit afraid of dying. I only wanted it to end."

She went on to explain that she was frantically trying to save some turtles from high tide the night before the Fourth of July celebration. "I didn't even notice Lizzie was there. You know how she had that way of standing and watching you, not saying a word. I was using the shovel to mound up some extra sand. I went back with it and hit something solid. I didn't even realize I'd hit Lizzie in the head until I saw her fall to the ground."

"You hit her in the head, Mrs. Harcourt, but you didn't kill her. You should've called for help."

Mary Lou's eyes were wet with tears that gleamed in the bright lights. "What are you saying? I checked her pulse. There was no heartbeat."

"There was sand in her lungs. That means she was still breathing when you buried her."

"No! *No!* That can't be true! I checked her. She was dead. I had to bury her to protect the turtles. Then when everyone was looking for someone to blame, I went to Millie and asked her for money for the turtle sanctuary. I was thinking if I could get everything set up, I'd confess. But she told me I had to wait until she died to get the land she promised me. That's when I thought of blaming *her* for what happened. Only for a while. Only until the turtles were protected. Then I would've told the truth. It was only an accident. I never meant to hurt Lizzie."

I thought I was shocked and horrified *before* Agent Walker explained about Miss Elizabeth's death. Knowing that she had been buried alive on the beach made everything so much worse. I started crying and covered my face with my hands. Kevin put his arms around me, and I cried into his shirt. How could something like this happen in Duck?

"You'll have to come with me." Agent Walker took Mary Lou's arm to lead her away.

I lifted my head to see her go, and she stared at me. "I'm so sorry, Lizzie," she sobbed. "I didn't know. I swear I didn't know."

I couldn't speak. What could I say anyway? I didn't know how Miss Elizabeth would've responded to that apology. But it was impossible to be forgiven by the dead. Mary Lou was going to have to live with what she'd done for the rest of her life. It struck me that the rest of us would have to live with it too.

Kevin took me home without any conversation. I went upstairs while he explained what had happened to Gramps.

I drew a hot bath and sat in it until I was completely pruny and the water was cold. I didn't really think about anything. I couldn't. My brain felt wiped clean of any information.

As I got out of the tub, I realized that even with all that water, I still hadn't scrubbed the makeup off my face. When I looked in the mirror, I saw that half of it must've come off on Kevin's shirt. I scrubbed off the rest until my face was clean and pink.

I stared at myself for a long time, questioning again if what I'd done was the right thing. Sometimes, there was a terrible price to pay for helping people. I knew if I had to do the same thing again, I would. But I knew this incident was one I would never forget. The look in Mary Lou's drowned eyes when she asked me for forgiveness would haunt me the rest of my life.

When I was in bed, staring at the dark ceiling, there was a knock on the door. "Dae?" Gramps said. "Are you still awake?"

"Sure. Come in and we can talk."

He sat on the edge of the bed, not bothering to turn on a

light. "I'm sorry you had to go through that. And I'm hurt that you didn't tell me what was going on. I thought we could tell each other anything."

I thought of all my youthful indiscretions that lay like old shoes in the closet of my mind. I hadn't shared any of those. But I knew Gramps and I had a good relationship and there had been enough sharing between us to keep it strong. "I knew you had a thing with Mary Lou. I didn't want you to have to be there when we tricked her. *I* didn't want to be there either, and she wasn't even my girlfriend."

He hugged me tight and kissed the top of my head. "You can tell me *anything*. No girlfriend can ever change that. I hope no boyfriend of yours ever does either. I'm sorry this happened to Mary Lou. I don't know what possessed her to go through all those lengths to cover it up. She's a good woman, Dae."

I knew he was telling the truth about Mary Lou. "I think she got carried away trying to save the turtles. She thought no one else could do it but her."

"You know, she's right. Once she's gone, the group will fall apart, and the turtles will have to fend for themselves. There won't be anyone as dedicated as she has been. But we all have to live with mortality and our mistakes. I waited an extra five years to retire because I thought my deputies needed me. I had to be hospitalized with that heart attack before I realized they could get along without me. The turtles will have to get along without Mary Lou. I'm sure they'll survive."

I swallowed hard. "Did you know Miss Elizabeth wasn't dead when Mary Lou buried her?"

He nodded. "I'd hoped to spare you that information. The chief kept it secret because he wasn't sure Miss Mildred was the right suspect. He'd hoped to use it to catch the real perpetrator. This can be an ugly business, Dae. I always tried to keep those awful details from you when you were growing up. I guess I still like to think I can protect you."

I hugged him and kissed his forehead. "You can spare me those details anytime. I don't know if I'll ever sleep again thinking about her being out there still alive and no one knowing. It's terrible to be so alone."

"I know how you like to worry these things, darlin'. But you don't have to think about it that way. You'll *never* be alone. I guarantee it. Which reminds me, there was an awful lot of white makeup on Kevin's shirt. I guess you owe him a new one, huh?"

Wednesday morning dawned bright and clear, and I was running late. I was surprised at first that I'd slept at all. I looked at the clock and realized I'd forgotten to set the alarm. It was after nine and the auction was at ten.

I hurried out of bed, glanced at my wig-flattened hair and groaned. Nothing that washing and some blow-drying couldn't help. I showered quickly and gave in to my impulse to wear something bright and cheerful. I paired a bright orange Duck T-shirt with white shorts, slipped my feet into tennis shoes (I figured I'd be running a lot today) and got out the door without Gramps yelling at me to eat breakfast.

I was surprised to find he was already gone and even more surprised he hadn't left a note about where he was. I figured he was probably trying to organize the members of the Turtle Rescue League, who would no doubt be missing their fearless leader this morning. Mary Lou was the heart and soul of that little group. Thinking about her brought on a quick bout of depression. But I had an auction to stop, and I couldn't let anything stand in my way.

I met Trudy at the end of the drive. She was riding her new red scooter and offered me a ride. It was small. I wasn't completely convinced it could hold both of us. But I strapped on the extra helmet and sat behind her. "Where are you off to?" she asked as she waited for a break in traffic.

"I'm headed over to Miss Mildred's house. They're planning to auction it off today, but I'm planning something different."

"Can you do that? Is that something mayors do?"

"I don't know yet," I yelled over the buzzing of the scooter engine. I'd ridden on motorcycles before. This was like a cross between a motorcycle and a bicycle. "I'll let you know."

"I saw you with Kevin Brickman yesterday. Is something going on there that Shayla should know about?"

"Shayla? I thought she was dating Tim again."

"She was. They broke up, like always. I don't know why they bother. Tim isn't going to be happy with anyone but you. And Shayla isn't going to be happy with anyone at all. But of all those losers, Kevin is on top of the pile, don't you think?"

I didn't want to dwell on that, especially not this morning. I wasn't sure whether there was anything special between Kevin and me. We'd gone through some extraordinary events together, and sometimes that kind of mutual experience created a bond. But bonds like that don't necessarily last. I didn't have enough information to make an informed decision yet. I'd have to think about it after the auction.

"I heard Mary Lou Harcourt was arrested last night," Trudy yelled at me. "Think she had too many overdue library books or something? I mean, can you imagine her doing anything illegal? I guess we'll have to wait and hear the rest of it. There have been some crazy goings on this summer. I'll be glad when fall gets here and everyone goes home. I know it's not good for business, but I like the quiet."

I knew everyone in Duck would be shocked when they learned the truth about what had happened to Miss Elizabeth. Some people wouldn't believe it even when they heard all the details. I felt sure we'd be talking about it way after Duck Road was quiet in winter. I wondered what would happen to Mary Lou. I hoped she'd receive a light sentence despite her desperate attempts to hide what happened. I believed it was an accident, like she'd said. No one really knew what they'd do until they were in the middle of that kind of situation.

Trudy dropped me off at Miss Mildred's house. A large group of cars, even a few limousines, were parked up and down the road. Plenty of people were interested in the auction. What Chuck had said was true—land was at a premium in Duck. It had to be because there was so little of it between the Atlantic and the sound.

"Looks like they have a good crowd," Trudy observed. "Good luck convincing them not to auction everything."

"Thanks. Say, would you do me a favor and check for UPS packages? You still have a key to Missing Pieces, right? Maybe you could throw them inside if there's anything there."

"You got it." She revved the scooter engine. "See you later!"

I tugged my shirt down and wished I'd worn some kind of official-looking jacket. There was a police car in the driveway to ensure that everyone else parked in the street. Not only would I have to argue with Chuck and Jerry, but I'd

also have to argue with police officers. But that was okay. I
was ready to take on whoever needed taking on.

As I started up the drive, a well-dressed older couple got
out of their Cadillac and walked up with me. The woman
was dripping with large diamonds, and the man was wearing a big cowboy hat. We see them all in Duck, from the
rich to the poor, from the cowboys to the slick city people.
I guess they all want to live here, at least part-time.

Officer Scott Randall was at the front door, his police
uniform freshly cleaned and pressed. He looked kind of
stiff standing there, nodding to everyone who came in. I
paused when I saw him, wondering if I should enlist his
help in what I wanted to do. Then I considered what would
happen if he said no and changed my mind.

"Mayor O'Donnell." He nodded to me without a smile,
obviously taking his duties very seriously.

"Officer Randall." I nodded back. "Fine day for an
auction."

"Yes, ma'am."

I mingled with all the other people there for the auction.
As Chuck had predicted, the champagne was flowing freely
and the brie on the sideboard was plentiful. I didn't see a
single face that I recognized, except Scott. How had all
these people even heard about the property being auctioned? Sometimes I was amazed at how many people were
interested in our little town.

Chuck and Jerry were in the living room where the furniture had been moved aside to make way for at least fifty
folding chairs. They were chatting and laughing like two
hyenas. It was going to give me great personal pleasure to
put an end to their partnership.

Chuck rang a bell, and people started moving into the

living room. Apparently that signaled the beginning of the auction. I kept my spot against the wall rather than take a chair. I needed to be in position to go up and question the legitimacy of the auction in light of recent developments. I didn't know how long I could hold them off, but I was hoping that no one would bid on the properties if they knew there was a question of legality.

When everyone was seated, except for a dozen or so still standing in the back of the room by Miss Mildred's armoire, Chuck cleared his throat and welcomed them all to the proceedings. "As you can see, this is a classic older home right in the heart of Duck within walking or golf-cart distance to shopping and restaurants. The second home, which we'll be travelling to for the next auction, is very much like this one. The two together represent a terrific value for anyone interested in property here."

He nodded to a white-haired man who I thought must be the auctioneer since he came prepared with his own gavel. "We'll start the bidding at two million dollars for this home and land. Do I hear two million?"

I took a deep breath, calmed my frantically beating heart, pasted on my big mayor smile and sailed to the front of the room. "Ladies and gentlemen, could I have your attention? I think you should know that the owner of these properties is going to be released from the hospital and will be back to claim them. Jerry Richards is not the rightful owner and can't legally sell this or the other house."

The people in the room began talking amongst themselves while Jerry and Chuck glared at me. Jerry recovered first. "I'm afraid sentiment over these properties runs very high here in Duck, but believe me, I have every right to auction them today. My grandfather is the sole beneficiary of the properties, and I have his power of attorney to dispose of them."

"Officer!" Chuck called and beckoned Scott. "Please remove this woman from the premises."

Scott looked at me and looked back at Chuck. "That's the *mayor*, sir."

I heard a faint siren sound coming from Duck Road, but I ignored it as I stood my ground. "Believe me, Jerry, you *don't* want to continue. This is only going to cause you more trouble."

The siren was getting louder, and I wondered if there was a fire close by. With the winds sweeping across town each day, fire was a frightening thought even with all the water so close by.

"Officer," Jerry responded. "Do your duty. This woman is disrupting our legal auction."

Scott looked at me again. "Excuse me, sir, but that is not a woman. That's Mayor O'Donnell. I can't throw her out. Maybe you should reconsider the auction."

"What?" Jerry was livid, veins popping out in his temples and neck. "Never mind them. Go ahead and proceed, auctioneer."

By now the siren was its own distraction. It sounded as if it were right outside. I couldn't smell any smoke, but that didn't mean there wasn't a fire. Scott and I stood between the crowd and the auctioneer. I could see they were confused and unsure what to do next. I was glad that Scott had taken my side, and I vowed that I would trust him with information if I was ever in a similar situation again. But in the meantime, the people in the crowd were looking at the auctioneer. I didn't know what else I could do to stop the proceedings.

"What in the world is going on here?" demanded a voice I'd feared I'd never hear again in this house.

I looked toward the open front door as did everyone else in the room. Nestled between Chief Michaels and Gramps, Miss Mildred was furious. "Why are all of you people here? I can't believe I'm gone for a few days and strangers enter my house and leave the door wide open." She turned to Chief Michaels. "Doesn't the town pay you to keep order in Duck anymore? This is totally unacceptable. And where is my furniture?"

Chief Michaels smiled, a really nasty smile that I loved. "I'm afraid this auction is over. The judge dropped the charges against Millie this morning. All of you are trespassing. Officer Randall, please show these people out."

"Not before they move my furniture back and get these ugly chairs out of there," Miss Mildred protested.

Scott smiled at me and nodded before he began herding people out the door. The expressions on Chuck's and Jerry's faces were comical. Jerry even took out his official power of attorney and waved it in the chief's face. "I have a right to be here. She can't waltz back in and screw everything up. My grandfather has some say over this."

Miss Mildred grabbed the paper from him and ripped it in two. "I'm embarrassed to call you my grandnephew. I'm going to talk to Silas about this. And I never really liked you on the news either. You're too tall, for one thing. And you have an annoying voice."

And just like that, things were set right for the most part in Duck. Of course, what had happened could never be completely forgotten, but the guilty had been punished and the people who wanted to take advantage of a bad situation were put in their places.

There was a memorial service for Miss Elizabeth at Duck Cemetery three days later. Everyone turned out for it, almost overwhelming the small graveyard. The minister from the Duck Presbyterian Church talked about life and death and the love that abides among those who are left behind.

I was pleased to see Silas Butler in a wheelchair holding his sister's hand at the gravesite. I'd heard a rumor that he was going to be living with her from now on. I hadn't heard what would happen to Miss Elizabeth's house, but I wasn't worried about it anymore.

I spent that afternoon and well into the evening painting the Blue Whale Inn. I'd brought help—Shayla, Tim and Trudy—to make the job go faster. If Kevin minded, he didn't say so. I presented him with a new shirt to replace the one he'd sacrificed when he let me cry on his shoulder.

"I heard Jerry Richards lost his job at the TV station," Kevin said as we painted side by side. "Something about the owner not liking him disrespecting the mayor of Duck."

"You have to be careful about what gets caught on tape nowadays." I smiled as I laid down fresh blue paint.

"Agent Walker told me he was wrapping up the investigation into Wild Johnny Simpson's death. Apparently, Bunk Whitley is going to take the rap for it."

"He isn't around to defend himself." I dipped my brush into the paint again. "I guess that makes him a good suspect. Of course, we'll never know for sure."

"As long as I don't find him in some secret closet, I'm good with that. I'm hoping this new coat of paint is signaling a new era in Blue Whale history."

"I like that." I smiled at him and stopped painting for a few minutes when he smiled back.

"And about your old nickname," he began, a devilish look in his eye. "Dizzy?"

"Hey!" Shayla came up from the other side and slid her hand across his shoulder. "Didn't I hear some promise about lasagna for dinner if we came and worked? It's getting late and I'm starving. Why don't you and I go inside and start dinner. Dae, Tim and Trudy won't mind going on without us."

Kevin looked at me, and I looked away. I had no holds on him and didn't want to talk about being called Dizzy. "Go ahead. I'm going around back to clean my brushes anyway. I probably won't be able to lift my arms tomorrow as it is, and Andy is expecting a repeat performance from the mayor for Tai Chi on the Green."

The two of them walked into the inn. I didn't see Trudy or Tim, but they were probably on the other side of the building. I'd never realized how massive the inn was until we started painting it.

It was that soft time of evening when it isn't day anymore but it isn't quite dark either. I washed out my brushes and stood looking out at the Atlantic as it rolled easily to the shore.

Everyone said this was the best time to see ghosts. Shayla told me once that twilight was like an opening between where ghosts lived and where the rest of us stayed until we joined them.

My eyes followed the smooth, empty sand that ran past Miss Elizabeth's house. There was someone out there, fuzzy, not quite formed. It looked like a man and woman. She was leaning toward him and his arm was around her. Had Wild Johnny Simpson finally made it back home to reclaim his abandoned bride?

"Dae? Where are you?" I heard Tim call from around the other side of the building and glanced that way.

When I looked back at the beach, the couple was gone. Was it my imagination or had I finally seen a *real* ghost? "Around back," I answered, wiping a tear from my eye. It wasn't my mother's ghost, but maybe there was hope for me yet.

GET CLUED IN

Ever wonder how to find out about all the latest Berkley Prime Crime and Signet mysteries?

berkleyobsidianmysteries.com

- *See what's new*
- *Find author appearances*
- *Win fantastic prizes*
- *Get reading recommendations*
- *Sign up for the mystery newsletter*
- *Chat with authors and other fans*
- *Read interviews with authors you love*

MYSTERY SOLVED.

berkleyobsidianmysteries.com

M2G0808